WHITEWING

FIRST ORDINANCE, BOOK 5

CONNIE SUTTLE

Subtle demon
subtledemon.com

To Walter, Joe, Larry, Sarah, Lee, Dianne and Mark.

Thank you.

ACKNOWLEDGMENTS

As always, this book is the result of collaboration. If it weren't for the support of my editor, my cover artist and my beta readers, it would be less than it is. All mistakes, as usual, are mine and no other's.

ALSO BY CONNIE SUTTLE

Blood Destiny Series:

Blood Wager

Blood Passage

Blood Sense

Blood Domination

Blood Royal

Blood Queen

Blood Rebellion

Blood War

Blood Redemption

Blood Reunion

Legend of the Ir'Indicti Series:

Bumble

Shadowed

Target

Vendetta

Destroyer

High Demon Series:

Demon Lost

Demon Revealed

Demon's King

Demon's Quest

Demon's Revenge

Demon's Dream

God Wars Series:

Blood Double

Blood Trouble

Blood Revolution

Blood Love

Blood Finale

Saa Thalarr Series:

Hope and Vengeance

Wyvern and Company

Observe and Protect*

First Ordinance Series:

Finder

Keeper

BlackWing

SpellBreaker

WhiteWing

R-D Series:

Cloud Dust

Cloud Invasion

Cloud Rebel

~

Latter Day Demons Series:

Hot Demon in the City

A Demon's Work is Never Done

A Demon's Due

~

Seattle Elementals Series:

Your Money's Worth

Worth Your While*

~

BlackWing Pirates Series

MindSighted

MindMage

MindRogue*

~

Black Rose Sorceress Series

The Rose Mark

Rose and Thorn

Black Rose Queen*

~

CHAPTER 1

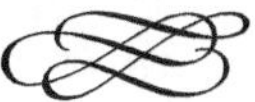

eth Alliance
Planet Gilvos
Lew Velker

Just a little farther, I silently begged the small treasure-bot. While passing a certain perimeter had raised the hair on my arms and caused my heart to pound unnaturally fast, the treasure-bot wasn't afflicted by those mortal difficulties.

The bot had dug deep and now had trouble climbing from the hole it had created. Clutched in its prehensile, metal fingers was a strange, glass ball. *This was what all the fuss was about? A marble?*

It must have some value—I'd watched from a distance as the Lord Mayor from the nearby city visited this spot several times.

Everybody knew how obsessive he was. It made me think that something of worth was buried there; why else would he keep coming back?

"Ah," I breathed as the bot's tiny fingers deposited the marble in my hand. Surely I could convince the Lord Mayor to tell me its worth; blackmail usually worked quite fine for that sort of thing.

Avii Castle, Le-Ath Veronis

Quin

"Director Kooper Griff, my King," Ardis announced as the long-legged Director of the ASD offered a proper bow to Justis. Justis nodded in return and lifted a hand, indicating that Kooper should approach us.

Justis and I sat at breakfast in Justis' private quarters, having nearly finished our meal when Ardis informed us that Kooper had arrived. Rather than keeping him waiting, Justis intended to offer breakfast.

A Yellow Wing poured tea for Kooper, while another set a plate in front of him when he took the offered seat.

"What can I do for you, Director?" Justis grinned at Kooper. Oddly enough, they'd become good friends.

"I was hoping Quin had heard from Zaria," Kooper blew out a troubled sigh.

"Nothing," I said, setting my fork down beside my plate. She'd promised to help me with several troubling things. So far, Queen Lissa was the one to get me from one poisoned planet to another, so I could call the poisonous creatures to the collection spheres I buried there.

I felt somewhat abandoned by Zaria's absence, although I had no desire to voice my complaints; Zaria had rid us of the menace Liron presented, as the rogue god he was. She'd also saved my life and many others—I had no right to complain.

The truth was, I missed her greatly.

I also knew that Caylon Black missed her as well; Cleo, his first mate, should deliver their child at any time, and he and Cleo wanted Zaria there to assist Karzac with the birth.

Caylon silently cursed Ilya, who'd left a hole in Zaria's heart and forced her into hiding to conceal her grief.

At least that was what happened shortly after Liron's demise. Months had passed and still Zaria had not appeared, leaving all of us to wonder how long she would suffer from Ilya's lack of faith and his dismay, once he learned she was both Karathian and Larentii.

None had seen him, either; his continued absence was nearly as puzzling as Zaria's. As nobody had heard from Zaria, there was no way to determine where she might be. Queen Lissa likely knew where Ilya was hiding, but she wouldn't say.

I imagined he'd found his way back to Falchan; he was happy there, fighting alongside the Falchani warriors in their constant war with a long-time enemy.

"Ilya's on Falchan; Dragon says so," Kooper said, confirming my theory. "The perpetual, stone-faced warrior, that one," Kooper shook his head. He failed to understand, just as I did.

"He has to make peace with this in his own time," Justis said, lifting his cup of tea and sipping. "People handle things in different ways. I hope he doesn't destroy his love by waiting too long."

"That's the problem right there—he's destroying his love," Kooper snorted. "He has to own his mistakes and then pray that Zaria takes him back when he comes to his senses. We have other troubles, too," Kooper said. "An entire shipment of replication bots has been stolen off the loading docks—before they ever made it onto the ship. Those bots can reproduce almost anything, and are heavily controlled and licensed because of it," he added. "I'm concerned that they're in the hands of Cayetes, since we have no leads. I was hoping you or Zaria could help with that."

I studied the images on Kooper's comp-vid and used my gift to search for the machines depicted. I found nothing. Somewhere, a Sirenali likely guarded them.

"Director Griff, I cannot find them," I admitted defeat in the matter. "If I hear anything from Zaria, I'll let you know," I promised. "Please, enjoy your meal and we will speak of happier things."

~

"When are you going out again?" Gurnil asked as he shelved a book in the massive library he kept at Avii Castle. The book made the soft, familiar hissing sound of cover against cover as it slid into its place with a quiet thunk.

"In two days," I flattened my wings against my back. "We will visit three more worlds before I return to rest."

"Elabeth always returned to Avii Castle exhausted after performing a saving in Fyris," Gurnil observed. "She would never speak of it afterward, as if the poison troubled her in such a way that she didn't wish to speak of it, or place that burden upon another."

"It is troubling," I lowered my gaze to stare at my shoes. "I can feel the planet itself groaning from the sickness that invades it."

"Camryn never said anything about that," Gurnil mused. "He would confide in me at times, but he never mentioned that Elabeth was so sensitive to the planet itself. I think it is your making by Liron that does that. No, do not lament your making, we are all richer for that and are grateful," he held up a hand. "You have done too many things to save not only this race, but too many more to count."

I'd blinked at him before opening my mouth to speak; Gurnil allayed my fears before I could speak of them. "At least something good came from Liron's betrayal," I breathed. "I hold more gratitude toward Zaria than I will ever have for Liron."

"I've wished to speak with you about that," Gurnil offered a smile. "I heard a rumor that Zaria remade you, and in doing so, removed all traces of Liron in you."

"I hope that is true," I was back to studying my shoes. "I would much rather owe my existence to her than Liron."

"Dearest, it is true," Daragar appeared beside Gurnil and me, a broad smile lighting his sky-blue face. "If the Vhanaraszh changes what was, it is authentic in every way. You are more hers than anyone else's, now."

"I've missed you," I returned Daragar's smile.

"And I you. Would you like to visit the falaca with me?" He spoke of the soft-bleating, mild-tempered, wooly creatures inhabiting the Larentii homeworld.

"I would," I said. "More than anything."

～

Earth

Caylon Black

My daughter would arrive soon. Karzac hovered and that was always a sign that the child was coming. Until now, I hadn't considered sending mindspeech in an attempt to find Zaria. She and Cleo still hadn't met, and I didn't want that meeting to take place at an inopportune moment.

That's why I'd chosen Dragon's dojo on Earth to do my pacing and cursing; I didn't want to upset Cleo with my anger and misgivings. While I was at it, I cursed my own heart for choosing Zaria as a second mate.

Once, I'd had no use for such things. Those decisions were no longer in my control, or so it would seem.

"I hope you're shielding this from Cleo," Zaria snapped as she appeared ten feet away from me. "You have no idea how difficult it is for me to come to you when you're cursing yourself and the need for mates in the first place."

"What kind of fool do you take me for?" I snapped back.

"One who is so afraid of getting hurt that he curses love?"

I went still. "Fuck," I mumbled in Falchani.

"I understand every language. You can say fuck in all of them. I'll agree with you."

"Will you—please—come into the house to meet Cleo? She needs an ally. You see what kind of ally I make."

"Caylon, I hope you allow the ice around your heart to thaw someday," she said with a sigh. "Lead the way. It's time I met your Cleo."

She is *my Cleo*, I reminded myself.

"And your first mate," Zaria read me as easily as a random road sign. "You love her."

"Yes."

∾

Zaria

"Cleo, my love, this is Zaria," Caylon introduced us.

"Caylon, are you running a fever?" Cleo asked. "I don't think you've ever used an endearment when introducing me," she teased.

"Zaria is showing me the error of my ways," Caylon said. "And you are my love. I'm just a fool of a Falchani who is too shy to admit it," he replied.

"There's not a shy bone in your body," Cleo grinned at him.

"True," Caylon agreed. An almost smile curled a corner of his mouth.

"How's that baby girl?" I asked.

"Kicking me every chance she gets," Cleo laughed. "I'm so glad you're here. I was about to beg Belen to come find you."

"I would have been happy to do so," Belen appeared in a flash of brightness. "I, too, have been waiting for Zaria to return."

"Is there something I didn't know before now?" Caylon lifted a dark eyebrow.

"There are many things you do not know," Belen beamed. "Where shall I start?"

"Alphabetically?" I asked.

Cleo snickered.

"Honey, don't look so dejected," I patted Caylon's face. "We're just teasing."

He shocked the hell out of me by grabbing my hand and kissing it.

Ilya's an ass, he sent to me, kissed my hand again and then let it go.

I know, I replied.

∼

Falchani Plains

Ilya

"What do you want?" My voice was sullen and it shouldn't have been with the former King of Karathia. It didn't matter that he called himself Wellend, now. For years uncounted, he'd led a dual existence, much as I had. He and his father Warlend, King before Wellend, had operated under two separate identities.

Like me, I imagined the Mighty Heart or one of the others had seen to that. It takes a great deal of power to allow someone to exist in two places at the same time. My two identities merged the moment I sat in my seat at the trial on Karathia.

Corolan and Warrik. Gale and Norn. I imagined it was the same for them; they'd all been present at the trial, too. What difference did it make in the long term? They were one and the same, now; all four had disappeared, leaving only Wellend and Warlend behind.

What did matter was this; Wellend should have been *her* father. Still counted himself as such, actually. He'd appeared inside my tent on Falchan while I cleaned my blades. He hadn't said anything, yet; he merely sat easily on my cot and studied the sparse furnishings around him.

"Surprised you don't let your horse sleep at the foot of your bed," he observed.

"Hmmph," I grunted.

"You're wondering why I'm here," he went on, while amusement lit his eyes. "Well, I have it on good authority from the current King of Karathia that Vardil Cayetes may be coming out of the shadows to reclaim his old empire."

"What's that got to do with me?" I growled. "You should go. I hear we may have a battle on our hands in the morning."

"Two small bands of marauders—that's from the current King's father, who can tell these things," he grinned. "You're not needed for that."

"Then what do you want me to do?"

"Go looking for Vardil." Wellend shrugged, as if any dolt would have figured that out by now.

"What's the ASD doing, sitting on their hands?"

"No. The ASD is hoping Zaria comes back to help with all this. They've exhausted their resources, looking for him already."

My heart constricted when he said her name. I'd kept myself immersed in blade work and battle to keep that name from my mind. Yet here he was, saying it as if it didn't make my soul bleed.

I'd fucked everything up with her until it was beyond repair. She didn't need me. She had other mates, or others who wanted to be her mates.

"She didn't sleep with them," Wellend picked those thoughts from my mind. "Still hasn't."

"Not my problem."

"You're delusional if you think it's not."

"Then I'm delusional. She doesn't need that."

"Say you don't want her," he said, "and I'll tell you how much of a lie that is."

"It's not what I want that matters. It's what she needs. Leave. Please."

"I've never met anyone so stubborn in my life," he shook his head. "The rumor is that Vardil was seen on Paricos II, if you'd like to follow up on that. The King would very much like regular reports, too."

"Is this a command from the King?"

"Will it get you to Paricos II?"

"That's the only way I'll go."

"Then it's a command. Leave in the morning. Get some sleep tonight; you'll need to be rested to handle what's likely to come your way."

I cursed him when he disappeared; at least I had the sense to wait until that happened. He was a trusted advisor to the current King, and I knew better than to fool with that. I'd fucked up everything else in my life except that, or so it appeared.

Fucking Vardil Cayetes, I grumbled mentally, *who is allied with fucking V'ili*. Not only could V'ili command Vardil's former villains to obey his commands, but together, they could be impossible for anyone to locate.

~

Earth

Zaria

Cleo went into labor late; with Karzac in attendance, there was little for me to do except coach Caylon mentally on what Cleo needed from him during the birth. He held her hand as her knuckles went white while squeezing the blood from his fingers. He soothed when she called him names at difficult times.

Reaching out with a Larentii's ability, I took the sharp edge from her pain on several occasions. Karzac offered mute appreciation for my efforts. At the end, he placed tiny, squalling Cle-Anne in Cleo's arms.

I could have told Caylon then what a determined warrior his daughter would become, but held back; that would be a happy revelation for his future.

After the baby suckled and slept, Cleo also slept. Caylon wanted to talk, but I held him off, telling him he should give all his attention to Cleo and his daughter. We could talk later.

"You're leaving?" Kyler, Cleo's twin sister had arrived but held her sister's other hand while Karzac and I coached Cleo and Caylon through the birth.

"Cleo needs his full attention," I shrugged. "He and I can discuss things later."

"Don't wait too long," she advised. "It wouldn't hurt to send him mindspeech, either. Regularly."

"I'll work on that," I said.

"He's a little lost," Kyler explained. "He never expected you or Cle-Anne."

"I know. He has to make some of this right himself. I can't do it all for him."

"I understand," her shoulders drooped. She wanted everything made right for Cleo. Things could be uneven at times, but Caylon was already trying to sort things out for himself. "Where are you going?" she asked.

"To Quin," I said. "I promised to help her, and I'm currently behind on that promise."

"They're all wondering where you are; I may have let it slip to Aunt Lissa."

"That's fine," I said. "You know we're related from way back. Sort of."

"Sort of is a good description." She smiled.

~

Avii Castle

Quin

Queen Lissa was scheduled to arrive in the morning for my three-world visit, to save those worlds from the poison spreading through them. Justis, Berel, Bleek, Barc, Terrett, Kaldill and I were having dinner together when Zaria appeared in Justis' private dining room.

"Director Griff is asking for you," Justis spoke first.

"I imagine he is," Zaria agreed with a nod.

Scooting my chair back, I rose and almost ran toward Zaria. She laughed when I flew into her arms, before wrapping me in a warm, delicious hug and kissing my cheek.

I missed you, I sent to her.

I missed you, too. Very much.

"Are you going with me tomorrow?" I asked.

"That's why I'm here," she smiled.

~

Zaria

"You know Vardil will be looking for Quin. She healed him of everything. He's obsessed with his health, now, unless I am mistaken."

Kalenegar, King of the Larentii in all but name, stood beside me on the Avii Library balcony. His large blue hands were clasped behind his back as he soaked in the morning sunlight to feed himself. He'd spoken his opinion on the one I sought.

"I think the same," I allowed my shoulders to slump. "With V'ili at his side, he can command almost anyone to do his bidding in order to get to her. Look what he did to Bleek and Barc, just to get Bleek's cooperation."

"Vardil and V'ili are still very dangerous, even without the aid of Deris and Daris."

"I doubt that's the half of it, too."

"You know something, dearest?" Kal turned abruptly, his gaze settling on my face while a frown wrinkled his forehead.

"I found a bulletin on those criminal webs. Somebody is putting treasure-hunting crews together."

"That is nothing new—those are constantly being formed." Kal turned his face back toward Le-Ath Veronis' sun.

"Yes, but these are targeting worlds where Quin has already placed her spheres."

Kal stiffened. He knew as well as I did that those spheres could be worth the price of an entire planet—if they were found and held hostage until a world paid a tremendous ransom for them. Yes, wards had been placed, but those wards were porous. They had to be, to allow the creatures to travel to the sphere and be caught inside it.

"We have trouble, then," Kal sighed.

"It'll be bigger trouble if we discover Vardil Cayetes at the bottom of all this."

∼

Queen's Palace, Le-Ath Veronis

Lissa

Connegar and Reemagar had come, telling me that Zaria and Kalenegar required a meeting. After hearing what they had to say, I was mad enough to throttle somebody. That's when Kooper arrived. I informed him of Zaria's suspicions.

"You know we've already cleared it with the worlds you're visiting, so there may have been a leak on those already," Kooper paced, his shoulders tight, his face set with worry. "I've figured out already that Cayetes may be hunting Quin; there are posts offering a reward for an unusual, black-winged young woman. There is a substantial reward for her return to him."

"Word gets around, apparently," I snapped. "He's got his balls and his resources back if he can offer a huge amount. Every slaver, kidnapper and half-competent criminal will probably jump on that.

At least she doesn't have black wings any longer, but how long will that protect her? Enough have seen her as she is now, and don't know not to say anything."

"And with V'ili, Vardil can command the best of them to look for her. It won't take more than five brain cells to connect a winged girl with the Avii," Zaria said. "It could put every Avii female in jeopardy as a result."

"Have you discussed this with Justis?" I demanded.

"Not yet. You know he'll want Quin locked away somewhere so she'll be safe. That's really not an option, when there are worlds in need of her help." Zaria frowned; I could see that she'd thought this through already. She was right, too—Justis would be bullheaded about this, once he learned of it.

"Then how do we inform the worlds that we're coming, when that information could be leaked to the wrong people five seconds later?" I asked.

"I suggest we don't tell them until after the fact, and the sites must be hidden carefully and perimeter ward nets placed—not just for people, but for robots and other treasure-locating devices," Zaria said.

"I'd like to get my hands on whoever leaked the information on what to hunt," I snapped.

"Then you may have to resurrect Liron and kill him again," Zaria sighed.

"We must direct our attention to Vardil Cayetes," Kooper said. "If we find him, I believe we find the source of all our current troubles."

"V'ili, too," Zaria pointed out. "We need both of them dead."

"Most certainly dead," Ildevar Wyyld appeared as if called. "Breanne sent me," he smiled. "Should there be a way I can help; I will most certainly offer."

~

Avii Castle
  Quin
  "Queen Lissa is here, with Ildevar Wyyld, Zaria, Kalenegar and

Kooper Griff," Dena announced after knocking on the door to my suite.

While I couldn't read Lissa or Zaria, I could see trouble in Kooper's face.

"We're postponing the next three worlds," Lissa said when she walked into my sitting room. "We think someone may be searching for the spheres you've already placed, and they may be hunting you as well."

CHAPTER 2

Quin

"But the empty spheres are locked inside these walls, and only I can use them," I argued. We'd moved our discussion to Justis' council chamber; he was angry as he listened to Lissa's and Zaria's words.

I hoped he wasn't angry with them; they had no fault in this. Vardil Cayetes, on the other hand, could be more than guilty.

"So. He wants my Quin, not just to keep him healthy, but to control the spheres, too?" Justis hit on the one thing that neither woman had voiced as yet.

"We're concerned, yes," Zaria dipped her head in agreement. "This way, he can have ultimate control over who lives and dies. Leave the poison to spread and it's up to him whether he provides relief, in exchange for money and power, in all likelihood."

"This gets more frightening as it goes along," Kooper pinched the bridge of his nose.

"Headache?" I asked him.

"Not enough to worry about yet," he held up a hand. I'd intended to offer healing, if it were necessary.

"I want Quin moved to a safer place," Justis demanded. I jerked my head to gape at his sudden decision.

"That could keep her safe, but what about the others here?" Ildevar swept out a hand. He meant all Avii women, and not just me. They could all become targets, if someone thought to dye feathers.

"What are we to do?" I squeaked. The thought of Dena captured in my stead squeezed my heart.

"We moved the castle here; it can be moved elsewhere," Lissa suggested.

"I am not sure I like that idea." Justis rose from his throne and rustled his red feathers in irritation.

"Let me think on this," Lissa held up a hand. "There may be good options and it could be made temporary, until Cayetes is captured."

Zaria

"There is an ocean on Avendor, but it's more than a thousand miles from SouthStar," Lissa said.

"There is a river that flows through SouthStar," Kal pointed out. "Very wide, at one point. With some work, a new riverbed could be formed to flow about the castle, and continue on its course, unhindered."

"So far, that's the best suggestion," Lissa agreed. "Harifa Edus is still open enough to place everybody in danger."

"Someone will have to ferry them in and out of SouthStar," Ildevar observed.

"True," Lissa said. "But that's better than the alternative."

"At least Justis can see his nephew," Quin said. I could tell she wasn't looking forward to seeing Farisa, the brown-winged guild master for the artisans, or Liron's mother Wimla and Jurris' other widow, Vorina, who were now technically married to Justis.

Justis isn't interested in any of them, I sent to Quin, who hung her head as if ashamed. *They tried to hurt you*, I added. *Pay them no mind.*

I made a mental note to make sure Terrett and Lafe went with

Quin; they would ensure that those three wouldn't harm Quin with word or deed.

"When?"

"We have to clear it with Ashe, first."

"Ashe approves," Trajan, the Mighty Hand's second-in-command appeared. "He's already altered the riverbed; he's just waiting for us to make the move."

SouthStar Groves, Avendor

Quin

"The castle is in very deep water here," Trajan explained. "The river is in a shallower bed that splits and goes completely around. Bear in mind this is fresh water and not saltwater," he grinned as he pointed at the wide, shining ribbon of water facing the Library's terrace. It disappeared in a far bend, surrounded by rows and rows of fruit trees in flower.

I hadn't been in the castle when it was moved in haste from Siriaa to Le-Ath Veronis; Justis said it was much the same this time, happening in a blink and barely moving a cup out of place.

"It's lovely here, but hotter than what I'm used to," I said.

"We'll make arrangements to cool the castle," Trajan said. "You may not sleep, otherwise."

"Thank you," I said. "For protecting us."

"You're welcome," he grinned.

Paricos II

Ilya

Even with both blades strapped to my back, a knife in my boot and a dagger up my sleeve, someone still thought to attempt robbery while I sat in a pub drinking pirated Refizani beer.

The culprit now nursed a broken nose at a table opposite mine.

The ass had the nerve to cast accusing glances in my direction, too. I hadn't resorted to power to do anything to the sorry sot; if I had, he'd be a thousand miles away and dealing with worse than a broken nose.

"I haven't seen you here before," the pub owner slid onto the bench opposite mine.

"I haven't been here before," I said.

"Been a flood of would-be muscle through here recently, looking for jobs."

"Not one of them," I stated flatly and sipped my beer.

"Not one of them, or merely not looking for a job?"

"Both."

"What if I offered to find you a job—at top credit?" he asked. "And all the Refizani beer you wanted?"

"Answer would still be no."

"I've been waiting for someone to catch Lightning Fingers over there. Nobody passed the test—until now."

"He works for you?" I lifted an eyebrow at the pub owner. He had hair going gray from blond and more than enough of it; males of some races kept their hair as they grew older. I suspected he was in his one-fifties, at least.

"He works for me. Gubb," he tapped himself on the chest.

"You fleece your own customers?" I growled.

"Nah, Lightning keeps what he takes. I just pay him in beer to scope out the best that come in here. *That* I have a stake in," Gubb said. "I can get you a job with just about any boss on Paricos II."

"For which you accept a fee," I said.

"My services are much sought after."

"I'll bet they are."

"If you plan to stay, I'd suggest a job. Assassins aren't well-received here."

"Not an assassin. Just looking for a place to stay for a while."

"Look, I'm warning you," Gubb said. "You don't want a job, not a hired assassin—the only other reason to come here is to set up shop. The bosses don't like that."

"So, taking a job will keep you happy?" I asked.

"It'll pay my fee and keep me from reporting you."

"I see how this works, now."

"I have three names of bosses looking to hire. You can choose who I send you to," Gubb leaned back, a satisfied smirk on his face.

I wondered, then, how many others had marked Gubb for death—eventually.

~

Avii Castle, Avendor

Quin

Just as I imagined, Farisa, Wimla and Vorina arrived quickly at the castle, to claim their old suites of rooms and allow Liron to visit Justis. At least Farisa went straight to her guild without a word; I left Justis alone while he visited with the other three. I had no desire to see anger or jealousy in the furtive looks from both women.

Terrett found me on the Library terrace later, gazing at the glittering river that split and moved constantly past the castle.

Don't worry about those women, Terrett came from behind and wrapped his arms about me. *I think it is safe for you to fly as far as these groves grow,* he added. *If you so desire.*

Terrett could speak aloud; I'd heard his voice. Still, he preferred mindspeech. I think he wanted his words kept private between us; it was something personal that we shared with one another.

"I never thought of that," I said. "I haven't stretched my wings in a while."

"There you are," Lafe arrived, an almost smile curving his lips. "Zaria says there's an invitation from the big house for dinner tonight. It includes her, Quin, Justis and Quin's other mates who are present."

Wimla and Vorina not included, Terrett chuckled mentally.

I turned in Terrett's arms and kissed him, then pulled away and smiled at his humor. *I love you,* I informed him.

I love you more, he said.

~

SouthStar, Avendor

Zaria

Trajan brought Bel Erland, Bekzi, Yanzi, Gerrett and Morrett shortly before dinner. Morrett had been hired away from New Fyris' King and now worked for the King of Karathia.

His official title was Chief Librarian, but everybody knew King Rylend depended upon Morrett to keep him and the Crown Prince safe from those attempting to locate either with spells or power.

Gerrett offered a grin the moment he saw me; Morrett's smile was more reserved but no less heartfelt.

"I miss," Bekzi came forward and lifted my hand to kiss it.

I didn't speak; I put my arms around his neck instead and settled my head against his shoulder. "What wrong?" he whispered against my hair.

"Too many things," I mumbled.

Take you to bed tonight, he sent. *We talk. And other things.*

I pulled away and nodded mutely; his green eyes held nothing but concern and love for me. *I love you*, I returned.

Know this, he dipped his chin in acknowledgement. *Love you big*, he replied.

~

Quin

The big house was a palace in anyone's estimation. It was built of white stone, with blue and gold-topped domes and trim. It looked to be something from a favorite story instead of the reality it was.

I was surprised about something else, too; Edden and Berel had come. Edden, Bleek and Barc stood with Zaria's other mates who'd come.

Bleek cared about me; I understood that—but his feelings weren't romantic. Instead, his gaze stayed on Zaria much of the time, and I think he was finally making his preference known.

Barc loved Zaria and me; that was easy to see. Young Liron, his eyes round with wonder, gazed about the big house's immense library, where Trajan had set us down.

"Someday, young one," Valegar, one of Zaria's Larentii mates, appeared and lifted Liron in his arms so the boy could see the tall shelves of books better, "I will take you to see the Larentii Archives."

Few know the magnitude of that invitation, Kaldill arrived last and smiled at me.

"Shall we?" A man appeared and motioned for us to follow him.

That is Fes Desh, the best master cook on Tulgalan, Kaldill offered his arm.

Justis went first; Kaldill and I followed, with Valegar carrying Liron behind us. The others followed suit as we walked down many stairs to arrive at the dining room. One wall was floor-to-ceiling glass, which allowed guests to see endless groves of gishi trees below the house.

"Welcome," a man stood at the head of the table. He was tall, with light-brown hair and blue eyes. I would have been a fool if I didn't notice the power that cloaked him, although I couldn't begin to read him.

Beside him stood a woman whose beauty was breathtaking. Black hair rippled down her back, while bright-blue eyes watched all of us carefully.

The man's power enveloped her, keeping me from reading her as well.

"Ashe," Kaldill dipped his head to the man.

This was Strength, who was also called the Mighty Hand. Queen Lissa spoke of him upon occasion.

A god.

One mightier than Liron could ever hope to become.

It made me wonder for a moment about Zaria, who'd killed Liron. What sort of power did she possess to accomplish that?

Wisdom lent her power, Ashe's voice sounded in my head. *He has yet to call it back. Wisdom says it is fine where it is,* he added. Ashe's comment was accompanied by a chuckle.

Then I thank him, and acknowledge his wisdom in doing so as it saved me, I sent back.

Perhaps you will tell him so yourself, someday.

I drew in a breath. Would I meet Wisdom eventually? That would be a true gift. I was sharing mindspeech with Strength, when I never imagined I would. Meeting any of the others would be an incomparable honor.

You have already met Love; you merely didn't recognize her.

I stood, unmoving, while those around me took their seats at the table. When had I met the Mighty Heart? I couldn't recall it.

Don't worry, Ashe nudged me toward my chair and pulled it out with power. *When she is ready, you will see her.*

Dinner was a wonder, and I still can't recall what I ate. Ashe talked and laughed with all his guests, as if he were the same as they. Kay, his beautiful mate, seldom spoke but she was kind and witty in turns when she did so.

Many times, though, Kay glanced from Zaria to me and back again. I wondered why that was, but didn't wish to pry.

~

Paricos II

Ilya

"A bidding war. Brilliant," Gubb was gleeful when I asked to meet all three prospective employers.

That meant he received a percentage of whatever the boss was willing to pay me as a yearly wage. Gubb's death was becoming more intricately painful in my imagination as time went on and I learned more about him.

Zaria's talents would have been welcome when I met with each of the three, but she wasn't here and I wasn't going to involve her in any of this. A part of me recognized the fool I'd become, and how proud that fool actually was rather than admit my mistakes and ask for help.

"First, I have to have a dossier to present to them," Gubb said, lifting a comp-vid and preparing to take notes. "Who have you worked for in the past? Where were you trained, if you were trained to use those blades you carry?"

"I worked for the Eagle Warlord on Falchan," I said. "I was trained by the Falchani Sursee for the Eagle Warlord. I am also trained to handle more sophisticated weapons."

"Have you ever used a ranos pistol?"

"Yes."

"Ranos rifle?"

"Yes." As I suspected, the criminal element on Paricos II had access to weapons they weren't supposed to have. Not that they followed the laws of either alliance, who only allowed ASD and CSD agents to carry the dangerous weaponry that employed ranos technology.

"How did you get training on those weapons?" Gubb pretended disinterest.

"Through a business associate."

"Do you have a name? Nobody on Falchan uses those weapons."

"Not a name I'm willing to give—for professional reasons, you understand."

"Of course. These bosses appreciate that sort of loyalty."

They wouldn't appreciate it if they knew the weapons I'd trained with were ASD issue and provided by Director Griff. "I can operate most hovercraft and fly small transport ships as needed," I offered.

"Licensed?"

"I was before I came here. Those licenses were issued by both Alliances and aren't accepted here, or so I'm told."

"You operated in the Alliances?" Gubb betrayed his rising interest.

"Until I came here."

"It takes talent to do that," a smile crossed Gubb's face for a moment. His price was rising and he knew it. "Can you elaborate on anything you've accomplished?"

"Well," I pretended to consider his request. "I may have been in the vicinity of a bank when accounts were emptied, and somewhere near where murders and kidnappings took place, but I really can't give more detail than that." All those things were true—I just didn't commit any of them.

"Excellent," Gubb's eyes lit with greed.

"And," I added, "I have saved the lives of my associates on many occasions." Some of those lives—Deris and Daris'—shouldn't have been saved. That singular act would leave a black mark on my soul for as long as I lived. They'd helped create and maintain the monster that Cayetes had become, and too many deaths were attributed to those three alone.

"Good. Very Good. I will transmit this information and arrange the meetings," Gubb shut off his comp-vid. "Where may I find you to let you know?"

"I'll be here tomorrow at noon for a meal," I said, rising from the scarred table in his bar. "I have fewer worries if nobody finds me unless I want to be found." Lifting my leather jacket off the bench beside me, I jerked my head at Gubb and strode toward the door.

～

The rooms I'd rented were cleared of insects and invasive animals through the spells I'd cast to eliminate them. The space was also cleaner and better furnished than it had been when I arrived.

The window in the room I'd paid for in the city of Fendala, Paricos II's capital, had a view of the bay where sleek, hover-yachts bobbed above the water next to smaller fishing craft run by locals. At least the oceans of Paricos II were clean, even if the hearts and morals of many of its citizens weren't.

I'd considered bringing in a boat of my own—after buying one elsewhere. Docking fees couldn't be more expensive than the rent I paid for a view of the harbor and little else.

If I were forced to work for a boss, I'd likely be housed at his compound. Many of those lay farther up the hills surrounding Jagged Bay, with high walls enclosing them and guards visible if you looked hard enough.

Word had it that the bosses were involved in everything from assassinations to smuggling. The evidence of smuggling could be seen in most shops, with higher prices on even the commonest of Alliance items.

Some items passed off as Alliance-manufactured were counterfeit, however, and that was another line of income for the bosses. I'd also heard several say that Paricos II was now what Campiaa had been under Arvil San Gerxon, minus the casinos, of course.

Wellend was correct; Paricos II was the perfect place for Vardil Cayetes to reform his empire.

~

Queen's Palace, Le-Ath Veronis

Lissa

Wellend arrived with Warlend, asking to have a private dinner with me. It was an unexpected visit, but they were family—my great grandfather and uncle, actually. They wished to tell me something; I merely had to wait to see what it was.

They no longer looked like Corolan and Warrik, Wylend's former guard and seneschal. They looked like themselves, as they had millennia ago. They'd served in those capacities for Rylend, too, before Zaria revealed their true identities. Ry still trusted both with his life, although they no longer served at the palace.

"We came to ah, clear the air," Warlend's forehead creased with concern. He worried that I'd judge him and Wellend, both.

"For sleeping with Wylend?" I lifted an eyebrow.

"Well, for appearing to sleep with him," the furrows deepened on Warlend's forehead. I'd hit the nail on the head with my first attempt. I was about to tell him that I wasn't concerned with what was in the past, but that would be a lie.

"We had to stay near the throne; I hope you understand that," Wellend began.

"I understand that. What do you mean, *appearing* to sleep?"

"Look, we're talking sex here, not sleeping, and we didn't," Warlend growled.

"How did you pull that off?" I demanded. "Wylend practically wrote poetry to Corolan, he was so good in bed."

"Because it was all in his mind, and that generally tends to be better than the real thing, as often as not. Not that I'm a slouch, you understand. Reah has no regrets, I believe."

"Jeez Louise," I rose from my seat at the table placed inside the arboretum for this private dinner. Reah. Corolan—Warlend—was mated to Reah. How had I forgotten that?

"We've talked. She's trying to come to terms with all this," Warlend said softly. I had my back turned to him and Wellend by this time. Like Reah, I imagined, I was having difficulty coming to terms with it, too.

"How did you pull that off?" I whirled to face them again. "Wylend is Fifth-level. You weren't—Erland said you were both Third-level or thereabouts."

Wellend coughed and looked guilty before ducking his head. It hit me, then. Corolan had been stronger than a Third level—I'd known that about him. It was why Wylend allowed him to act as a bodyguard, or disguise himself and sit the throne. *A fake throne*, I reminded myself.

"Zaria did that," I blinked at both of them.

"The ones we resembled—when she changed us to look like them, their power was added to our own," Warlend admitted. "She didn't tell us to fool Wylend after that; we came up with that on our own, to stay close to the throne."

"We worried at first that someone would attempt a second coup— there were still angry factions among the population. We acted as members of Wylend's personal guard at first, until our—ah—talent at diplomacy came to his attention," Wellend added.

"He wanted us as lovers after a while; we accommodated that request—in our own way, of course. By giving him the best sex dreams he'd ever had."

"An unusual talent," I said dryly. Taking my seat at the table again, my eyes wandered from Warlend to Wellend. "I wish Wylend hadn't done what he did to you," I nodded to Wellend. "Removing your ability to father a child—that's treasonous. I feel it was karma biting his ass when he didn't find Griffin until thousands of years later."

"The universes turn in strange ways, at times," Warlend said. "I'm grateful to my granddaughter that I'm alive and have more power than before. Together, Wellend and I have protected the Karathian throne, even when we didn't always agree with Wylend's decisions or actions."

"The perennial problem of serving royalty," I agreed, allowing my shoulders to sag. I realized I'd been holding myself stiffly and had an aching neck and shoulders for my trouble.

"Let's have some wine," I suggested. "I think this has been difficult for all of us and we need to loosen up. Let's leave the past where it is." I gave both a fake smile; I secretly hoped we could leave the past behind, but that is often much more difficult than it sounds.

I lifted the bottle of white from its wine bucket as Wellend and Warlend exchanged troubled glances and sighed.

~

V'ili

Vardil rolled three spheres in his fingers, as if they were mere baubles instead of precious items worth perhaps trillions in Alliance credits. He stared hard at the one who'd come to bargain for his planet.

"Not enough," Vardil hissed. "You can do better than that. Where do you think you'll go when the poison kills everything?" he demanded.

Devarr, King of Carek Prime, shuddered imperceptibly. Already, hospitals on his non-Alliance planet were filling up with those afflicted by the poison disease. He needed to do something quickly, to save what was left of his dying world.

I wanted to laugh at the situation. Inadvertently, Vardil had accomplished what most criminals only dream of; creating a problem, then charging as much as he could to fix it. Devarr, perhaps, was paying now for his refusal to join either Alliance, although his world would qualify. Isolationistic, most called Carek Prime.

"This is all I can afford," Devarr handed a comp-vid to Vardil. The revised amount was larger than the previous offer, by a third.

"Much, much better. Transfer that, and this will be yours," Vardil held up one of the spheres. "Guaranteed to work. I'll give a full refund, too, if you can bring me this." He lifted his own comp-vid from the desk and handed it to Devarr.

"A winged woman? How is that even possible?" Devarr's voice broke.

"As I said, find her, deliver her to me, your wealth will be restored." Vardil leaned back in his chair while still toying with the spheres. "In the meantime, transfer those funds to me now, and you'll have your salvation."

~

Paricos II

Ilya

I disliked Weir of Paricos II the moment I met him. Tall, thin, nervous; he unsettled even his seasoned bodyguards. This was why he was willing to pay a high price—he had trouble keeping employees.

"No," I told Gubb after the meeting was over and Weir and his guards left Gubb's small office over the bar. "Absolutely not."

"Ah, I see you have discerning taste," Gubb grinned. I wanted to punch him for it. "Perhaps the next will be more to your liking, then," he added.

Zarbec of Paricos II was a simpering, conniving sphincter. I had no use for him; he only spoke of himself in the grandest of terms, as if his underlings didn't carry out every miraculous thing he ascribed to himself.

"No," I hissed at Gubb once the meeting had concluded.

Gubb's eyes widened; he'd been so sure of this one. He'd deliberately put Weir first, knowing the effect he'd have on anyone with more than one brain cell firing. He'd put his money on Zarbec as a much better alternative.

"If the next is no better than the first two," I hissed a warning at Gubb. I didn't have my blades with me, but that didn't matter. I had my warlock skills, and I wanted nothing more than to send Gubb to the sea for a good dunking.

Several good dunkings, actually.

Gubb's mouth hung open and worked for several seconds before he could form words. "I—I could only arrange for a subordinate from Master Tamp," Gubb whispered. I realized then that Gubb's shirt was twisted in my hand and my eyes bored into his. He was outmatched and he knew it.

"What subordinate? Who is Master Tamp?" I demanded.

"Master Tamp keeps to himself and only goes out in disguise," Gubb warbled. "He specializes in treasure hunting. Sells things to— certain collectors. The subordinate—I didn't recognize the name when it was given to me."

I released Gubb's shirt, then, and stepped back before nodding. "Bring him in. I'll speak to him."

"I'll go get him. Now." I'd unsettled Gubb.

Good.

~

Lew Velker

He was Falchani trained. My eyes strayed to that particular line in his dossier as I studied him. Not Falchani, mind you, but anyone the Falchani agreed to train was formidable, or they wouldn't have agreed to the training.

This is a warrior, my mind warned me.

Subtle.

Deadly.

They all were who'd passed a Sursee's tests.

I felt as if his dark eyes assessed me. Read in me that I was university-trained in antiquities.

That I'd lost my credentials by obtaining artifacts by less than scrupulous means. I wanted to squirm under his gaze, but that would be unprofessional, besides allowing my insecurities to dictate my actions.

Breathe, I reminded myself.

Master Tamp wanted this one—to protect me on Alliance worlds while I searched for more of the spheres. I was now in charge of his treasure hunting operations, and he wanted the best security for me, since I had experience the others lacked.

I'd been well-paid for what I'd I brought to him; in the past, I'd never seen him in person. He'd taken an interest in what I held this time—a great deal of interest. Enough that I'd actually met him, although I couldn't be sure whether the face he showed me was disguised or genuine.

It didn't matter; I now had a steady, generous income and the ability to do what I did best—with guards at my back to protect me while I did it.

~

Ilya

Lew Velker. I intended to research that name the moment our meeting was over. A criminal treasure hunter, no doubt, but there was culture in his voice, if not in his weathered face and unruly, sun-bleached hair.

The name could be fake, I reminded myself. It broadened my search parameters, but that was of little consequence. It wouldn't be the first time a trained archaeologist had succumbed to the lure of treasure, ill-gotten or otherwise.

"May I ask what it is you'll be searching for?" I queried.

"Not until you are in Master Tamp's employ," Velker attempted to appear bored. He was anything but—his body language spoke volumes of how tense he actually was.

"Then name your terms," I said, dipping my chin to show my interest.

"Ah, uh, a quarter of a million credits per sun-turn, if the work is satisfactory," Velker stumbled over the word *satisfactory*. What he didn't say was that Master Tamp would order me killed—or attempt to do so, if the work was anything but satisfactory.

"I was hoping for twice that," I countered. I knew what elite bodyguards were paid by their criminal bosses. Loyalty and ability came at a high price.

"I am only authorized to offer up to four hundred thousand," he flinched under my hard gaze.

"Then four hundred thousand will have to do," I snapped. "Until you recognize my worth, that is."

So many emotions crossed his face, chief among them fear. He was afraid of me.

Good.

~

Queen's Palace, Le-Ath Veronis

Lissa

"How long before they learn your replacement for the Avii Castle is fake?" Gavin asked at breakfast. "You moved all the Black Wing guards with the real thing. Nobody is left, now, to pull idiots out of the water when they jump off a boat."

"Crap." I rubbed my forehead. "I suppose I'll have to ask Justis to provide volunteers to stay at the fake."

"You could send some of ours to stay there, in case anybody gets the idea to try to get in and do a kidnapping or two."

"ASD or from our army?" I asked. Gavin was making sense; I just hated that I hadn't considered this to begin with.

"How about both?" Gavin shrugged and reached for another biscuit.

"My gosh, you're handsome when you're right," I said, studying his face and the line of his jaw.

I watched as his mouth pulled into a slow smile. He buttered the biscuit as he considered a reply. "I wouldn't say no to a bit of fun before the council meeting," he said as if he were discussing the weather.

"Honey, let me put in a call to Kooper, and then I'm all yours."

"Exactly what I wanted to hear," he chuckled.

~

Avii Castle, Avendor

Quin

"Ardis is taking most of the Black Wing troops back to Le-Ath Veronis with him—to make the replacement castle Lissa put up appear authentic in every way," Justis informed me over lunch. "They're leaving this afternoon."

"But what if they're attacked?" I breathed. Dena wouldn't like it if she and Ardis were parted—their baby was barely three moon-turns old.

"The ASD and Queen Lissa are providing troops to help guard the castle. I hear that she's planning to give them a device that will make it appear as if they have wings when they stand on the terraces and such. Dena, ah, she elected to return with Ardis."

"No," I began.

"Quin, she gets to make her own decisions. It isn't an unreasonable request. Servants will be provided by Queen Lissa to look after all of them. The ASD and the Queen's troops will be well-armed. A few other wives are returning with their Black Wing mates, too. They understand the dangers, my love."

His words unsettled me. How could he say they understood? They'd never been flung onto Vardil Cayetes' ships, or seen the death and destruction he was capable of dealing.

He'd destroyed Siriaa, their home planet, for the gods' sake.

"It's their choice," Justis stroked a hand down my feathers, which had risen and ruffled with the anger and frustration I felt. "The others are happy to be here and appreciate the freedom to fly unhindered as far as they want."

"I can't help but believe they are placing themselves in unnecessary danger," I said, setting my napkin on the table and looking into Justis' dark eyes.

"I know," Justis continued to stroke my wing. "I have seen you fly into danger many times, my love, and every time you do that, my heart stops and my feathers rise. Do not deny these that same freedom, I beg you."

He was right. "I only want to keep them safe," I mumbled and dropped my eyes to my hands, which trembled in my lap. "I know you want the same," I admitted. "I hope they come to no harm."

"As do I."

CHAPTER 3

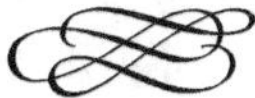

vii Castle, Avendor
Quin

"Three spheres are missing." Queen Lissa's voice was flat. She reined in her anger at this setback—I could see it in the stiffness of her shoulders and the stern line of her mouth.

Three spheres I'd placed had been stolen. "By whom?" I felt close to tears. Three worlds were back where they were before I'd placed the spheres to save them. "Do they know?" My voice trembled.

Justis' hands gripped my shoulders and pulled me against his chest. This was the worst of news. "They know," Lissa's shoulders drooped. "I told them this morning. It seems the Lord Mayor of a nearby city on Gilvos was blackmailed to reveal what the sphere was to a treasure hunter. He gave information on the other two worlds we visited in that three-world trip. We're attempting to track the treasure hunter now, and the Lord Mayor is in custody, but that gets us nowhere. We don't have the true identity on the treasure hunter and he's off everybody's radar."

"You think he's been hired by Cayetes, don't you?" Justis' chest rumbled against my wings as he spoke.

"Or someone just as bad—there are plenty of criminals on non-

Alliance worlds who deal in ill-gotten treasure and antiquities. They have a full list of buyers, many of them not considered criminals and possibly living on Alliance worlds, who are wealthy enough to place these things in private collections that the public has no knowledge of."

Zaria, who stood nearby with her arms folded tightly against her chest, was flanked by Bleek, Bekzi and Edden. Her face was pale and grim; she didn't like this turn of events. She'd suspected that treasure hunters were searching for the spheres; to learn that three had already been stolen was more than upsetting to her.

"Do we have enough to replace those three?" Edden asked. As always, the diplomat among us searched for a viable solution for the problem we faced.

"We do, unless those bastards steal more, or more worlds are found that are poisoned. If that happens, any surplus we have will disappear and worlds will die anyway," Lissa replied.

"We have to modify the shields around what has already been placed," Zaria grumbled. "And we have to do that now, instead of hunting the filth stealing from us."

"We have others to hunt, too—don't forget that," Bleek offered.

He was right—we'd never found the wealthy captives that Cayetes had kidnapped. Who knew where they were? The ASD was still looking; they'd merely had few results in their search.

The banking accounts and holdings for all those people were still intact for now, but with Cayetes healthy and back in business, that could be temporary.

"Kooper is tracking all their business concerns," Lissa said as she practically read my mind. "So far, it's business as usual and not even a ping from all that."

"He can afford to wait," Edden said. "We don't know those kidnap victims are alive. Cayetes can wait years—until we lose interest and he has time to plot and take that wealth in a single move."

"Frightening," Lissa breathed.

"What if somebody beats him to it?" Zaria asked.

"What?" Lissa's head turned swiftly in Zaria's direction.

"Cayetes wants the black-winged woman. He also wants to destroy her pirate ships. He doesn't let go of a grudge—we've all seen evidence of that. I think we should wipe out as many accounts as we can, funnel that money back to the families discreetly under different names and business concerns, and then let the ASD put up their new most-wanted list, with a black-winged woman at the top of it."

"You think it'll deflect his attention from the spheres—if he's the one hunting them?" Lissa's eyebrows lifted and the dim light of hope grew stronger in her eyes.

"He never forgets things like that," Zaria shrugged. "He'll come after the BlackWing pirates; you can count on it."

"He'll redouble his efforts to find Quin," Justis voiced his concern as he pulled me tighter against him.

"The Orb is no more," Zaria reminded him gently. "She wouldn't be susceptible to it even if it still existed. It cannot appear and fling her wherever it wants any longer. She will be protected, Lord King."

"I say we do it," Lissa said. "I'll have to meet with Kooper, Ildevar and a few others, but that's the best option I've heard in a while."

"You cannot take everything," Edden spoke a sharp reminder. "Remember, if those victims are alive, we have to hold something back to ensure their lives continue."

"Then let's start with half," Lissa grinned at him. "I think that should be sufficient, don't you?"

Zaria

Lissa wanted me to look at the family members who could be trusted to keep the secret of the transferred funds, but to present their case to the media that the funds had been removed suddenly, indicating theft. They would also say they'd been interviewed by the ASD afterward, to collect evidence in the supposed thefts.

Shortly after, the ASD would make their announcements known— that the BlackWing pirates were their prime suspects.

I handed her a list of names—most often second or third in line who only wanted their family members returned safely. We were throwing the dice, and they accepted the possibility that their loved ones could already be dead.

This was a way to track Cayetes and leave half the family funds in their complete control. The ones I chose were grateful for that; they'd worried the accounts would be emptied, leaving their families in poverty.

After all, half of enormous wealth was still enormous wealth—in most people's eyes.

"You're pensive this morning," Edden placed a cup of coffee in my hands as I sat on the Library terrace at Avii Castle.

"Just thinking," I looked up at him and offered a smile. Already, the power of SouthStar was making its presence known—small age lines in his face had disappeared, leaving only youthfulness behind.

"Mind if I sit with you?"

"Of course not," I patted the seat of the covered porch swing beside me. I'd placed several of them on the Library terrace—Gurnil was using them to read and eat lunch, now, since the weather at SouthStar was so fine.

"It's almost like the wake of a large boat, flowing in the wrong direction," Edden sighed as he looked out at the split river flowing around Avii Castle. "Have you had breakfast?"

"Well, I was soaking up sunlight," I said. "Although eggs would be nice."

"Good, because I ordered for both of us. It should arrive soon."

"You are an amazing man," I lifted my cup to him. He smiled. He had a nice smile. I learned that morning that he also had a nice kiss.

Very nice.

"If you two will stop necking," Bleek set a tray on the table in front of us and pulled in another swing with only two of his four hands. "We can have breakfast," he added. "I commandeered the tray from a Yellow Wing," he waved away Edden's comments before he could make any.

"Bleek has ah—news," Edden said, smoothing my hair back. A light breeze had swept the terrace, lifting my hair as it passed.

"What news?" I turned to Bleek.

"That my photograph has been included with the others of the BlackWing pirates."

"You really want to infuriate Cayetes, don't you?" I blinked at him.

"Yes," Bleek settled on his seat and lifted his plate from the tray to eat. "He owes me—for the lies he told and what he did to Barc."

I didn't disagree—Bleek was right. Vardil Cayetes didn't care that Barc would die if pulled from the glass coffin. He held the boy hostage to keep Bleek under his command. If Quin hadn't healed Barc, the boy would have been destroyed.

"Besides—my image alone, and the fact that I defected to the enemy will ensure that Cayetes comes out swinging. I want to make that first punch against him."

"That's a long line you're standing in," Edden pointed out and dipped into his food. "It'll take strategic jostling to get the first spot."

"Six lobes," Bleek tapped his head.

I laughed.

~

Paricos II

Ilya

I found no information on Lew Velker. I even tried variations on the name and nothing came up. Whomever he was, his real existence was successfully covered up. I entered new search parameters on the comp-vid; at least it was protected against use by others, as well as detection by others.

The device was ASD issue, with a DNA passcode and undetectable. I preferred it that way. *Search for ousted archaeologists, any institution*, I entered the command. I wanted as much information as I could get before reporting for my first day at work the following morning.

Gubb had gotten his fee; I knew that much. He'd smiled at me when I showed up at his bar earlier for dinner, and didn't charge me for what I ate and drank.

"Generous of him," I muttered while the comp-vid worked on my latest request.

Velker hadn't told me where Tamp kept his compound; he'd merely asked me to meet him at Gubb's bar the following morning. Transportation would be arranged for us from there. I figured the compound was large enough to house more than it actually held; I'd asked Gubb about Tamp.

"A recluse," he'd said immediately. "Changes disguises often. Has an extensive collection of artifacts himself, besides what he sells—if the rumors are true. Don't cross him," Gubb added. "Nobody knows exactly where his compound is. He does business with others at predetermined locations."

I gave no indication to Gubb that crossing Tamp was certainly on my agenda. We'd see who came out on top. Meanwhile, it was my duty to size up his compound, determine what he held to keep it safe (both in manpower and weapons), find whether he'd had contact with Cayetes and follow any leads I uncovered.

If Cayetes were on Paricos II, it made sense that the bosses would know of it by now. He threatened their very existence, if they knew anything about what happened to Vic'Law.

For now, I hadn't heard rumblings of a turf war, but that could change, once I got inside Tamp's quarters.

Time to let my current landlord know I was moving out.

~

Avii Castle, Avendor
Quin

"These three," Zaria tapped the names of three planets on a comp-vid. "They won't know we've been there until we're gone, and we certainly won't tell any of them where their sphere is buried."

The worlds she'd chosen weren't the three I was previously scheduled to visit. Those—the information that they were next on the list could have been told, sold or stolen.

We understood that.

"We'll hit those three separately on later dates, so nobody will suspect," Zaria said, reading my concerns easily. "BlackWing VII, in disguise, of course, will house us while we're away from SouthStar."

"Who will come with us?" I asked. I couldn't expect Queen Lissa; I'd already used up a great deal of her time, and she had her own planet to rule. Besides, she was in charge of strengthening the wards around the remaining spheres I'd placed—in an attempt to keep future thieves away.

"Kooper is sending one of his agents," a smile lurked about Zaria's lips. "Jana asked for this assignment."

Jana had barely finished her ASD training. We would be her first official assignment. I felt joy and apprehension at the same time. I worried that she'd be in as much danger as Dena could be, merely by association.

She understands the danger—perhaps better than most, Zaria's voice entered my mind. *And she deserves this—Cayetes killed her family, remember?*

Now I understood why Zaria sent those words in mindspeech. The ASD had a rule against any agent being directly involved in an investigation, if the agent's family were involved in the crime—either as victims or perpetrators. Likely, that information had been kept from ASD files and Kooper had turned his head when Jana asked for this assignment.

I understand that, I returned. It was what I would do in Jana's place. "When is she coming?" I asked aloud.

"We leave tomorrow morning for BlackWing VII. She'll meet us aboard ship. Salidar is also coming—to keep up with your training and to take command of the ship, since Caylon is currently unavailable."

~

Queen's Palace, Le-Ath Veronis
Lissa
"Are you going to tell Zaria that we have Ilya working this

assignment from another angle?" Erland set his empty bourbon glass on my desk, after producing a coaster he'd *Pulled* from the kitchen.

"Not unless she asks a direct question," I said, making a face at Erland. "What's the latest word?"

"Ry says that Ilya's latest report indicates he was forced to accept employment with one of the local bosses, as a bodyguard. It may be fortuitous—the bosses will know better than anyone whether someone else has joined their ranks uninvited."

"Then I hope this bears fruit soon," I said. "He won't like it if he's forced to do something that's less than ethical."

Neither Erland nor I said the word murder, but it was at the forefront of both our thoughts. Granted, Paricos II was a lawless world, but innocents could be sprinkled easily among the criminals. Cooking or cleaning wasn't a crime, even if it were done for the worst of the worst.

"He's been instructed to use his best judgment, and to get away if he's threatened or required to do something that goes against his conscience," Erland said. "Let's hope he understands to take good advice when it's given, this time."

"Yeah." I leaned back in my chair and forced tension from my shoulders. Erland's eyes narrowed as he studied me from across my desk. "You know something I don't," he accused.

"Erland, now isn't the time," I said. "It isn't anything I can discuss—with anybody."

"Outside the original Three." His guess was shrewd. Not many could hide something from my Karathian warlock mate.

I mimed locking my lips and tossing an invisible key over my shoulder.

"Very well," Erland sighed. "I'll keep you updated, as requested."

"Thank you," I said, grateful for his patience. I had a feeling that after a while, everybody would know what I did, and the fates of more than one would be settled for all time.

~

Paricos II

    Ilya

The chopper was fast; even so, it took nearly an hour to reach Tamp's compound. I blinked at the ingenuity of it; a massive, high rock, surrounded by a rough sea, bore Master Tamp's quarters. Built into the rock itself, the compound began halfway up the monolith, above the point where crashing waves couldn't reach it.

The side facing the land gave no indication that the rock was inhabited—one had to fly to the other side to see lights shining from the recessed windows carved into it.

I felt it, too, once the chopper passed the perimeter—Tamp had warding spells up to fool more mundane visitors. He already had wizards or warlocks in his employ.

It made sense, if Tamp were the wealthy, reclusive collector and bargainer that Gubb described.

The chopper lowered to a wide, flat heli-port, jutting out near the monolith's top. The pad was still hidden from the landward side, but large enough to hold a small fleet of choppers or hovercraft.

"Come," Velker motioned for me to follow him, once we'd disembarked from the chopper. Winds keened and blew fiercely about the rock, strong enough to rock even the heaviest of hovercraft parked about us as I wound my way through them, following Velker toward the cave-like doorway. Heavy mist, flung by the wind, nearly blinded me several times before we reached that destination.

Once the auto-doors closed behind us, the absence of wind, water and sound felt like salvation to my battered ears and body.

The inhabitants were used to getting wet; Velker and I walked over a heat-grate, with warm air blowing away the chill and moisture before we'd finished crossing it.

"Tamp is waiting." We'd crossed another threshold, to find a woman waiting there for us.

"Master Tamp wishes to see us?" I heard surprise in Velker's voice, although he attempted to hide it.

"He does." She was tall, dark-haired, beautiful and as hard as a diamond. Her eyes settled on me and lingered for longer than I deemed necessary.

I wanted to tell her that she could keep her interest to herself. I'd had the best; she could never compete with that, or even the memory of it.

"Thank you, Arna," Velker's voice turned silkier, as if he could draw her attention to himself by changing his voice. She'd dismissed him already, in favor of what she considered more dangerous prey. Perhaps I should feel flattered.

What a useless emotion.

"You may be surprised when you first see Master Tamp," Arna informed me as Velker and I followed her to a waiting trans-vator. I didn't fail to hear Velker's low snort. "He understands that others find him—unusual," Arna's lips thinned in anger as she glared at Velker.

"In other words, don't make a big deal out of it," Velker hissed as Arna instructed the trans-vator to take us to level twenty-seven.

❧

Karathia

King Rylend Morphis

"Tamp is a pod'l-morph?" Attempting to keep my eyes in my head rather than allowing them to bug out at this news wasn't as easy as someone might think.

"They're rarer than female vampires," Dad huffed. "Can mimic anything—animal, vegetable or mineral, as your mother is so fond of saying."

"He sent the images, or I may have been skeptical," Wellend blew out a breath. We sat at the breakfast table; Wellend let us know he had news, so I'd invited him to join us.

"It's my understanding that only his mother may know the real image he was born with—and we thought chasing Vardil when he was switching bodies was difficult," Wellend scraped butter across a croissant before taking a bite.

At times, I missed him as Warrik, but Warrik had served the crown long and well. This was a former King of Karathia, even if his rule lasted less than a month.

He bequeathed the throne to me, I reminded myself. I held the rule of Karathia by his initial permission. Bel Erland was my heir and next in line, with Zaria's permission. It made me uncomfortable upon occasion; how could it not? Still, he'd taken his vows to protect the throne and the King. That should be enough.

I think he and Warlend knew, however, that things just weren't the same. Everybody tiptoed about the subject of their dual existence for years uncounted. As for Wylend, word had it that he seethed with the knowledge of what he considered their duplicity.

They'd protected his behind for years, and this was their thanks for that loyalty and effort on his behalf. I wanted to sigh at the injustice of it.

"No wonder Tamp has been able to survive so long to do what he does," Dad observed, drawing me away from my thoughts. "Who knows how many times he's changed locations to stay in business? Did Ilya say whether he'd seen any of Tamp's treasures?"

"Nothing yet; he's been forced to follow his immediate supervisor around, listening to what this treasure-hunting servant of Tamp's wants in the way of protection. Apparently, this one considers himself Tamp's finest and expects Ilya to bow to his every whim."

"Anything else to note as yet? Nothing on whether Cayetes has infiltrated Paricos II?" I asked.

"No, but he's barely been in Tamp's employ for a day. I'm hoping for more news later, as he settles into the job." Wellend cut into his eggs and ham, carefully—and correctly—placing a bit of each on his fork and bringing it to his mouth.

How many times had I watched him eat with Grampa Wylend, with the same impeccable manners? This was my great uncle, after all. Yes, he and Warlend had explained how they'd gotten around coupling with Wylend. It made me wonder how Wylend felt about that, too.

It concerned me, actually.

Wylend couldn't be accused of always employing the best of

judgment in matters of the heart. He'd lost Reah that way—by overreacting.

A part of me was glad. Reah was having some difficulty coming to terms with things as they were—with Warlend. She certainly shouldn't have to worry about Wylend, too, and his reaction to the entire mess.

"Things can't help but be complicated, can they?" Wellend's guess was shrewd as he studied me.

"Please, continue your meal," I waved a hand. "Things will get sorted or they won't."

"I'm hoping for sorted." Wellend frowned and went back to his food.

~

Avii Castle, Avendor

Quin

"Everybody ready?" Trajan had arrived to take us to BlackWing VII.

"I think we're ready," Zaria answered. We were—packed bags lay all around us, ready for transport. Only a few knew our destination, and none of those would reveal that information to anyone who shouldn't have it.

It was my hope that the spheres we were prepared to bury on affected worlds would be safe from predation this time. I studied my shoes as my feathers rustled, revealing my anxiety.

Justis and I had taken flight only that morning, to say a private good-bye away from the castle. Nowhere else was that possible—Avendor was safe for the Avii King to fly as he willed.

"We can only do our best," Zaria tipped up my chin. I blinked into bright-blue eyes; she offered comfort with her touch and I was grateful. In seconds, I was wrapped in her arms while warmth and healing surrounded me.

Stop worrying, she breathed into my mind.

I can't help it, I replied.

I know.

We were still embraced when Trajan moved us.

❧

BlackWing VII
Zaria

James and Nathan were piloting the ship, still, and enjoyed their work. Sal had taken charge of the ship already, and was in contact with Director Griff concerning our position and course.

Lafe, Quin and Terrett had gone to sort out their berths, which lay next to one another. Yanzi was across the hall. Kaldill hadn't joined us for this short trip, although he would come if Quin sent mindspeech.

Instead, Daragar was the one to shield the ship for us. I could have done it, but he was more than willing.

"Tea," Edden handed a cup to me as I sat in the empty dining hall, watching stars shoot past us as we traveled toward our first destination.

"Sit with me," I invited.

"That's why I'm here," he grinned. "Bleek is on his comp-vid, speaking with Master Morwin on Avendor. He's quite particular about keeping up with Barc's studies."

"Already? We haven't been underway for twenty minutes," I sipped the tea Edden brought. It was hot and welcome; already I felt cold as the black emptiness surrounding the stars passed us by.

"I, ah, believe Barc wasn't pleased that his father was leaving without him," Edden coughed.

"Oh. Now I get it," I said. "Everybody Barc likes to hang out with is on this ship."

"Hang out?"

"It's an old Earth term. It means associate with, or be with."

"I see. Want to hang out with me?" he grinned again.

"Of course."

❧

Paricos II

Ilya

If I hadn't seen Tamp changing in front of me without the use of any wizard's or warlock's power, I'd have doubted his words.

He was, in all ways, a pod'l-morph. Striding this way and that as he'd spoken, he'd shifted to many forms while I watched, struggling to keep my thoughts behind a mask of indifference. The most disconcerting of his changes involved a large, talking succulent.

Yes, I'd heard of pod'l-morphs. Children's stories were written about the rare beings. I never thought to see one. It made sense that he was running a criminal operation—he could disguise himself as anything and escape the notice of authorities.

I wondered what Zaria and Quin would make of him. Would they see through his shifting to the real creature beneath?

I wished for one or both of them during my brief interview with Tamp. As for Velker, I already wanted to strangle him. He'd constructed complex scenarios, each of which involved an attack upon his person while he was involved in his treasure-hunting. I was supposed to outline my reaction to his attackers, so he would know what to expect.

I wanted to laugh in his face. Every attempt to kill him or take him into custody would be different. Location, terrain, whether it was local authorities, ASD, CSD, or even another treasure hunter, would change the scenario.

I didn't bother to tell him that. It came as a surprise that he'd survived as long as he had, in my estimation.

Fool's luck, I reminded myself.

"We have teams hired on several worlds. They're scouting for the treasure now. If they find something, they're instructed to hold back and wait until I arrive. It requires delicate maneuvers to extract it."

My concern that other treasure hunters could be our main opponents rose significantly. He'd babbled on about everything except what I wanted to hear—that Cayetes had somehow appeared on Paricos II, or figured into the equation in some way.

"So we have buyers already for the treasure?" I ventured during a lull in Velker's one-sided conversation.

"Of course," Velker lied. "Tamp wouldn't bother if there were no money in it. That's all for today—I'm waiting for word from two of my teams. Be ready to go quickly if that word comes, even if it's received in the middle of your sleep period."

"I understand." I turned to go; I'd been assigned quarters on the lowest level of the compound, where the booming of waves could be heard, even through thick rock. At least I had a window to look out at the sea.

I wondered, too, why Velker lied. It was easy to read his body language in this. Likely it didn't matter—he was being paid well enough, I think, to hunt whatever Tamp wanted.

"If you need additional clothing, weapons or armor, send the message through the comp-vid mounted on the wall in your quarters. You'll find a ranos pistol and rifle waiting there already."

"That should be sufficient," I said. "Thank you, Master Velker."

It irritated me greatly to call him that, but he was puffed up and pleased with the title when I left him and strode toward the transvator.

~

BlackWing VII
Quin

"We have this." Sal set a comp-vid on the table. He'd called a quick meeting after hearing from Director Griff. Zaria, Bleek, Edden, Berel, Terrett and Lafe sat at the table with me, waiting to hear what Sal had to say.

There was no mistaking the images on the comp-vid. Bleek's photograph, next to mine in my former disguise, were very prominent. "These were found on the assassins' sites," Sal informed us. "They're offering a substantial reward for both of you—Bleek dead, Quin alive."

"Good." Bleek folded all four arms across his chest with a satisfied grunt.

"I really don't like that you're a target," Zaria informed him quietly. He turned toward her, then. I could tell he was touched that she cared.

"I can cross my arms over my chest, too," she told him, her voice tart.

"Yes, but two arms just don't have the same effect," he grinned.

"Oh, sure, pull out the four-arm card," she snipped. "Followed by the six-lobe card."

"It works," he chuckled.

"You're insufferable," she swatted one of his arms.

"No—if I had two cocks, I'd be insufferable. As it is, I'm merely confident."

I watched Sal attempt to suppress a laugh. A snicker escaped anyway. Lafe turned his head to hide the grin; Edden, Terrett and Berel didn't bother to hold back their laughter.

"We'll be in orbit around Benvali tomorrow morning," Sal said when the laughter died down. "We'll wait until darkness falls on the proper side of the planet before sending our team down to plant a sphere. Queen Lissa will come to help Daragar lay better wards around it."

"I hope they work," I breathed a sigh. I couldn't help thinking about three worlds that had already been stripped of their salvation. The feeling of helplessness that came with those thoughts overwhelmed me for a moment.

"It'll all come right," Lafe reached out to massage my neck. "We'll make sure of it."

"I hope you're right," I mumbled before laying my head on my arms at the table. Lafe's massage felt good on muscles tightened by worry and stress.

CHAPTER 4

envali

Zaria

"The biggest concentration of the poison is in this area," Quin spoke softly. A large city wasn't far away, which made our operation that much more dangerous—I had tight shields up as a result, so the local inhabitants couldn't see us or what we were about to do.

Without *Looking*, I knew the nearby city had been hit hardest with sickness and death related to the poison. *I feel it too,* Lissa's mental voice informed me; she'd arrived the moment Daragar transported us to the surface of Benvali.

"We must plant this one deep," Daragar said. "Perhaps that, in itself, will discourage any from looking for it."

"And protect it from those looking to build upon this surface in the future," Edden observed. Already, he was seeing the city's growth in years to come, provided the poison was stopped and the planet allowed to continue on a normal path.

"I'll set the wards far enough below the surface to allow for that," Lissa acknowledged.

"Quin," I said, "I'll link with you, so you can tell me how far down to open the hole."

"All right."

Extending my hand and my power, I began to create a narrow hole between Quin and me. At more than six hundred fifty feet, she asked me to stop. "There," she breathed. I pulled away from her then, to watch what she did next.

Pulling a sphere from her jacket pocket, she whispered to it in the language spoken by the Avii.

"Come," she instructed, before dropping the sphere into the hole. I made sure it made its way to the bottom before sealing the ground around it, as if a hole had never been made.

Light formed about Lissa, then, as she set the wards. The area sang with her power as she lay them; far enough below the surface that treasure hunters wouldn't feel it.

That was our mistake before, she informed me in mindspeech. *Setting the wards nearer to the surface so that anyone getting close could feel them. How could they not know something was there? Combine that with a Lord Mayor who has a strong case of OCD and you have disaster waiting to happen.*

He knew about the other two worlds done during the same trip, I guessed. *What did they blackmail him with?*

Embezzlement, Lissa replied. *He'd lose his job. Turns out, he lost all that anyway, and will spend time in prison for his shenanigans.*

Too bad for him—and for us, I replied. *He sentenced those worlds to death a second time, too, unless we get the spheres back.*

Those worlds' leaders haven't made the announcement to the general population, yet. I imagine there'll be rioting when the truth is discovered.

Amazing, isn't it, how one man can kill so many?

Are you talking about Cayetes or the Lord Mayor?

Both.

Yeah. I think we've both seen their kind before.

Yeah.

"Wards are done, let's hope this isn't a useless gesture," Lissa announced aloud.

"I second that," I said. Daragar transported us back to the ship so we could plan our next stealth mission.

~

Paricos II

Ilya

My life as Velker's bodyguard looked to be a boring one between treasure hunts. I had too much time to think—on past mistakes and such. That's why I went looking among those who provided security for Tamp, hoping at least one of them knew how to fight with blades.

"You know how to fight with a knife?" The chief of security studied me in speculation.

"Yes. And with swords, poles and anything else you have at hand. I can also make the blades in question, should the need arise."

"Falchani-type blades?"

"Yes, but those take time to make properly."

"Tamp has a market for those things," Chief Darkins said. "Properly made, as you say. He has no patience—and no market—for poorly-made fakes."

"You'll need a forge, and I haven't seen one on the premises," I pointed out.

"That would be nothing," Darkins waved a hand. "Make a list of what you'd require, and I'll present it to Tamp. I doubt he'll turn the opportunity down, but he'll examine the blades you make carefully afterward. If they're not up to his standards," Darkins warned.

I wanted to laugh in his face. I'd spent nearly twelve hundred years, a century at a time here and there on Falchan, making blades for the Warlord's army. Some I'd made had been passed down through the generations. I knew what I was doing.

"I'll need apprentices or those willing to help—a love for the making is a necessity, because of the time involved."

"I'll leave you in charge of hiring them," Darkins said. "Mind, Tamp will either approve or disapprove. Make your choices wisely."

~

Tamp's approval came swiftly and forced any complaints Velker might have to stay behind his teeth. I'd been given permission to hire as many as six apprentices, too, at an adequate compensation.

I wanted none from Paricos II—I'd seen the riff-raff that wasn't already employed by this boss or that. I was forced to send mindspeech to King Rylend, asking for suitable recruits.

After all, six spies were better than one; I could be called away to who knew where by Velker at a moment's notice, leaving the compound behind and a potential gap in information.

Apprentices could be left behind to keep their eyes and ears open for news of Cayetes.

Let me think on this. I'll let you know tomorrow, Rylend's reply came shortly after I sent my request.

At least two Falchani, I returned. *The rest are your choice, as long as they know what they're getting into.*

Noted, Ry agreed.

∼

Le-Ath Veronis
Lissa

"We need either Quin or Zaria there, and Quin is needed to place spheres," I said. Ry and Erland stood in my private study, informing me of the latest from Ilya.

"Ilya will likely balk when we send Zaria," Ry pointed out.

"Ilya is under orders from his king," I shot back. "Tell him to suck it up and behave professionally."

"Who is going to help Quin, then?" Erland asked.

"I had an unusual offer," I said. "About ten minutes before you got here."

"From?" Erland lifted a well-shaped, dark eyebrow. He's gorgeous, even when he's skeptical.

"From Kay." I said it. I still didn't believe it. The most unbelievable part was that Ashe agreed to let her go. She held sufficient power to help Quin, and if she didn't, Ashe would lend her something to make it so.

"You think Ashe is taking a personal interest in all this?"

"Hell, several people are taking a personal interest in all this," I huffed. I'd included myself in that statement, I just didn't say it aloud.

"So, Zaria and who else?" Ry asked.

"He said two Falchani. I'd ask Caylon, but he's a new father so that's out of the question. How about Turtle and Flyer?"

"Those two sound good. We have Zaria, Turtle and Flyer. Who else?"

"Send the Blevakian." Charles, also known as Wisdom, arrived in my office and settled on the edge of my desk with a grin. It was now official—all three of the original Mighty had taken a personal interest in this.

"Why?" I asked. I couldn't help myself.

"We'll see if Tamp has a close relationship with Cayetes, first off. If he's interested in Cayetes, or willing to do anything Cayetes asks, then Bleek will be handed over right away, don't you think? If that's not true and Tamp makes his own decisions, then Bleek should be safe enough."

"Bleek doesn't have power," I began my argument.

"No, but Zaria does, as do Turtle and Flyer. Bleek is also adept at using blades—with all four hands. I doubt he'll be in danger long, especially if Zaria has a way to locate him, should he be abducted."

"You've thought this through, haven't you?" I made a face at Charles.

"Bleek likes to meet the enemy head on. This is a good way to do that."

"Then who else should we send?" I asked as pleasantly as I could. "We have four. We can send up to six."

"Don't be too quick to fill the roster," Charles warned. "If more are needed, we can always add them in."

"Ilya will be pissed about Zaria," I sighed.

"To use your own words, Ilya can suck it up."

Paricos II

Ilya

They'll meet you at Gubb's tavern, Ry informed me. *We're sending four now. If you need more or have a specific request, let me know.*

I will. Thank you. Which Falchani are you sending?

Flyer and Turtle.

Good. When will they arrive?

Tomorrow morning. I hope you can arrange for transport.

I'll make sure of it. Chief of Security Darkins and two guards intend to come with me.

Making sure of your hires?

Something like that.

Then don't reject any of them, Ry warned. *That's a command.*

As you will it, my King.

~

BlackWing VII

Zaria

"This makes my heart hurt," I muttered, flinging clothing into a trunk. Edden Charkisul sat on the end of my bunk, watching my near-tantrum with a calm expression. "I know it makes sense to let me see this pod'l-morph and figure out what he's up to, but the—other part of this is upsetting."

"Dearest, don't trouble yourself," Edden said. He didn't point it out, but I could have easily packed using power, it was merely more satisfying to expend the physical energy. "Bleek will be with you, at least."

He expected Ilya to reject me, just as much as I expected Ilya to reject me. Bleek would be waiting to smooth metaphorical ruffled feathers. At least I'd be the first Larentii to step inside Tamp's compound. Nefrigar had already asked me to transmit images and information to him for the Archives. Valegar offered to drop in, too, while keeping his presence shielded.

"Have you prepared a dossier for Tamp's security team?" Edden continued when I didn't say anything.

"Yes. Lissa says to list my talent as a Third-level Karathian witch. Not powerful enough for Tamp to get his underwear in a twist over. Ilya says Tamp has five Fifth-levels working for him, but they keep to themselves and are housed higher up."

"You think bringing in a Third-level will coax the Fifth-levels out of hiding? Just to make their own assessments?" Edden's assumption was correct. The man truly was a diplomat of the highest order.

"Yes. I hope they're not bullies."

"If Tamp can't keep order in his own house, then he isn't much of a leader or a boss, even by Paricos II's standards."

"Agreed, but even a pod'l-morph can't be in all places at once."

Paricos II

Ilya

After leaving the hover-chopper behind and guarded by Darkins' guards and pilots, the Chief and I made our way to Gubb's bar. I still wanted to grasp Gubb's throat and squeeze, but that would have to wait—by necessity.

At least the streets were paved and clean enough—even in the worst areas. The bosses saw to that. I'd seen few begging; I had the idea they didn't last long on Paricos II. I wondered at times why the bay wasn't full of floating bodies, but decided early on that investigating murder among thieves and murderers could be a hopelessly recurring task and wasn't included in my mission.

"You know these and trust them?" Darkins asked as we made our last turn to reach Gubb's.

"I do." I knew two of them, at least, and imagined that King Rylend wouldn't send someone I wasn't familiar with.

"Tamp gave me authority to pass off on them," Darkins said.

"Good enough," I shrugged. "They can help me set up the forge if they meet your requirements."

Gubb's place was close enough to the water that a thin mist and fog hung about as I pushed the door open ahead of Darkins. It may have been the hardest thing I've ever done to force my feet not to falter as I walked toward the table where my apprentices waited.

～

Paricos II

Zaria

Bleek had a beer in one hand, both upper arms spread across the back of the bench and the fourth was occupied with drumming his fingers on the thick, wood-planked table. He looked as comfortable in this land of murder and malevolence as anyone could.

I took up the corner next to the wall, wedged between it and the back of the bench so I could see everyone coming and going. Turtle and Flyer sat opposite us, each nursing a beer they swore was Refizani in origin.

I wasn't surprised—Paricos II was known for its piracy. When Ilya walked in, followed closely by another man, I forced myself to breathe, although it wasn't normal breathing by anyone's definition.

I almost forgot to read the man with him, my reaction to Ilya's nearness was so consuming. Yes, I was much surprised to see an honorable man working for a boss on Paricos II.

Stranger things have happened, I reminded myself. I didn't miss the thin, hard line of Ilya's mouth, or the refusal to show emotion. The Falchani had taught him well.

"You found Falchani," Chief of Security Darkins breathed the moment he caught sight of Turtle and Flyer. "Tamp will be very pleased."

～

Ilya

Darkins didn't seem to care that I had a Blevakian and an apparent Third-level witch as apprentices; he was fascinated by the two

Falchani who'd come. It became obvious that a Falchani had never been to Paricos II before.

I wondered what Darkins would do if he knew Zaria was also Larentii, but squashed that thought immediately.

Zaria, though, kept her emotions hidden behind a mask as I introduced her to Darkins. The entire interview, if it could be called such, was mostly directed toward Turtle and Flyer and their exploits on Falchan.

It amused me that they had plenty of stories to tell. I was grateful, too, that Darkins didn't seem to question my hiring of any of them. "Where are your bags and trunks?" Darkins asked eventually, indicating that he was ready to leave and that all had passed his evaluation.

"At the inn two doors down," Turtle replied. Zaria was happy to have Turtle and Flyer answering questions; I imagined she wanted to strip off a layer of my skin with caustic remarks.

"Lady witch, do you imagine your power strong enough to bring the bags and trunks to the hover-chopper, once we arrive at its berth?" Darkins turned to Zaria.

"Of course. My power is sufficient for that."

"What do you suppose you'll be doing for our Bladesmith, here?" Darkins rose and stretched.

"I'm talented at keeping a forge at the proper temperature; that will be needed as the location is open to the mist and weather," she shrugged, as if she'd done that very thing before.

"I see. I hadn't considered that," Darkins admitted. "Shall we? I imagine Blade, here, is anxious to get started."

Yes, I'd employed an alias for my stint on Paricos II. A slight frown tugged at a corner of Zaria's mouth, but she didn't say anything. How was I going to get through this? Being stabbed in the heart would have been preferable.

Darkins led the way out of Gubb's bar after tossing money on the table. I followed behind. I also didn't fail to notice the flash of anger from Bleek as he placed himself between Zaria and me for our trek to the hover-chopper.

~

Zaria

I employed what would be a Third-level's power to bring our things to the hover-chopper, and even managed to place everything inside the chopper under Darkins' watchful eye. He was testing me, now, although his questioning had been brief.

He wasn't expecting much from a Third-level, that was easy to see. It made me wonder about the five Fifth-levels Tamp had working for him. Darkins would have looked suspiciously at anyone with power; I could easily see the distrust in him.

It made me all the more eager to meet the warlocks, the treasure hunter and the pod'l-morph. The sooner we sorted everything out about them, the faster we could leave this place. Ilya could stay if he wanted; I'd found little that was redeemable on Paricos II.

I'd already read Gubb. He should change his name to Grasping, he was so greedy and self-centered. Turtle and Flyer had complimented him on the Refizani beer he served. Gubb puffed out like a proud bird and smiled as he served a second round.

I could see what he'd done to Ilya, too; I imagined that Ilya wanted to kill Gubb for it, although I hadn't tried to read him yet.

That was pain waiting for me and I wanted to put it off as long as I could.

Stop worrying. Bleek patted one of my hands when the hover-chopper lifted from the pad and made a wide, banking turn to take us to Tamp's compound.

Bleek seldom used mindspeech, so his mental voice made me jump. I was grateful Darkins sat at the front with the pilot so he didn't see my unease; he'd have questioned that, too.

I couldn't help thinking that the long trip in the hover-chopper could have been avoided; most Third-levels could have easily transported everyone. *Next time*, I promised myself, after realizing that Darkins wouldn't expect anyone to read the location of Tamp's hollowed-out rock, just by staring at him for a moment.

I was used to being around those who not only knew about that talent, but were comfortable with it. Here, I'd have to hide almost everything about me. I found it confining, after months of freedom among the Larentii and a few others.

There was something else I knew, too. Darkins intended to ask Flyer and Turtle for blade-fighting lessons.

I wanted to laugh at the prospect; any Falchani would force a student to learn how to care for a blade, first. Darkins probably wouldn't like that.

What kind of space will you have for the forge? Turtle pointed his mindspeech at Ilya, but included everyone in the question.

It's a cave below the lowest level of quarters for employees, mine included, Ilya admitted. *It is plumbed and such, but little else. Equipment and supplies will be brought in, including a quantity of good iron ore.*

Is the space large enough? Flyer asked.

More than large enough. We could run two forges if we wanted. I'd prefer not to do that. It's cooler where we're going; that's fortunate in some ways as we'll be depending on the sea mist and outside temperatures to cool us while we're working the forge. It would be foolish to attempt to provide air conditioning.

Ilya said what I'd already guessed—nature would have to cool the workers down; the forge would remain hot.

That was my job—to keep it that way. I'd already volunteered, when I answered Darkins' question.

~

BlackWing VII
  Quin

Kay arrived before dinner on the same day that Zaria left before breakfast. I wasn't surprised to see that two had come to help guard her. She held power of her own, but the Mighty Hand was more than solicitous regarding her safety.

Franklin and Trace introduced themselves when they arrived with Kay. Franklin called himself a healer; Trace, Trajan's younger brother, said he was third-in-command at SouthStar.

Kay was comfortable with both, I could see that easily, although she shied away from conversations with most men. There was a story —and a good amount of pain behind that behavior, but I couldn't read her to see what it could be.

It left me mildly curious, but if I were destined to know the reason, it would come. There was no sense fretting about it; we had work to do.

"It'll take two more days to reach our next destination," Sal announced at dinner. "Quin, if you'd like to spar in the morning, I'd be more than happy to see you in the dojo."

"I'd like that," I said. "Jana, too, I think."

Jana nodded with enthusiasm; I imagined she'd be bored, otherwise. I could see Jana had a desire to leave with Zaria and Bleek, although she understood that she had nothing to offer in blade-making.

Perhaps if two more were needed, Jana could go as a beginning apprentice. Zaria, on the other hand, had been hoping for a short period of time on Paricos II.

For her sake and mine, I hoped that were true. I missed her already, and she hadn't been gone a full day.

～

Paricos II

Ilya

I had to ask questions; Zaria refused to speak with me otherwise. Her quarters, as well as Bleek's and the Falchani's, weren't far from mine. I'd worried that Darkins would separate us, but he hadn't bothered.

Is it safe to talk here? I asked as she and the others stood inside my suite of rooms.

I'd checked for power and for listening devices, but still I worried that something could be overheard.

"Yes," Zaria sighed. She shook her head, as if she couldn't believe how she—we—had been tossed together in this.

"What did you see in Darkins?" I demanded. My words sounded harsher than I'd intended. She turned away from me, then. I couldn't say I blamed her.

"He doesn't know what Velker or Master Tamp are hunting," Zaria said. "He knows nothing of anyone fitting Cayetes' description arriving to set up shop here on Paricos II."

"Do you think that it has been Tamp all along?" Flyer asked.

"I won't know until I see him," Zaria replied. I could see the tension in her shoulders as she crossed arms over her chest. Her back was still toward me, but I knew these things about her, even after so many centuries had passed.

"The one I really need to see, I think," Zaria added, "Is the treasure hunter—Velker."

"Oh, you'll likely see him soon enough," I said. "He can't help himself, and blathers on about anything and everything, chief among them his safety."

"Except," she pointed out shrewdly, "He hasn't told you what he's hunting."

She was right. He hadn't said.

"There's something else," Zaria said.

"What's that?"

"Darkins' security detail is going through all our things," she said. "Before they get to our rooms."

"It's to be expected," I began.

"But he's asking one of the warlocks to place spells on everything," she snapped and whirled to lock eyes with mine. "Your things are fine. Why are they going through ours?"

Zaria

It angered me that a warlock of any kind had handled my things. None of them had been spelled and I certainly hadn't brought any weapons with me.

Can you dampen those spells, if they're dangerous? Bleek's mindspeech held concern.

Yes, and they'll never know it was done, I responded. Too bad they wouldn't know; I'd like to see warlocks sweat about what a Larentii might do to them, if they intended harm to me or mine.

Bleek and both Falchani had brought blades with them—none of them spelled, just in case they were inspected. I had no idea what sort of mayhem would occur, should Flyer's and Turtle's Grey House blades be discovered by curious warlocks.

I wondered if the blades would be taken away, but all that had been declared when I pulled the trunks and bags to the hover-chopper. Darkins hadn't said anything about those weapons; he'd asked about pistols, instead.

We had nothing like that.

Darkins hadn't recognized Bleek, either. If he'd been trolling the assassins' sites, he would have. Bleek and Quin's rewards were the largest being offered.

It gave me hope that Tamp wasn't familiar with the price on Bleek's head, too. It reinforced the idea I had that Tamp didn't do business with Cayetes.

My love, Bleek said then, *Please tell me you have a way to locate me if I am taken away.*

I do. Your DNA is written on my heart, I told him. *Were a Sirenali standing beside you, I would still know where you were. Barc, too, if he is ever in danger.*

His dark eyes turned soft as he blinked at me. He loved his son more than anything. *I would die for either of you—and for Quin,* he stated.

I know, I replied. *I hope it doesn't come to that.*

Amusement lit his eyes, then. The Blevakian had a wicked sense of humor, and it was making its presence known more and more as the years he'd spent working under Cayetes' thumb wore away.

Ilya cleared his throat, then, to regain our attention. "We'll spend the afternoon in the cave, working out schematics. We'll have lunch, first. Follow me; we eat in the regular mess."

~

Tamp couldn't be accused of racism; he had all sorts in his employ. It took a great many people to keep his operation running smoothly; from housekeepers to techs to security.

I noticed that only low-level employees ate in the regular mess, which was located three levels above our suites. Ilya still didn't know where those higher on the food chain ate, but I saw it in several cook's assistants, who worked there but were forced to eat with the rest of us.

The others eat on the fourth level from the top, I informed the others. Food here was served army-style, with a tray and a long line.

"This soup is terrible," Flyer muttered. He'd know—he reportedly made the best noodles on Falchan. Turtle agreed with him; he was no slouch at cooking, having owned a bar on Falchan for more than a century.

"So cooking isn't the cook's strong suit?" I lifted an eyebrow at Flyer, who offered a grin.

"It looks that way," Turtle pushed his bowl of soup aside and attacked the meat on his plate. "I hope the ones upstairs are getting something better than this."

"How difficult would it be to do our own cooking?" I asked. Ilya's eyes were on his plate; therefore, my question surprised him and he glanced up to meet my gaze.

"It wouldn't be difficult," Flyer insisted. "Get me a few pots and pans—we'll already have a fire. The only thing left is getting supplies."

"I'll ask Darkins," Ilya said and went back to his plate of food.

~

Darkins didn't care that we wanted to cook for ourselves; he shrugged and told Ilya to make a list of necessities. Equipment was already arriving on the second day; Ilya barked orders on where he wanted everything and the rest of us went about making it happen.

Several times I employed power to move something heavy and

position it correctly. Slowly, Ilya's forge was taking shape. We expected the iron ore to arrive last, when everything else was in place.

"I didn't expect this," I studied the stove we'd been sent. It was huge, had ten burners and two ovens. It was any cook's dream, provided they had room for the behemoth. Shelving, pots, pans, a fridge, freezer and food supplies were also brought, in addition to a grocery list of meats and vegetables to last us an eight-day.

"We'll use the fish, first," Flyer said. "I understand you don't eat meat?"

"True," I agreed. "But there's plenty here to suit me."

"I suggest you eat at least three meals in the mess, so the others don't get upset." Darkins walked into the cave, followed by a warlock. As expected, the five had sent one of their number to check things out.

"Loor Blackmantle," the warlock offered a hand to Turtle, first. I stopped breathing for a moment.

CHAPTER 5

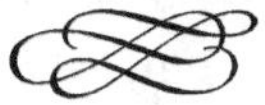

*P*aricos II
    Ilya

He has four brothers, Zaria hissed into my mind. *I've already sent mindspeech to Nefrigar. He's checking their lineage now.*

As old as I was, I imagined that nothing could surprise me.

This surprised me, and not in a good way. I'd thought the Blackmantle name dead. Where had these five come from? Why were they working for Tamp?

What were they doing for Tamp?

How long will it take Nefrigar to send an answer? I returned.

He's going backward in time to search for an answer, she informed me. I could hear the concern in her mental voice—it was tinged with a healthy dose of fear.

How old are they? I sent, struggling to keep my own worry at bay.

Old enough.

Fuck.

Smile and grip his hand, Zaria reminded me as Loor came to me after greeting Flyer. I did, allowing a congenial mask to slide into place.

"I never expected a Blevakian," Loor went to Bleek after exchanging pleasantries with me.

"My mother said the same thing," Bleek took the offered hand. Loor laughed.

Last of all, he went to Zaria. Yes, he'd bypassed her by greeting Turtle, first. I imagined he wanted to size her up, and this was his way of doing it.

"I hear you're Third-level," Loor held out his hand.

"It says that on my assessment," she agreed and took his hand. I could feel the wash of power as he made his own assessment, grunting his satisfaction afterward. I praised whatever power the Larentii held to make that happen. He had no idea whose hand he held or what she could do to him, should she choose to do it.

I preferred it that way. However, if he intended harm in any way toward her, I'd blast him myself for even thinking it.

Does he recognize Bleek as someone with a price on his head? I thought to ask.

No. Not yet, anyway. I worry that they'll look into our backgrounds, though, and come up with Bleek's reward as a result.

Will you keep us informed?

As much as I can.

Gods, I'd missed her. She stood there, looking small against Loor's taller bulk, making trivial conversation with him while answering my mental questions. From lengths away, I could read his interest in her.

Who wouldn't be interested? She was beautiful, Larentii or witch. It only drove home the idea that she was much too good for the likes of me.

If Loor gets any ideas, I intend to smash his face in, Bleek broke into my thoughts.

As will I, brother, I replied.

~

Phrinnis Tampirus

"I distrust them." Those words were spoken by my seer, Mayyab.

"Yet you tell me yourself that all their readings are not threatening," I reminded him.

"They want something; I just know it." He drew his falaca-wool cloak tighter about his shoulders as he turned his back toward me. His gaze settled on the view through my wide window; the sea was choppy today instead of angry, as it usually was. Mayyab felt the cold of the sea inside the Rock, most of the time.

"Everybody wants something," I said. "I want something. I want Falchani-type blades to sell on the black market. They draw a very high price. It will be nothing for my warlocks to make them appear ancient, which draws an even higher price. You like getting paid, I assume?"

"Everyone wants that. It's why we take jobs. This one is better than any other," he was quick to add.

"I know why you work for me," I said. "And your skills at mollification are lacking."

"A lack of manners often goes hand in hand with my talent," he said.

"A sound excuse," I agreed. "Your last fear should be allayed—Loor reports that the woman's talents are mid-Third-level, just as reported."

"Loor could be thinking with his genitals," Mayyab retorted.

"I very much doubt that," I said. "If she were stronger, he'd view her as a threat. Loor and his brothers are more than satisfied on that quarter. A Third-level cannot harm the shields and spells my warlocks have placed. We are safe, here."

"Very well. Just remember that I voiced my concerns."

"Noted. Leave me now; I'd like my bath. Inform Arna on the way out."

"Hmmph. You should watch Arna, too. She has her eye on your Bladesmith."

"I care not if she dallies."

"Yes, but he is unwilling. I can see that much, at least."

"Then I'll have a word with her regarding the rules of the Rock."

"She'll attempt to confront the witch," Mayyab said as he strode toward the door. "I know not whether the witch can withstand her."

"I'll see to it," I waved Mayyab through the door. I wanted to become a jungle plant and stand on the balcony to soak in the mist.

∾

Ilya

Velker found me as a work crew was placing the furnace the following day. The furnace took up a great deal of space, but unless we wanted to build and rebuild stack furnaces to smelt iron ore, then the furnace was a necessity.

It also made it easier to control the carbon burn, so carbon dioxide wasn't produced during the smelting process.

"Master Velker," I acknowledged Velker's arrival while lifting two sets of tongs to place near the anvil.

"It'll be cold here until you get the fires going," he remarked, as if I didn't already know that. One side of the cave was completely open and faced the sea. Mist clung to the outer walls and the balcony space outside the cave. That would disappear in the heat the furnace produced.

At the back of the cave, there was a trans-vator and stairs leading to the upper levels; Velker had ridden the trans-vator down after breakfast to keep from walking the distance.

"Is there something you need?" I lifted an eyebrow instead of responding to his inane comment.

"We'll be going out tomorrow, so you'll have to put this on hold. I've been given permission to take your entire team with me as added security."

Zaria, I sent, *please come and meet Velker*. She was with Bleek, who was talking with a second crew about delivery of the iron ore. I wanted her to verify what I suspected from Velker's tone and body language—he was going into a dangerous area to collect something.

I wondered what it was, too. Zaria would know just by looking at the fool.

∾

Zaria

I was happy to leave; some of the work crew wanted to stay and talk. Bleek had already planted himself between me and two of the men who kept moving toward me, half a step at a time.

"I'll be back," I excused myself.

"We ah, have to go, too," one of the men said the moment I turned to leave. Just what I needed—amorous admirers.

Bleek could see them off; Velker was there with Ilya and I needed to see him. Once inside the stairwell, I folded space to the bottom and walked out. The man standing beside Ilya gaped as I walked toward him.

His hair was bleached, as if he'd spent hours digging in the dirt with the sun high overhead. His face confirmed that notion; it was weathered and made him appear older than he was.

He bore an obsession, which made my heartbeat irregular. I could see Tamp's orders easily enough—Tamp hadn't placed the obsession or directed that it be placed. I learned two terrible truths, gazing at this treasure hunter who was supposed to be dead.

First, the obsession prevented me from knowing whether he'd had anything to do with the stolen spheres. Second, what Tamp ordered him to hunt was just as bad as hunting those spheres.

Tamp was looking for Marid of Belancour's spelled containment spheres—the ones holding poison that Marid stole from Siriaa.

I immediately sent an image of Velker to Queen Lissa; if this man blackmailed the Lord Mayor from Gilvos, then I hoped the Lord Mayor could identify him. I also told her what else I'd learned—that Tamp was searching for the poison itself.

Velker had no idea what Tamp wanted with the stuff; he'd merely been instructed to search for the containment spheres.

He'd described them in detail, too.

As if he'd actually seen them before.

All of us had gone about our business, tending to other things and forgetting that Marid had taken more than enough of the poison away from Siriaa to sell to one criminal faction or another.

It made sense that Vardil Cayetes wasn't his only buyer. Not only had Marid hidden whatever was left, but it was possible that other criminals had buried or hidden what they'd purchased from Marid, just to keep the leaking poison from affecting them.

We're fucked, Lissa's reply came swiftly.

I hear that, I agreed.

I'll start Looking, *but I'm worried that there may be Sirenali involvement with this, too,* Lissa added.

I need to speak with Terrett, I said. *I just had a terrible thought, but it needs to be verified.*

You're worried that there are dead Sirenali buried or hidden with those spelled orbs, aren't you? Lissa was on the same wavelength.

Yes. It appeared that their talent extended beyond death, if my suspicions were correct.

Being employed by an experienced treasure hunter may be fortuitous, then. He has criminal contacts and could be our best bet in actually tracking that filth, Lissa said.

Yeah. I can't say I'm thrilled about continuing my employment here, but it just took a more ominous and necessary turn.

On another note, why is Velker not on anybody's radar?

He's supposed to be dead. He worked for a famous university, used less than legal means to obtain something for them, and they found out. Rather than reporting him, they opted to keep their record clean and sent him on an expedition, from which he didn't return. In other words, they faked his death and sent him on his way, probably threatening to send him to prison if he didn't cooperate.

We'll work on that after we get the rest of this handled, Lissa replied. *For now, we need him where he is.*

Understood.

Velker was asking me to dinner by the time I finished my conversation with Lissa. "She already has a dinner date," Bleek's hands gripped my shoulders from behind. I imagined he was frowning deeply at Velker, too.

Velker took a step backward.

Smart move. Anybody with any sense would back away from Bleek. Quin had aptly named him the Blevakian Mountain. Velker held no power and had no weapons training. Bleek would have him tied in a decorative knot in no time.

"Where are we going tomorrow?" Ilya asked to lessen the tension between Bleek and Velker.

"Can't say—need to know," Velker waved a hand. "Remind your employee," Velker jerked his head at Bleek, "that he is under my command, just as you are."

He doesn't know where we're going, either; Tamp hasn't told him, I explained to Ilya and Bleek. *He's been told it's somewhat dangerous, that's all. I can give him hemorrhoids, if you'd like.*

Bleek ducked his head as if he were acquiescing to Velker's words. Ilya and I knew he was suppressing laughter, instead.

~

Ilya

"The furnace will be brought in while we're gone," I said as I placed my blades in their scabbards. Turtle and Flyer had done the same, although we wouldn't wear them until they were needed. My crew, Zaria included, stood about me inside the cave while we waited for word from Velker.

We'd head upstairs to the heli-port then. I had no idea how long we'd be gone; Velker hadn't said, so we'd all packed a small bag of clothing to last us on our journey by ship.

It made me wonder where Tamp kept his ships, or whether he merely paid another boss for passage. At least two bosses on Paricos II had a fleet of star cruisers; Zarbec, who'd wanted to hire me, was one of them. He'd boasted that his were the best, however.

I distrusted his opinion.

All my crew except Bleek could fold space; I figured Zaria would take Bleek with her if it became necessary. As for Velker and the ship's crew—I didn't give a damn about any of them.

Frankly, all we had to do was alert the BlackWing ships and the closest one could take our vessel. That sounded infinitely better than being in close quarters with Velker for who knew how long.

"We're ready to board," Velker's voice came through the communicator I wore on a wrist. "Have Zaria bring you and your crew."

"We'll be right there," I said as civilly as I could. He was tossing Zaria's name about as if he were a familiar friend. He had no idea what I wanted to do to him because of it.

"Ready?" Zaria asked. When I nodded, she transported us to the heli-port.

~

Zaria

We're going to Kelburr, I informed Ilya and the others after reading the destination in Velker's face. He'd gotten instructions from Tamp less than half an hour earlier. For now, we were headed to the small spaceport orbiting Paricos II, where ships belonging to this boss or that were docked.

Who owns the ship we're taking? Ilya asked.

Zarbec, according to Velker, I replied.

I was afraid of that, he sent a mental sigh with his words. *Zarbec is a conniving asshole,* Ilya added. *I interviewed with him and refused to accept his offer of employment.*

He and Gubb have a special arrangement—I saw that in Gubb when he waited on us the other day, I sent.

No surprise. I'd like to kill Gubb with my bare hands. He expected me to take Zarbec's offer. Now I know why.

We were in our seats after stowing bags in the hold. Velker had many crates and boxes to bring with him and supervised the placing of those things in the hold. I imagined he had everything from the latest in treasure-bots to technology designed to map caves, rivers and any other thing that could present a navigational problem.

Which university did Velker work for? Ilya asked. It surprised me that he was so willing to have conversations with me.

Hoph-Rill-Poldar, I replied. It was the pre-eminent university that trained archaeologists in the Reth Alliance. *I'm sure they've gone to great lengths to bury Velker's murderous involvement in obtaining those ancient shields they're so proud of.*

He killed someone?

Several someones.

I knew he was an asshole.

He still is an asshole, I pointed out. *At least he's more honest in his criminal activities.*

Easier to admit it, when you're surrounded by other criminals, Ilya observed.

True. And safer, too.

Has Nefrigar gotten back with you yet? he asked.

Not yet. This may take some time. Family trees often have deep and twisted roots.

I understand.

I watched as Velker finally took his seat at the front of the hover-chopper and buckled in. I could have transported all of us, bags and equipment included, to the space station, but that could be seen as taxing a Third-level's ability.

I wondered why Loor or one of his brothers hadn't offered. Nevertheless, we had a long ride ahead of us, merely to reach the space station in question. I wanted coffee, too, but that would be frowned upon.

I was having trouble sleeping. Ilya's suite wasn't far from mine.

Neither was Bleek's.

Too many times I'd considered folding space just to get away from Paricos II for a little while. The entire planet bothered me in a way I couldn't define. After all, ghosts walked other worlds. Paricos II's ghosts were in a league of their own.

My love, you look tired, Bleek offered. I sat between him and Ilya; Ilya had settled into the third seat in my row before Turtle or Flyer could take it.

I was just wishing for coffee, I answered Bleek's mindspeech. *Paricos II blows.*

Blows?

Vomit-inducing, I explained.

I agree with that assessment. Velker also blows.

I wanted to laugh. I didn't. It wouldn't do to reveal our talent of mindspeech to anyone on Paricos II. Things could become dangerous in a hurry, and, as Lissa said, this could be our best chance at finding Marid's stash of the poison, in addition to any other containment spheres held by someone else.

Kalenegar and Nefrigar had already warned me about bending time to search for Marid before he died; not only did he have Terrett with him in the past, which could prevent that very search, but the timeline was more than fragile. I understood that. Upset any part of it and things could turn out much worse.

Liron could be alive instead of dead.

I wanted no part of bringing him back.

For now, we would do our search the old-fashioned way.

With an obnoxious, murderous treasure hunter.

~

V'ili

Vardil had a new assistant. This one wasn't in love with him, although she was most anxious to please Vardil in every way.

I'd seen to that for him.

I'd waited two days before bringing him the news that the ASD and CSD were currently hunting the same people we hunted. When I'd shown him the rewards offered for the black-winged woman and Bleek, he was angry and silent.

In fact, not only were both security details offering rewards for those two, it also offered rewards for information on the entire BlackWing fleet of pirates.

"We need another mole inside the ASD," Vardil hissed after several moments. "I want their information as it comes in."

"I will see to it, Master Cayetes," I nodded to him. "It may take some time; I will return only when the task is completed. The mute clones will conceal you while I'm away."

"Good. When are the next customers due?"

"I can put them off until my return, if you'd like."

"I'd prefer that."

"It will be done."

~

Queen's Palace, Le-Ath Veronis

Lissa

"You think he'll try to obsess someone else, so any information we get will be sent straight to Cayetes, don't you?" Kooper leaned back on the sofa inside my private study. "He did it last time; it makes sense," Kooper nodded.

"I don't want to interfere; we know Kay can remove an obsession by changing the victim's aura lines. What we need to do is identify who bears the obsession and watch them until we have Vardil's contact information. We'll send him whatever we deem safe while attempting to track him that way," I said.

"At least Ashe is willing to let Kay participate. He wouldn't let her out of his sight for the longest time."

"I know. He's terrified he'll lose her, somehow."

"That's what Bree says."

At times, I forgot that Kooper was one of my sister's mates. The original Three answered only to themselves and most often didn't respond to mindspeech sent by anyone else, mates included.

"How else will the rest of you grow if we swoop in to solve all your problems?" Bree arrived and teased Kooper and me at the same time.

"Baby," Kooper was on his feet immediately and pulling Bree into his arms for a quick, determined kiss.

"Uh, okay," I said, preparing to fold away from my study to give them some privacy.

"No," Bree waved a hand and pulled back from Kooper. He was disappointed, I could tell.

"You're about to have other difficulties," Bree turned her gaze on me, her cobalt-blue eyes shining from the depths. "Just remember, not everything is how it seems on the surface."

With that, she and Kooper disappeared.

"Great. I have questions and she's making whoopee," I muttered.

~

Paricos II

Ilya

Velker supervised the loading of his equipment a second time—on the star cruiser that would transport us to Kelburr. Velker hadn't given us particulars, including the location, so I refrained from asking questions.

I and my crew were merely bodyguards—muscle for Velker's excursions into thievery. I worried that we could be getting in over our heads—at least according to the abilities we reportedly held.

If Zaria or I employed our true talents to obtain anything Velker wanted, or to save ourselves if it became necessary, it would blow holes in our cover.

We need a vampire, I informed Zaria.

What?

To lay compulsion if Velker sees something he shouldn't.

I'll consider that—and who might fit the bill, she replied. *Larentii can lay a form of compulsion, but it's almost never employed because of the interference rules.*

I know. Let's hope we get through this first assignment with no trouble, and we'll hire a vampire who can walk in daylight.

~

BlackWing VII

Terrett

I received mindspeech from Zaria last night, I told Quin at breakfast.

"How is she?" Quin asked right away.

She says fine, although she sounded tired, I said. *She wanted to ask an unusual question—about dead Sirenali.*

"Why?" Quin's brow furrowed. "She didn't frighten you, did she?"

No, love, nothing like that. She wanted to know what most Sirenali are reluctant to tell—that the ability to conceal things from the powerful continues after our deaths. We hold that secret close to prolong our lives, you understand. Why feed and house a live Sirenali when his moldy bones will do just as well? My kind often lie, to perpetuate the belief that a dead Sirenali is of no use whatsoever.

"Terrett, that's frightening." Quin was suddenly terrified.

Dearest, the mute ones are in the greatest danger—those who speak can prevent someone from taking their lives, unless they are taken by surprise. I patted Quin's hand to calm her fears.

"But your brothers," she whispered, her eyes locking with mine.

I know. I worry that it would be too much to ask those powerful enough to restore their speech. Once this becomes known, however, it could be prudent to do so anyway. I hope they have earned the trust of those around us well enough to have their speech returned.

"Is there any way to prevent this—a dead Sirenali from concealing something?" Quin asked.

The body must be burned completely and the ashes scattered. That is the only way I know.

"Terrett, this frightens me," she said.

Dearest, I wouldn't have told you if it weren't so important.

"Heads up," Sal strode into the dining hall, crackling with energy. "The ship's being fired on. The shields are holding; that's why we don't feel it, but somebody out there needs a lesson in manners. Who wants to board a real pirate ship with me?"

"I will go," I said aloud. Sal looked at me for a moment before jerking his head in a nod. I could command the pirates to tell Sal everything, and forget my commands afterward.

~

Star Cruiser Hellion
    Zaria

Kelburr was two days away at Hellion's best speed. Ilya moved like a restless cat in the small dining room as we waited in line for lunch.

He didn't like traveling this way, and he certainly didn't like being at the mercy of an unknown crew in Zarbec's employ.

Few worth saving in this lot, Flyer informed me as we inched forward in the food line. Flyer was a member of the Saa Thalarr. He'd *Looked* into the background of the crew members.

All were considered criminals, like the criminal who paid them.

They're paid to get us to and from Kelburr in one piece, I told Flyer. *If they decide to go rogue, we'll handle it.*

I worry that Zarbec will want whatever Velker finds, Ilya huffed.

I haven't seen that in any of them; they have their orders and that wasn't included, I said. *Tamp has hired this crew before—I know that much. They're experienced and reliable, at least.*

Are you comfortable sleeping while surrounded by murderers? Flyer asked.

No, I answered truthfully. *I haven't slept well since I got to Paricos II. You have no idea how many ghosts walk that planet. At least I can place a shield to keep the live murderers out of my bedroom.*

You just raised the hair on my neck, Bleek muttered.

I hunched my shoulders and stopped talking. Bleek noticed. Two hands dropped onto my shoulders before he pulled me back against him. Those hands remained where they were; the other two arms circled my waist to hold me close.

His warmth reminded me how cold I felt. I wanted to turn into that warmth and let Bleek take my worries away for a while. I couldn't. Not with the cook and galley crew watching.

Tales would find their way to Velker, who hated Bleek already. If Velker made one wrong move toward the Blevakian Mountain, the treasure hunter would have no idea what I could unleash against him.

Larentii were allowed to protect their mates. Velker's life meant nothing to me. Another treasure hunter could be found, I'm sure.

Too bad Velker didn't know that.

∽

BlackWing VII

Terrett

Any of them obsessed? Sal sent.

None that I can see, I replied. It had been ridiculously simple to take the pirate ship firing on us; there were only twelve crew members on board, and they hadn't been expecting an attack from behind.

The prisoners stood against a wall of their ship as Sal, Lafe, Jana and I studied them. *Quin will see through them well enough,* I added.

Lissa's sending some of hers; she'll be transported here soon, Sal said.

Quin arrived a few moments later, flanked by Lissa's Falchani twins, Drake and Drew.

"They want the reward and intended to sell us twice," Quin turned to Sal after reading the pirate captain's intentions.

"How?" Drake asked.

"By splitting the crew. They already have another woman they've disguised as me," Quin sighed. "With black wings and everything. They want nothing to do with Cayetes; they want to fleece the Alliances instead. The captain isn't concerned that Bleek isn't here. Cayetes would demand that, I think."

"That gives me an idea," Drew's lips curled into a smile. "Quinnie, where are they holding the black-winged decoy?"

~

Le-Ath Veronis

V'ili

I stood with the crowd as the black-winged woman and her pirate crew were herded toward the holding cells at ASD headquarters. They'd be questioned and a date for hearings and judgment set.

Word ran through the crowd that they'd been captured by the ASD while firing on another ship.

Fortuitous for Master Cayetes and me. Here was his black-winged healer that he desired so much. The only one missing was the Blevakian, but that could wait. I would work my way through the holding cells, one obsession at a time, until I reached the girl.

She would tell me where the Blevakian was hiding, or whether he'd died in the fight for their ship.

Either way, I'd have news for Vardil. It could take a few days, but the search for the girl was over.

She'd be under my thumb very soon.

CHAPTER 6

Queen's Palace, Le-Ath Veronis
Lissa

"Anyone with power, from the Powers That Be and upward, will be immune to V'ili's obsession," Belen explained. "King and Queen vampires, some vampires that are very old, pod'l-morphs and the Larentii are also immune."

"We'll make sure enough of ours are disguised and sprinkled throughout the holding cells after V'ili places his obsessions. The Sirenali will be fooled into thinking he's placed an obsession on the ones who'll replace the original guards," I said. "Once V'ili arrives to take Quin's decoy, we'll strike. He'll die and Cayetes will then be easier to find if everything goes as planned."

We'd used the crew from the actual pirate ship as decoys for BlackWing VII's crew, and found the woman they'd disguised as the black-winged Quin. I'd employed power to tweak their disguises so that nobody would know they weren't real.

I'd gotten mindspeech from Rylend, too, asking for a vampire capable of walking in daylight. Ilya had sent the request. It was a reasonable one.

"Are the location chips hidden well enough on the prisoner, in case

V'ili gets away with her?" Merrill asked.

"As well as a Larentii can hide them," Connegar acknowledged.

The plan was sound. The execution of it would either fail or succeed, depending upon the fake Quin and V'ili's ability to sniff out our deception.

If he became suspicious at any time and left the woman behind—we'd be no better off than we were before. It was a huge gamble, and the odds fluctuated from one moment to the next.

"How long will it take him to attempt to place obsession on those we plant in the holding cell facility?" Kiarra asked.

"Three days at most," Trajan appeared. "Ashe says so."

"Then we have three days," I tossed out a hand. "Let's hope this works. We kill V'ili, we find Cayetes. We find Cayetes, we find those stolen spheres. Then we can concentrate on finding those leaking containment spheres that Marid hid or sold."

"Has anyone spoken to Morid?" Dragon asked.

"At length. He can't tell us a thing. He only said that Marid disappeared, taking Terrett and the containment spheres with him. He has no idea where his father went before he ended up on Siriaa. We do know, through Quin, that he didn't have those things with him when he landed on that world. She read him before he killed himself and said that he'd released hundreds of containment spheres on hundreds of worlds, but Morid reported that his father held hundreds, if not thousands, at the least, of those spheres. He held some in reserve, so he could sell them later, no doubt."

"They could be anywhere, then," Kiarra shook her head. She knew, just as I did, that we should have been hunting those things all along.

～

Star Cruiser Hellion

Zaria

"That's not Quin," I said, gazing at the images of a shackled pirate crew being led to ASD holding cells on Le-Ath Veronis. "The entire crew is from an actual pirate ship that fired on BlackWing VII. They intended to sell their victims twice, to the ASD and CSD. The decoy that looks like Quin was their insurance to collect both rewards."

Ilya had brought his comp-vid to me to show me the images on the news-vids sweeping both Alliances and all networks outside them. This particular feed had come from Carek Prime, which was likely the most reliable of outside sources.

"Good. I hoped she wasn't in danger." Ilya sat on the side of my bed—the berth was small and the bed only large enough for one person. I'd gotten a private berth; Ilya and the others had to share.

"You think she'd be in danger on Le-Ath Veronis?" I blinked at Ilya.

"Now that you say that, no."

"Lissa would never stand for that. I can see the sense in allowing this lie to go forward," I tapped the woman's image. She looked exactly like Quin. "I think this is a trap, to draw V'ili and Cayetes out."

"That makes sense," Ilya raked fingers through his dark hair. "Bleek wanted to know, too. I'll go tell him now."

I watched Ilya walk toward the auto-door. It swung open to allow his exit. He'd come, and still there was nothing from him about our past, or what we'd be in the future—either together or separately.

I'd blocked myself from reading him; I didn't want to see the mix of emotions that boiled inside him.

I was terrified he had no care for me any longer, and that, in itself, would break my heart.

"Where's the Ilya I met long ago on Earth?" I whispered. I wanted him with me so badly.

～

Carek Prime
  King's chambers
  Devarr

"My King, this is all I can do on such short notice," Hulce handed the packet of identification chips to me.

"These will get my troops onto Le-Ath Veronis?" I demanded.

"There is no difference between these and what the Reth Alliance produces," Hulce claimed. "This will gain them passage on any Alliance ship. They will arrive on the vampire planet in a day and a half if we move now."

"Then we move now. Captain Lenk has chosen those he trusts. They will release the winged woman and bring her to me. Carek Prime's wealth and well-being are depending on your abilities," I held up the packet he'd given me.

"They will work," Hulce asserted.

"Good. Send for Captain Lenk immediately."

∾

Star Cruiser Hellion

Ilya

Tamp waited until we were three quarters of the way to Kelburr to reveal our target, which gave Velker and his team half a day to make plans.

I was glad, because the target wasn't one I would ever have chosen, or have taken on willingly after I knew.

Yes, I thought we'd be digging in the dirt or among ruins. Tamp pointed us toward another criminal compound located on the non-Alliance world of Kelburr.

Velker prattled on about the gadgets he'd brought with him that would fool any surveillance system. I wanted to laugh in his face. His gadgets wouldn't get past a wizard's or warlock's boundary if they held any sort of power at all.

Tamp had the Rock warded; I could feel the wards every time I walked past their perimeter. I imagined that this would be no different and we'd either be thwarted in our attempt or forced to employ power Velker didn't know we had.

I wanted to curse as my team and I stood around the three-dimensional image Velker displayed at the meeting table and described how we were going to break into the massive compound. We would then make our way to a basement treasury, where the thing Tamp wanted was placed.

Unless the containment sphere has been warded by a better wizard or warlock, it will have leaked poison on everything in that treasury, Zaria pointed out.

We don't know that's what Velker is hunting here—do we? Flyer asked.

We do. Zaria sounded defeated.

Can we check the people inside the compound for poison sickness before going in? Turtle asked silently.

I can do that, Zaria agreed. *I'll wait until we're in orbit around the planet, first, in case I need to fold into the compound.*

You think they may have Sirenali protection, don't you? I asked her.

It makes sense. We really need to find out who is manufacturing all these clones for Cayetes and who knows who else, she grumbled.

That will have to wait—we need to do this first, I pointed out.

"Zaria," Velker barked, "Repeat what I've said."

Without a hitch, Zaria repeated his words verbatim. I wanted to kill Velker for picking on her, thinking she was our weakest link. Why would he think she'd be interested in him after that?

If he'd come after me, which is what he wanted, I'd have strangled him, Bleek informed me. *I now want to strangle him on Zaria's behalf,* Bleek went on. The Blevakian answered the question I had; Velker would attack the one he could be sure wouldn't fight back.

How little he knew.

∾

Le-Ath Veronis

Captain Lenk

My instructions were clear. Take the winged woman. Get her to the ship and make our way back to Carek Prime as swiftly as possible.

The king had paid dearly for our passage, and for no questions asked. That meant we traveled on a ship that occasionally accepted bribes and smuggled items. This time, the items were members of the King's guard and a winged woman.

Should we be captured or some of us killed, the instructions were also clear. Disavow any connection to the King of Carek Prime. We were outlaws looking for reward money only.

Devarr had placed his trust—and the fate of our world—in my hands. I was determined not to fail him.

Hulce, on the other hand, had placed one of his latest devices in my hands and instructed my men and me on how to employ it.

So far, it had gotten us past customs at the space station. I hoped it worked as well at the ASD facility. If not, I had visions of being killed the moment we walked past the first level of guards.

Shoving my ranos pistol into its holster beneath my jacket, I looked around the Casino City hotel room at my men.

Live or die, we were in this together.

~

Le-Ath Veronis

Casino City

V'ili

The ASD guards are falling for my charms like leaves in a whirlwind, I informed Vardil via secured comp-vid.

As expected, Vardil responded. *Bring her to me swiftly; I want her to examine me. I worry constantly the poison disease will return.*

I understand. The moment she is in my grasp; I will fold space to you.

Good.

~

Queen's Palace

Lissa

"The trap is laid," Kooper said. "He placed obsession on six of our human guards, as you know. He intends to go straight into the holding cells and get out alive. We've replaced those six obsessed guards with the ones who won't be susceptible to his charms. Kay has removed the obsessions already, and the humans are at the facility on the light side."

"Are the rifle-bots hidden and set to fire?" I asked.

"They are—the moment anyone else appears inside the woman's cell or tampers with the lock outside it."

"Good. I know it's barbaric to display your dead enemy's carcass on the palace walls, but I've never been so tempted to do it in my life. V'ili is responsible for too many deaths to count, and I want to show Vardil Cayetes what's coming his way."

"You can always put images on the criminal sites. Offer a price for Vardil Cayetes after that; he'll no longer have V'ili to place obsessions for him. He'll be left with mute Sirenali who can't do anything for him except hide his sorry ass." Kooper wasn't mincing words.

"Agreed. The moment we have a confirmed kill, we let Vardil know he's vulnerable."

"I'm off, then, to supervise the killing of someone who's had it coming for a very long time," Kooper rose and stretched.

"Keep me informed," I said.

"Will do."

~

Star Cruiser Hellion

Zaria

"Nobody at the compound has the poison sickness," I said shortly after I'd folded back to the ship. There were Sirenali somewhere in the compound; probably dead, since I didn't see any of them as I swept invisibly throughout the place searching for anyone affected by the poison.

I could have appeared inside Juut of Kelburr's treasury and pulled everything he kept there away with me, but that wasn't following the plan.

I'd gone to the six-bed berth where Ilya and the others were staying to deliver my news—after adding my shields to Ilya's so nobody would hear.

"What sort of protection does he have?" Flyer asked.

"He has three warlocks and strong spells laid on just about

everything," I said. "Crime pays very well if you're Juut of Kelburr."

"We need a vampire mister," Flyer muttered. "They can get past all of that easily."

"Too late for that now," Ilya said, his words dry.

"I know. I have no idea how Velker thinks he can get in and out unscathed."

"It's his funeral, not ours," Turtle pointed out. "I just can't come up with any reason to go back to Tamp with the news that he didn't survive and we did. We have to stick with this unless there's no other choice. Getting rid of those containment spheres is now considered top priority."

I didn't say what I was thinking, and honestly, I wouldn't consider *Changing What Was* for filth like Velker under normal circumstances. The thought of expending that power on him if it became necessary made me ill.

"We'll follow his lead," I said aloud. "To see where he takes us."

"We don't have a choice," Ilya agreed.

~

Le-Ath Veronis
ASD Criminal Detention Facility
Kooper Griff
Those replacing the humanoid crew were in position and carefully disguised. We were merely waiting for V'ili to either walk in or fold in, depending on how confident he felt regarding the location of the decoy's cell.

Our plan concerning V'ili was flawless.

Lissa has a saying about best laid plans.

~

Kelburr
Ilya
As much as I hate traveling by starship, I hated the small, onboard

shuttles more. They were generally cramped with six people aboard. Velker crammed the five of us plus two of his treasure-hunting assistants into the one selected to take us to Kelburr's surface.

Zaria ended up on Bleek's lap, with no safety belt wrapped around her. She could fold space, but I silently cursed Velker anyway for ignoring her safety like that.

I didn't add what else I was thinking—that Zaria could have sat on *my* lap. My stubbornness and false morals were coming around to face me head on, and I didn't like what I was seeing.

Velker's assistants never complained on the ride to the surface, but spilled out of the shuttle first, once we landed in a secluded spot.

"Witch, you'll transport us to Juut's compound," Velker turned toward Zaria. I'm sure she already knew what he intended, but he'd said the word *witch* as if it were a curse. He'd been spurned and he didn't like it. I worried that he'd attempt to harm Zaria and Bleek as a result.

He could ask Tamp to release them.

I needed her.

That revelation shone a light on the starved parts of my heart and brain. If she went, the rest of us went, too.

Velker's only redeeming quality was his experience and treasure hunting ability. Fuck him; we could hunt the containment spheres on our own.

≈

Le-Ath Veronis

ASD Criminal Detention Facility

Kooper

V'ili walked right past the guards as if he owned the place. They'd been instructed to go about their business as if he weren't there.

That's exactly what they did. Nothing looked out of the ordinary to V'ili, who was so comfortable walking in that he could have danced a jig and nobody would have paid attention. He walked straight to the trans-vator, pressed a button and stepped into it.

The doors jerked once before closing; I had no idea at the time what had caused that, other than the usual mechanical malfunction. I made a mental note to have the trans-vator checked later and sent mindspeech to Lissa, telling her that V'ili had just walked into our trap.

I folded space down to the holding cells after that, setting myself down at a location near the end of the hall where the decoy's cell was located.

I was out of range of the rifle-bots, but placed a shield about myself anyway. Getting hit by flying debris is never comfortable.

I heard the trans-vator come to a stop. A few moments later, V'ili strode down the hall, heading straight for the decoy's cell.

It's working, I sent to Lissa, and that's when everything blew up in my face.

~

Le-Ath Veronis

Queen's Hospital

Quin

"His life is hanging by a thread. Will you help?" Lissa pleaded. She wanted this outlaw kept alive, so she could ask questions, no doubt.

I could likely read most everything in his face, but a life was a life. Besides, Queen Lissa had done so much for me, I would do this for her.

At least it wasn't V'ili.

That coward had folded space the moment the rifle-bots opened fire, killing eleven of the twelve men who'd walked in with V'ili. The twelve had been so heavily shielded by some sort of new technology that even the vampires on duty had failed to hear or scent them as they passed.

Kooper, who walked with Lissa and me toward the hospital room containing the prisoner, looked as if he'd attempted to tug his hair out by the roots.

The twelve men were clearly not connected to V'ili. They'd merely arrived at the same moment and were caught in the trap that Kooper and Lissa laid for the Sirenali.

My wings rustled at my back at the thought of how close we'd been to killing V'ili. With him, there was no thought of capture; he could fold space in a blink and had done so to get away from the detention facility.

Somewhere, I imagined Vardil Cayetes was furious and plotting his revenge against the ASD and Le-Ath Veronis.

"Here we are," Lissa led me into the room where the man lay, barely clinging to life. In a short while, without powerful intervention, he'd die. I went straight to him, laid my hands on his chest where the greatest damage was and went to work, filling the room with light as I did so.

~

Lissa

"He's sleeping," I held up a hand to answer Kooper's question before he asked it. "Quin says we should treat him well, and no, she didn't elaborate further."

"Name?" Kooper barked.

"She wouldn't give me that, either. Says it's important that she be there when he's well enough to be questioned."

"Fuck," Kooper settled his tall frame onto the sofa inside my study, his bulk making the leather creak as he shifted into a comfortable position and crossed his legs. I could see his exhaustion from where I sat.

"Tell me about the technology they used—Tony didn't hear or scent them when they walked past his station."

"It's something I've never seen before," Kooper raked fingers through his hair, which already looked wild and unkempt.

"Did you recover any of it?"

"Hell, no. It got blasted to bits, like the eleven other bodies the rifle-bots fired on. Bloody mess left behind, too. We've gone through the security images a hundred times. Nothing was recorded, other than the trans-vator doors bumping back open, probably because the last of them were angling for positions around V'ili without crowding him."

"We need that technology," I said, before realizing that Kooper was already ahead of me on that quarter. He was on a mission, now; I could see the determined look in his eyes.

"How long before the prisoner wakes?" Kooper asked.

"No idea—Quin said to let him sleep until he woke on his own. She's staying at the hospital with Berel, Lafe and Terrett. She wants to be there when he wakes."

"I'll give her a few minutes, but afterward, either she or he has to answer my questions," Kooper gruffed.

"I'll come, too," I said.

"I can control myself," Kooper insisted.

"And I'll make sure that remains true," I said.

~

Queen's Hospital

Quin

I'd fallen asleep with my head on Lafe's shoulder. Sleeping while sitting is always uncomfortable when you wake.

"He's waking," Terrett walked up and handed me a cup of tea.

"How do I look?" I asked, shoving back hair before taking the cup Terrett offered.

"You look fine. Beautiful. Shake out your wings, love, and let's see what the prisoner has to say," Berel grinned.

I did shake out my wings—the feathers tended to flatten whenever I slept on them. Some mornings, I felt like a hen who'd just gotten off the nest when I rolled out of bed and ruffled my feathers.

The four of us walked past the vampire guards at the prisoner's door and into the room, where the prisoner was just discovering that he'd been shackled to the bedrails.

"Don't worry about that," I waved a hand at the concern on his face.

"Who are you?" he demanded.

"Captain Lenk, I'm the one you were actually hunting," I replied. "The black-winged woman is just a disguise I wear at times. Vardil Cayetes has only seen that version of me."

Lenk's face drained of color when I said his name. The identity chip he'd worn had another name attached to it, but it was a disguise, too.

"Why are you telling me this?" I could see easily enough that he expected to die on Le-Ath Veronis. "What about my men?" he whispered.

"There wasn't enough left to save," I admitted. "I'm sorry. The ASD were hoping to kill the man you got on the trans-vator with. They had no idea you were there at all."

"Who was he?"

"Vardil Cayetes' right hand," I snorted. "If we'd taken him down, Cayetes would be vulnerable. Now, I imagine that Cayetes is plotting to kill all of us because we laid a trap for V'ili."

Kooper and Lissa walked into the room at that moment. "Are you ready to talk?" Kooper directed his words to me, first. He knew I could read Captain Lenk as easily as a book.

"Yes. Captain Lenk may have done us a favor, Director Griff," I said. "If we handle things correctly, we may be able to get to Cayetes from another direction."

~

Kelburr

Ilya

Zaria had her shields up and tight about the five of us as Velker employed the gadget he had. He claimed it would get us past everything in Juut's compound, including his warlocks.

I had no faith whatsoever in that gadget.

As for Zaria, I could see she was skeptical, too.

That's why all our jaws dropped when Velker strode confidently through the front gates of the compound, past guards armed with ranos rifles and right through the invisible shields placed by Fourth and Fifth-level warlocks.

Velker veered around the front of the fortress, heading for a side door, no doubt. I learned quickly that he was walking toward the side kitchen entrance, where food deliveries were taken.

We strolled right past kitchen helpers accepting a load of fresh produce and into the kitchen itself.

Fuck me, Bleek breathed into my mind.

I hope that's not an invitation, I replied. *Although I was about to say something similar.*

Not an invitation, I assure you. Juut's got some spoils of war, wouldn't you say? Bleek nodded toward a sword collection covering an entire wall of the room we walked through.

Two of those may be Falchani made, I said. *I'd have to get close to know for sure.*

Velker now led us toward a staircase that would take us down to the lower level. *The treasury is on the next floor down,* Zaria informed us. *It has major spells and security equipment around it. This will put Velker's gadget to the test.*

It was obvious when we walked through the kitchen that Velker's contraption muted sound as well as hiding us from sight. The stairs creaked as we went down them—they weren't used often, because a freight-vator stood next to the door to the stairwell.

The freight-vator was locked and likely keyed to only a few in Juut's employ. I'm sure Velker could have gotten past those measures with another of his gadgets, but the elevator opening would have given us away immediately. The stairs were a much better option.

Yes, we were passing guards, servants and concubines on the way to the treasure vault. None of them realized we walked right past them. Whoever designed Velker's device was a genius, and the first person I intended to tell about it was Director Griff.

After all, if this was available to criminals, he needed to know about it. Something like this could put all his agents in danger. Hell, it could put anyone in danger.

I hoped the ASD could devise something to circumvent the

technology, or we'd all end up losing, I think. The thought of this technology in Cayetes' hands concerned me greatly.

Here's the door, Zaria said, breaking me away from my morbid thoughts. Velker had stopped outside the door. I waited to see how well his unlocking mechanism worked.

Calling this a door was like calling a Fifth-level warlock a magician. It was huge, made of a titanium alloy if my guess were correct and had to be as thick as Bleek's shoulders were wide.

There were six separate locking devices on it, too.

Smart of Juut to install this one; if Velker opened one lock, the others would send a warning to the guards. I imagined that only Juut held the proper combination for this door, and in a separate location, to ensure that thieves who'd gotten this far would get no farther.

That's when Velker turned to Zaria and motioned her forward. He intended for her to get him inside the vault.

I didn't like it that he only intended for the two of them to go inside. *Keep your shields up, baby*, I warned as Zaria moved forward. I watched her hesitate and her shoulders stiffen when I spoke the endearment, before she moved forward again and grasped Velker's arm.

They disappeared.

~

Zaria

Leave it to Ilya to unsettle me just as I was transporting asshole Velker into Juut's treasure vault. I wanted to shake off the memory of grasping Velker's arm to get him inside; I wanted no part of him on my skin, including the cloth and leather he wore.

He was no rugged, rogue archaeologist like I'd seen in motion pictures from old Earth. He was a murderous jerk who'd collect his own mother's bones if she had any worth as an artifact.

I watched Velker carefully as he walked from shelf to shelf, drooling over what Juut had stashed away. I'm sure Tamp had instructed him carefully to only take what he'd asked for. Velker's pockets would be bulging if that weren't the case.

He was searching for the containment sphere and so far hadn't found it. I hadn't found it either, and that meant Sirenali involvement in some way. That's why I went looking for bones. With the time Velker was taking, carefully examining each bit of treasure and cataloging it in his mind, we could be there for a week.

~

Queen's Palace, Le-Ath Veronis

Lissa

"You asked for me, my Queen?" Halimel, one of the Rith Naeri, stood before my desk. Yes, Kooper and I were allowing our prisoner some rest, and Quin time to gather her thoughts and present her case for him in a meeting later tonight.

In the meantime, I had a request for a mister to fulfill. Kell would have been the ideal candidate, but he was on a separate mission. Halimel was my second choice. He'd already received my blood; he only needed misting ability before I sent him to Ilya and Zaria.

"Halimel, I have a sensitive assignment for you. I've gotten a request for a misting vampire who can walk in daylight, so his vampirism won't be evident. I believe the ability to place compulsion won't go amiss, either."

"I don't mist, lady Queen," he bowed respectfully.

"Yet," I pointed a finger at him. He blinked at me in surprise.

~

Kelburr

Zaria

Why would Juut keep bones? I sent mindspeech to Velker. He knew even the weakest witch or warlock had mindspeech, it's just that he'd never gotten anything from Tamp's warlocks, who held him in contempt.

He couldn't send back, but his head jerked in my direction when the words settled into his brain.

He immediately came to see what I'd meant.

Juut had carefully placed the containment sphere, upon which his warlocks had placed layer after layer of shielding spells, inside a nest of Sirenali bones he'd set inside a sewn-leather bowl. It was a macabre nest where they rested, and it made me wonder what Juut intended to do with all of it.

The bones were worth a ransom, if you wanted to hide something from the powerful; the containment sphere and the poison inside it could be used to blackmail or kill—people or planets, it didn't matter which.

Velker drew in a breath before pulling a gadget from a pocket and tapping a button on the small device.

He was deactivating the security mechanism the nest rested upon. Otherwise, an alarm would be triggered when those things were removed. Velker's gadget worked efficiently, deactivating the electronic security employed.

Once the security was shut off, Velker moved in to reverently touch the bones before reaching in to lift the treasure away.

Velker's hands gripped the nest while a jubilant smile lit his features. Too bad he hadn't counted on the more mundane and ancient mechanical measures Juut had employed as a backup.

When the hidden, small caliber pistol fired, it hit Velker right in the forehead. His eyes widened in surprise before they glazed over in a swift, almost painless death.

I stepped out of the way to allow his body to crumple onto the floor. A trail of blood leaked off his forehead and into an open eye, making me gag. Turning away, I considered my options while working to settle my stomach.

I could either *Change What Was,* or take Velker's body and get the rest of our crew the hell out of there before Juut's security came running.

CHAPTER 7

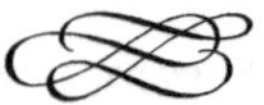

*S*tar Cruiser Hellion
   Ilya

Velker's body and the containment sphere nest of Sirenali bones were locked inside Velker's berth after Zaria transported all of us to the ship. Already the crew had the ship underway—Deen, one of Velker's assistants, had barked orders to the captain.

Yes, Juut's alarm had sounded because Velker hadn't considered anything other than high-tech measures to guard what the criminal had in his vault. Velker paid for that mistake with his life. Zaria, wisely, hadn't employed what she had to bring the bastard back.

I have a vampire mister to send, King Rylend's mental voice broke into my thoughts.

Hold onto him for a couple of days until we see how Tamp reacts to his treasure hunter's death, I responded. *If I give the all-clear, then send him.*

How did the treasure hunter die? Rylend asked.

By his own stupidity. He imagined that Juut of Kelburr only employed electronic protection for his treasures. A simple, ancient method of hooking up a pistol to a tripwire did him in.

You're right—that was stupid, Rylend agreed. *Any feedback yet from Tamp, or has he been notified?*

Velker's assistants are asking Zaria questions now. I believe Bleek is ready to breathe fire, they've been at it so long. That tells me they want their story straight before they give Tamp the news.

Understandable, since the bosses of Paricos II aren't known for their tolerance of stupidity or failure.

There wasn't any failure; Zaria brought the Sirenali bones and the containment sphere back with Velker's body. It was Velker's stupidity that got him killed and sounded the alarm. Juut knows his compound was breached and something taken by now. I'm hoping he doesn't have a clue who was involved. I doubt he's a reasonable person if somebody steals from him.

Few would be, if they'd been robbed, Rylend said, his sending dry. *Let me know whether to send the mister or not.*

Who is it? I thought to ask.

Halimel, member of the Rith Naeri and former King of Hraede, Rylend replied.

～

Zaria

"We have a meeting scheduled with Tamp the minute we get back," I flopped onto an extra bunk in Ilya and the others' cabin. I was exhausted. Velker's assistants, either of whom would have known to look for what Velker hadn't, were terrified of Tamp.

Yes, they'd finally sent the message that they'd gotten the treasure, but that Velker had been killed while obtaining it. As a result, Tamp insisted on meeting with all of us when we arrived on Paricos II.

"Head hurt?" Bleek laid a large, warm hand over my eyes.

"Yeah."

"Those two should have thanked you for getting all of us off the planet," Bleek grumbled softly. "If they grow any sense, maybe someday they'll remember that."

"Here." Ilya handed something to Bleek. It turned out to be a warm, wet cloth. Bleek removed his hand and set the cloth over my eyes instead. It felt like heaven.

"You want to stay here with us?" Bleek asked softly.

"Yes, please."

~

Queen's Palace, Le-Ath Veronis
Lissa

"This is a delicate situation, so please hear me out before you make objections," Quin said. Her wings were ruffled, as if what she was about to tell us upset her. I understood that. Her mates had all come to the meeting, including Justis, who was already frowning.

Bel Erland had come from Karathia with Erland, leaving Rylend guarded by Wellend and Warlend. Zaria trusted them; therefore, I was compelled to trust them, too. After all, they'd done the same thing for ages, employing different names and faces. I pretended that their circumstances hadn't changed in my eyes, but the truth was that things would never be the same—for any of us.

"What do you have, Quinnie Bee?" I asked, moving away from those thoughts and attempting to make Quin more comfortable.

"It's not just Captain Lenk that I want to talk about," Quin began.

"Who else, then?" Kooper asked.

"His King, Devarr of Carek Prime," she replied.

~

Quin

For a moment, everyone in Queen Lissa's library forgot to breathe. Carek Prime had a spotless reputation, although it was a non-Alliance world. Its newsfeeds were trusted and respected; in fact, many Alliance worlds used their feeds to report on events outside the Alliances.

Before the meeting, I'd done my research on Carek Prime with Berel at my side, pointing out this fact or that bit of information. Most texts referred to that world as an isolated entity, with little desire to interact with any other world.

It was self-sustaining, well-governed and had a standing army. Few outsiders had ever been allowed to visit, so tourism wasn't a strong point.

"What the hell does Carek Prime want you for?" Kooper exploded. Justis was demanding an answer, too, and their anger made me feel faint for a moment.

"Calm down, she's doing the best she can," Lissa scolded both. "I don't think she rested much after the healing she did, and that's not a good thing. Somebody get her a chair, for Pete's sake."

For a brief moment, I wondered who Pete might be, as strange a name as that was. "It has to do with this," I said after taking the seat Lissa's Falchani brought to me. "Carek Prime has been poisoned. Devarr emptied his treasury to pay for one of the spheres Vardil stole."

"So we know for a fact that Cayetes has them?" Lissa asked as calmly as she could.

"That's what I saw in Captain Lenk," I said. "He knows what the King was forced to pay to save his people and Carek Prime, as he was one of Devarr's guards who went with the King to meet Cayetes."

"That's it?" Kooper asked. "Did he know where the location was? Is Cayetes still there?"

"They met at a neutral site," I said. "He has no idea where Cayetes is hiding."

"Then what do you expect us to do about this?" Kooper asked, tossing out a hand in frustration.

"I'm not done," I told him. Exhaustion and fear were making me shake. I felt as if I were on trial in the Queen's library, and Captain Lenk's survival, along with that of everyone on Carek Prime, lay in my hands.

"What else do you have?" Lissa asked.

"Vardil made one last offer to Devarr before he left. He showed Devarr an image of a black-winged woman, and told the King that he'd refund the money if he found the black-winged woman for him."

"Fuck me," Kooper breathed. "That's why they were here."

"And now eleven of the twelve are dead," I pointed out. "The situation is delicate, Director Griff. Carek Prime is a non-Alliance world. The ASD holds no sway over it, and Devarr will deny Captain Lenk's very existence if we tell him we have him as a prisoner. We must approach this cautiously. I am willing to act as bait to get us to Cayetes; I only need someone to restore my disguise."

≈

Star Cruiser Hellion
  Zaria

I slept for the better part of the two days it took to travel back to Paricos II. I wasn't looking forward to meeting an angry pod'l-morph for the first time. I also wasn't looking forward to sleeping—or attempting to sleep—while surrounded by uneasy spirits.

I should have worried more about Arna and Mayyab, Tamp's assistant and seer.

They met us first on our way upward through the Rock; Arna couldn't help but sneer at me and gaze hopefully on Ilya. She didn't want another female who could compete for the best males the Rock had to offer.

She ignored most of the Rock's female employees; they weren't pretty enough to compete with her.

She had no idea I could see right through her; she had Elemaiyan blood and a few of their talents. I made a promise to myself, then. She would play a part in all this—I knew that. At the end, however, I would make her pay if she attempted to harm any of my party.

Mayyab, on the other hand, could be dangerous. He'd misinformed Tamp in the past if he didn't like this employee or that, telling Tamp they were dangerous. Velker was just an asshole. Mayyab was a dangerous asshole.

Mayyab's eyebrows lifted at the sight of the wrapped bundle that Deen, Velker's chief assistant held. Tamp was taking delivery of the treasure personally. Velker's body had already been transported to the top of the Rock by one of Tamp's warlocks. I figured we'd get to see all five of them, once we arrived in Tamp's penthouse.

I'd read in Velker early on that the gadgets Velker held were on loan from Tamp; I couldn't see Tamp letting that sort of technology run amok through the Rock—that would be foolish. That's why Velker's body had been locked inside his berth. I'd made sure it remained undisturbed by placing a shield myself; it wouldn't do to be accused of theft.

Turtle and Flyer wore the stoic, Falchani non-expression as we rode up the trans-vator to the penthouse. Bleek stood behind me, so I had no idea whether he was smiling or frowning.

Ilya barely suppressed anger as Arna leaned in his direction, forcing contact between the two. Mayyab was disturbed because he couldn't accurately read any of us. He itched to tell Tamp about it, too.

What are you? Mayyab's voice sounded in my head. Arna chose that moment to lean against Ilya, creating a clear path between the seer and me.

❧

Ilya

There are tales of Q'elindis in the past in King Rylend's library. Tales of a few who could bend the will of another to theirs, merely by leveling the full, unfiltered gaze of the Q'elindi upon them.

I didn't look into Zaria's eyes; it was enough to see their effect upon Mayyab, seer for the outlaw pod'l-morph, Tamp. He huddled against the wall of the trans-vator as if wishing to escape her gaze at first, but before it was over, he was already relaxing and nodding at her.

I doubt she'd have done it if it hadn't been necessary; that led me to believe that the seer intended to harm us in some way, or discredit us with Tamp.

Will he trouble us after this? I sent while attempting to extricate myself from almost full-body contact with Arna.

He'll be fine, Zaria replied. I understood that we needed to talk about us; I'd merely put it off until after the ordeal with Tamp was concluded.

The trans-vator doors opened into Tamp's private quarters instead of one level down, where I'd met him before. Evidence of his treasure-gathering was scattered throughout the luxurious space, as if designed and decorated by the best anyone could hire.

"Welcome to Master Tamp's suite," Arna stepped out first and regally swept out a hand.

~

Zaria

Tamp stood beside a wide, metal table made of bands and swirls of gold, silver and copper. For a moment, it reminded me of the edges of Quin's wings. Behind Tamp stood all five of his warlocks, just as I'd expected. Tamp held one of the gadgets Velker had carried with him; I recognized it as the device he'd used to get us past all of Juut's security measures.

As for Tamp, images blurred through my mind of all the forms he could take, until I looked past them at the creature he was. Tamp looked up, then, and his eyes met mine. He set the device he held carefully on the table before drawing in a breath.

~

Ilya

Today, Tamp chose to appear human and didn't morph into a multitude of shapes while inviting us in. Arna was puzzled; I could see it in the frown that played about her lips.

I imagined Tamp enjoyed watching the reactions of strangers when he revealed himself to them.

You're lucky, Zaria informed me. *There are some here at the Rock who've never seen him. They only have stories from a handful of others, and are told only that he's a master of disguise.*

That's what Gubb told me, I acknowledged.

He's the last, she added. *He's spent his entire life searching for others like him. He's never found any.*

This isn't the time to feel sorry for a criminal, Turtle broke into our conversation.

I wasn't saying that, Zaria countered.

"Come, bring me what you have," Tamp motioned for Deen to come forward with his bundle. "Set it here on this table, so I may look."

Deen stepped forward and laid the wrapped bundle he carried near the center of the wide table. Tamp motioned for him to step back, then, before touching the cloth wrapping.

The leather nest filled with bones was revealed, with the containment sphere at the center. "Does anyone here know what sort of bones these are?" Tamp asked aloud. "You, Zaria, do you know?"

I held my breath.

~

Queen's Palace, Le-Ath Veronis

Quin

"I refuse to lie to my King," Lenk stated flatly.

"I'm not asking you to lie," Lissa said. "I'm merely asking you to act as an envoy, so Ildevar Wyyld and I can approach him with our offer."

Neither Lissa, Justis nor Kooper had liked my proposal of returning to Carek Prime with Devarr. Therefore, they were offering a different tactic.

"Wyyld has offered a place in the Reth Alliance before," Lenk snorted.

"We're not offering that. We're offering a sizable reward, permission to keep the sphere that will save Carek Prime and the chance to get rid of Vardil Cayetes, before he kills other worlds by stripping them of the spheres we've already laid."

"He stole that sphere from another poisoned world?" Lenk's eyes widened.

"He did," Lissa confirmed. "What you may not know is that Vardil Cayetes is responsible for the poison spreading through the universes in the first place."

Lenk, who'd been holding the cup of tea a comesuli had brought to him during this meeting, set it carefully on its saucer as he processed that information.

"How?" he asked.

"The poison was contained on a single world, which was dying, as you can imagine," I said. As I'd seen it firsthand, I felt more than qualified to provide the answer to Lenk's question.

"A rogue wizard, who often worked with Cayetes, took some of the poison away and sold it. Cayetes was one of the first buyers. The wizard's containment spheres weren't well-made and leaked. Cayetes was stricken with the illness. He sought revenge against the wizard. The wizard returned to the poisoned world to escape the ASD, who was hunting him by that time. Cayetes, in a terrible act of revenge against the wizard, destroyed the entire planet with a ranos cannon, effectively sending poisoned debris flying into space. It has taken a toll on every world the debris has landed upon."

"You say Cayetes was ill, though. Surely he should be dead by now."

"He should be," Lissa huffed. "Have you ever heard of a transference spell?"

Lenk paled.

"How many lives?" he whispered.

"Too many to count," Lissa replied. "Eventually, he found a way out of that and no longer needs fresh bodies to keep himself alive. He is strong and well, now, and back to trouble all of us by stealing what will heal the dying worlds he created."

"Devarr never deals with this sort—and wouldn't have if there'd been any choice," Lenk's gaze dropped to his hands.

"We understand that. We're offering to let him keep the sphere that will save Carek Prime," Lissa reiterated. "We have a limited number of those spheres, Captain. We can replace that one, but few others. Cayetes steals too many, well, you understand what will happen."

"I can only present my opinion to the King in this matter," Lenk sighed. "I cannot make the decision for him."

"There's something else you don't understand, too," Kooper said. "It isn't only the spheres. Quin, here, has to place them. She calls the poison to the spheres. Those two things, working together, save poisoned worlds. Now do you see what Quin is willing to entrust to you and your king?"

Lenk raised his head to gaze at Kooper. They were both soldiers, burdened with the safety of worlds and leaders. "If she dies, the universes die?"

"Yes."

"I feel small," Lenk whispered. "Your people are right to call us isolationists. I had no idea."

"Please, let me talk with your king," I begged. "Perhaps together, we can cure what is killing so many."

"I will ask, Lady, as you saved my life and that of many others."

~

Paricos II

Zaria

Tamp wasn't his real name, and he knew the bones were a Sirenali's. He was testing us. I was about to surprise him.

"Those bones hold power," I said. "To defeat others who hold power from finding what they are meant to conceal."

"You feel this?" Tamp lifted an eyebrow at me.

"Yes."

"Surprising—and gratifying."

The five warlocks who stood at his back had no knowledge of a Sirenali's power. I found that unusual for anyone carrying the Blackmantle name. I wondered if Nefrigar had learned anything of their lineage, yet. I was determined to ask him later, provided there wasn't an emergency and I didn't have to haul my group away from Tamp's stronghold.

"Mayyab, what do you think of these now?" Tamp swept a hand out.

"I still hold reservations, as always, Master Tamp." It was the appropriate answer to the question.

"Of course you do. Do you see any difficulties with inviting the witch to have dinner with me?"

"She's only a Third-level," Mayyab snorted, as if a Third-level couldn't send his ass halfway across Paricos II's ocean and drop him in it.

He'd been instructed (by me) not to harm us in any way. I never told him he couldn't speak his mind regarding most matters.

"Yet she had the presence of mind to remove Velker's body, the crew and the prize he sought for me, before being discovered by Juut," Tamp frowned at Mayyab.

"Luck," Mayyab insisted. If I hadn't instructed him not to harm us, he'd be even more insufferable.

"What say you, Nyarr?" Tamp turned to the oldest of the Blackmantle brothers.

"Unlike Mayyab, who trusts nobody including himself, I see no problem with her," Nyarr replied.

I wanted to laugh—none of the warlocks were fond of Mayyab. It was his ability and position with Tamp that kept him from being a target of their power, because of his nastiness.

At least Tamp was able to control them. Arna, on the other hand, could become a problem if she weren't watched carefully.

"We have concluded our examination of the body," Darkins announced as he stepped off the trans-vator. "Death was caused by a single, ancient pellet fired by an even more ancient weapon. Devious, on Juut's part, to set that up."

"Have you reclaimed all the devices I sent with him?"

"Yes. They are locked away in the armory, as instructed, except for the one you have there." Darkins jerked his head at the device Tamp had held when we first arrived.

"Good. Very good," Tamp gave a slight nod. "I appreciate your efforts in this," he swept a hand over the bundle of bones and the containment sphere. "Deen, how confident are you that you can take Velker's place?"

"Very confident, sir," Deen replied. "I have one request, however."

"What is that?"

"That Zaria goes with me whenever I'm sent after treasure. For safety only," Deen was quick to hold up a hand.

"I think I can arrange that, as I was thinking in a similar fashion," Tamp agreed. "In fact, you may take any or all of Master Smith's crew with you when you go; it seems they are quite calm in sticky situations."

"I was grateful," Deen admitted. "Jin and I questioned Zaria at length. She was very calm and thoughtful with her answers. It would relieve me to know she can transport me away from trouble whenever it becomes necessary."

"Zaria, do you fight with blades?" Tamp turned to me.

"No, Master Tamp. I have had brief instruction in hand fighting, but I am not very good at it."

Ilya, the swine, ducked his head to hide the smile.

"Dinner is at eight bells," Tamp offered a smile. "Be here on time for drinks."

"Yes, Master Tamp."

~

Ilya

"You have Tamp's permission to hire two more; one will not be a problem," Chief Darkins said. He'd taken the trans-vator down to the lower level with us, so I'd asked about bringing one more in.

"I think I can have him here in two days; I'll instruct him to meet us at Gubb's," I said.

"Good. Zaria and I will come with you."

"I can transport us back and forth, to save time," Zaria offered.

"I'll take you up on that," Darkins smiled. "I was hoping you'd offer."

"It's no trouble," Zaria said.

"Tamp likes to keep his warlocks close, so it's not an option with them. I'm hoping he'll allow you to transport me when I have to leave the Rock," Darkins said. "Provided you aren't on assignment or otherwise engaged."

"I enjoy traveling," Zaria said. "Whenever I'm available, I'm at your service."

Don't get too friendly, Bleek warned.

He doesn't like women in that way, Zaria returned.

Good.

He thinks you're interesting.

I wanted to laugh.

Feel free to transport him away as often as possible, Bleek replied.

"Your furnace is in place, you only need to inspect it," Darkins said when the trans-vator reached our cave and opened. He was right; the new furnace took up nearly a third of the space.

"I'll check it over, including the connections to the solar power," I said. "It won't be lit until I'm satisfied that everything is as it should be. If all is well, I should have decent blades for Master Tamp in a few eight-days."

"Be sure to add treasure-hunting days into that schedule," Darkins warned. "Master Tamp may have another target very soon."

"That's fine," I shrugged. "As long as he's not unreasonable on the deadlines if I'm interrupted."

"If the work proceeds at a steady pace, he will be pleased enough. I will leave you, now, but know this; Tamp seldom asks anyone to his personal suite. He has never invited anyone to dinner."

~

Queen's Palace, Le-Ath Veronis

Lissa

To say Justis wasn't pleased with any sort of plan that involved luring Cayetes in with Quin as bait was like saying the Avii King only grew a few feathers as mere decoration. He'd ruffled his red wings and glared at all of us as we attempted to hammer out a plan.

That plan was to travel to Carek Prime in two eight-days, hoping that King Devarr would acknowledge Lenk and allow us inside his palace. Getting him to listen would be the frosting on the cake.

We can send Halimel in two days, Rylend's mindspeech broke into my thoughts. *And, just so you know, Garwin Wyatt, Travis and Trent just won the Founder's Prize for Diplomacy in the mock trials.*

Seriously? They won?

I think Garwin Wyatt was leading the charge, but yes, they won. Teeg wants to send Wyatt as a diplomat somewhere; I think he may be ready, now.

Well, after so many years of school, I'd expect something in return, I said. *Does this mean my twins are coming home, or are they going to hare after another adventure?*

You need to talk to Drake and Drew, Ry's mental voice held laughter. *I think they may have mentioned a life of piracy.*

So soon? I expect their diplomacy skills are going to rot quickly. Which ship do they have their eye on?

They want to sail with Amos Thompson and Bear Wright.

Of course they do. They wanted BlackWing I, because it was the fastest in the fleet, no doubt. *Your stepson and your younger brothers are going to get in trouble, I just know it,* I added.

They are adults, although you can't always tell that, Ry observed.

So are their fathers, I said. Ry's mental laughter made me smile.

~

Quin

Justis was angry and refused to speak to me. Instead, I watched him pace back and forth inside the guest suite Lissa provided, his red wings plastered tightly against his back and his movements stiff with displeasure.

I'd asked him if he wanted to go with Queen Lissa and Deonus Wyyld. He didn't reply. Justis, the Black Wing Commander, wouldn't have hesitated—he'd have insisted on being included.

King Justis wasn't happy and didn't care that it made me unhappy, too.

I saw no other way to find Cayetes than this. Kooper's attempt had been well-planned and should have succeeded. It didn't, because of unforeseen interference.

"What do you want me to do?" I flung out a hand when I couldn't take Justis' anger and pacing any longer.

He stopped and leveled a dark gaze upon me. His jaw worked and he shook his head before turning aside for a moment.

"It isn't just you I want to protect," he muttered before turning back to me. "My heart cannot take another beating where you're concerned."

"Justis," I struggled to hold back tears as I ran to him. He wrapped me in his arms and his wings as he kissed me and told me he loved me, many times.

~

Paricos II

Zaria

"Please, come in," Tamp held out a hand.

I stepped off the trans-vator into his suite, where he stood, waiting for me to arrive right on time.

He was dressed comfortably, although the fabrics were rich and well-designed. I'd had to pull what I wore from the bottom of my trunk, never thinking I'd have a use for the long, blue gown.

The color of the dress matched a Larentii's skin—and a sunny sky in summer. When I'd walked past Ilya in the cave to reach the trans-vator earlier, a frown had appeared on his lips.

Perhaps this was penance for his making me suffer. Perhaps it was something else entirely.

I preferred the second option. Seldom does anyone walk into an opportunity the likes of which I'd found. It was my hope that the opportunity would not fail, based on such a massive amount of hope as it was.

"Master Tamp," I held out my hand to him.

"Call me Tampirus," he said. "There is no need for anything else."

~

Vardil Cayetes' Private Quarters

V'ili

"I've heard the woman was moved afterward," Skyf, Vardil's spy reported. "There are no records of where. The Criminal Detention Facility has been emptied and repairs are under way."

"What in the name of the bloody god happened? They almost killed V'ili," Vardil hissed between clenched teeth.

"I heard it was an attempt by another band of pirates, looking to collect the reward. I believe the ASD is frantic that so many breached their security."

"How many?" Vardil demanded.

"At least a dozen. All killed, of course. Their deaths saved V'ili's life."

"I did not see or hear them, either," I said, surprising Vardil. "It has to be a new technology, to get past the ASD. I did not instruct them to ignore anyone else."

"Then search for that device," Vardil snapped at Skyf. "I want it in my hands within three eight-days, understand? I want to walk into the palace on Le-Ath Veronis and let everyone know who I am and what I want."

"Of course, Master Cayetes."

"Leave me," Vardil waved Skyf away. "I wish to speak with V'ili alone."

"What is it?" I asked, once the door closed behind Skyf.

"I believe the black-winged woman is either in the palace dungeons on Le-Ath Veronis, or in the cells inside that infernal Avii Castle. I want both searched if at all possible. Find a way to make that happen. I care not if those who may stand in our way are killed, you understand."

"I do understand," I said, smiling at Vardil. "In fact, it will be my pleasure."

"There is one other thing," Vardil said.

"What is that?"

"I want the ranos cannon built. Those fools on Vic'Law provided more than enough extra parts to repair the one which was destroyed. That means we have everything we need to build a new one."

"I will see to it," I said. "If we do not have enough engineers, I'll find more."

"Good."

CHAPTER 8

Queen's Palace, Le-Ath Veronis

Quin

I woke with my head on Justis' shoulder. "Want breakfast, love?" Justis murmured before kissing my forehead.

"Yes," I snuggled closer to him. "Do I have to move to get it?"

"I can send for breakfast, but I'll have to move to do it," he teased.

"We should get up," I said. "I just don't want to."

"I know. Let's get up together, and go to breakfast together."

"Sounds perfect."

Paricos II

Ilya

"Did he discuss what he is?" I asked over breakfast. Turtle and Flyer had cooked for us, although they'd already eaten. Zaria, Bleek and I were having our morning meal in the small space we'd reserved for our makeshift kitchen.

"He worked around that. I think he's worried I'll find him

disgusting if I learn he likes to become a tree, a rock or a cactus now and then."

"Do you find him disgusting?" Bleek lifted his cup of tea and drank, although he kept his eyes on Zaria to watch her expression.

"Not because of that," she shrugged.

"So part of him is disgusting?"

"I didn't say that. Like any of the bosses on Paricos II, he's done away with his share of people—mostly criminal employees. He doesn't drag it out, though, like some of the others. He likes to acquire things —and sells most of them—but you already knew that. He prefers to get a team in and out with no losses, or at least a minimum of losses."

"What does he want with you?" Bleek asked.

"To talk, mostly. He gets sex from Arna."

"She wasn't pleased about his dinner invitation, I know that much," I dipped my toast into poached eggs and bit off a corner. Turtle and Flyer were excellent cooks.

"She wants to kill me," Zaria said casually.

"Are you worried about that?"

"I'm only worried about what she might do to everybody else. I can feel her coming from miles away."

"Can you give me some of that?" Bleek asked.

"Probably, although it might make you uneasy until you get used to it."

"I'll take uneasy. I worked for years for Cayetes, and I'd have settled for being uneasy. Constantly watching your back does strange things to people."

"I hear that," I agreed.

"What are we doing today?" Zaria asked.

"Lighting the furnace. I checked everything over last night while you were at dinner. We're ready to start the smelting process."

~

Queen's Palace, Le-Ath Veronis
   Lissa

"Tell me about the device you used to get past my men," Kooper said. Captain Lenk was having breakfast with us in the kitchen. Gavin and Tony were with us, listening to what Lenk had to say.

Tony had been at the detention facility when Lenk and his men had strolled past, with no sound or scent to indicate their passing. Of course he was interested in the answer.

"The chief scientist for the King created it," Lenk admitted. "It worked too well this time and got my men killed."

"You're telling me you have this technology on Carek Prime?" Kooper sounded incredulous.

"We do. Devarr controls the number of devices produced, because he sees this as a necessary evil—somewhat like ranos technology. Extremely dangerous in the wrong hands, you understand."

"I can see that," Kooper agreed. "I'm concerned that Vardil Cayetes will come looking for it, if he learns of its existence. Along with every other criminal in and out of the Alliances. I have a meeting with Teeg San Gerxon scheduled to discuss it."

"Devarr will never allow the technology to leave Carek Prime," Lenk insisted. "He will destroy all devices and the plans before he'll let that happen."

"While that sounds more than altruistic, things like that often find their way into the worlds regardless of our best intentions," I pointed out. "We'd be working on something already to counteract it, if we had one of the devices to work with."

"Devarr will never agree to that," Lenk said. "He trusts Hulce and everyone else involved in manufacturing those devices. Carek Prime will never allow them to fall into the wrong hands. My apologies, Queen Lissa, that came out wrong," he said quickly.

"No, I understood your meaning. I'm merely pointing out that not everything is always as we wish it to be, Captain Lenk."

Kooper, I sent, *find out what Carek Prime's vulnerabilities are. If word of these devices gets out, I can honestly see the planet being attacked, just to get the technology or kidnap the scientist involved.*

On it, Kooper acknowledged.

"Captain Lenk, I understand that you think this technology will be kept secret," I said. "However, you and your king gave up that fantasy the moment you employed it to walk into an ASD facility."

∼

Paricos II

Zaria

We spent the day heating the furnace and bringing in barrels of iron ore to smelt. We had a use for the barrels afterward, too; to hold slag—the glass-like substance formed by the smelting process. The furnace would divert the molten slag away, cool it and then grind it to fine granules, which could be recycled for other purposes.

The cave warmed and then became hot. I employed power to keep the temperature down; Bleek had his shirt off and was sweating already as he moved hover carts loaded with iron ore toward the furnace.

I'd already changed to a tank top and short, close-fitting pants to accommodate the heat produced by the furnace. My hair was piled in a bun atop my head and I wasn't looking my best when Loor and Nyarr arrived to watch us work.

"We've never seen this before," Nyarr grinned as Ilya shoveled iron ore into the furnace.

"Want to help?" Ilya turned and grinned at both.

"No," Loor laughed. "We were just curious, that's all. It looks as if we've been taking the production of our metals too lightly."

"An industrial furnace will be larger and better controlled," Ilya wiped sweat off his face. "It's still hot work, no matter how you look at it."

"Those tattoos for real?" Nyarr asked as Turtle and Flyer, both bare-chested, rolled empty barrels out of the way to make room for another load Bleek brought in.

"They're Falchani. Of course they're real," Ilya said. "Want water or something else to drink? I'm ready for a break."

"No," Nyarr declined. "But we'd like to have dinner with you and your crew tonight—in the supervisors' mess."

"Sure," Ilya shrugged. "Especially if the food's better there than what's in the regular mess."

"We have trouble getting decent cooks," Loor said. "The best ones go upstairs, as you probably have guessed already."

"What time?" Ilya asked.

"Seven?"

"We'll be there. We'll even clean up, first."

What's that about? Bleek sent the moment both warlocks disappeared.

Curiosity, mostly, I told him. *They want to size all of us up, and want to get in on the ground floor, since we're Tamp's new favorite toys.*

Worried they'll be replaced? Turtle asked.

No—they've seen many come and go; Tamp isn't looking to replace any of his warlocks. They keep him happy; he keeps them happy. We're still an unknown quantity, and those five learned long ago not to put stock in anything Mayyab says.

What do you really think? Ilya asked.

I think they're looking for friends. Nobody here has similar interests, and, as I'm a certified witch who's apparently worked with all of you before, they believe we as a group may have something in common.

Does Tamp use them to carry out executions? Flyer asked.

No. He does that in a more tradition fashion. He has several spies and two assassins on his staff; we just haven't met them, yet.

Great, Bleek said. *Why didn't you say that before?*

Because I didn't want to scare you.

You think I'm scared?

Honey, please stop, I begged. *I'm getting a headache.*

"Come here," Bleek walked toward me. He lifted me up and placed my legs around his waist with both lower arms while holding onto me and rubbing my back with the top two.

I dropped my forehead against his shoulder with a sigh.

I'd seen the spirits gather inside the cave once the warlocks appeared. They stayed when the warlocks left, and now studied Bleek and me as he held me and rubbed my back.

I sighed again—deeper, this time.

~

Ilya

Deen and Jin joined us for dinner with the warlocks. I imagined that once Velker was out of the way, the warlocks were more than happy to approach the two assistants. Velker had hired both after Tamp employed him; that came out during dinner conversation.

"Tamp asked us to place Velker's body in stasis, so we did," Nyarr shrugged when Deen ventured to ask the warlock about his former supervisor. "He has it in his personal vault—until he decides what to do with it."

"I hope you didn't care for him," Loor grinned. "He treated everybody else like dirt."

"He cared more about dirt," Jin pointed out. "Especially if it had artifacts or something valuable in it."

"Are we bad-mouthing the dead?" Zaria asked. "Because if you are, I want in."

Nyarr laughed. Loor and the others struggled to hide huge grins. Deen chuckled and slapped Jin on the back.

"Not to change the subject," Deen said, "but Master Tamp says he has another target for a treasure hunt. If everything goes as planned, we'll leave in two days."

"Turtle and I can stay and start working the metal," Flyer offered. "That way, it won't just sit there," he added.

"We'll have Hal on board by tomorrow, so that should be fine," I said. "We'll take him with us and leave you two here."

"Actual Falchani, working a forge? Tamp may come to watch for himself," Kear, one of Nyarr's younger brothers, said.

"He'll be welcome to watch, but we'll only be hammering out the metal and beginning the folding process, to make steel blades," Turtle said.

"He'll be interested," Nyarr said. "We'll probably bring him down for a while. He is fascinated by your tattoos."

"It's the highest art form on Falchan," Turtle grinned. "And they all have to be earned in battle."

"Are there any research materials on the subject?" Loor asked. "Tamp would be overjoyed if there were."

"There is only an archive of the artists who served Falchan's warlords through the ages," Flyer said. "And very little about their techniques or the art itself."

"Too bad; he'd be captivated for days with that sort of research."

What Flyer didn't say was there were tales, passed down in an oral tradition, regarding many of those artists. I'm sure he wanted to keep the Falchani storytellers safe by keeping that information away from Tamp.

The Larentii have it in their Archives, Zaria informed me.

I wasn't surprised. It would surprise me if the Larentii *didn't* have it in their Archives. *Tamp would go nuts if he were to see those Archives*, I sent back. Hell, *I* wanted to see them. Not many who weren't Larentii had.

I'm sure he would, she agreed.

~

Zaria

I was ready to transport us to Gubb's bar the following morning when Chief Darkins arrived. Hal was waiting there for us already; Ilya received mindspeech from Ry, saying that his father had transported the vampire to Paricos II.

"Ready?" I asked Darkins. He grinned and nodded. We were walking into Gubb's moments later.

"Tamp sends his greetings and this," Darkins tossed a small bag of local currency to Gubb, who was hovering about Hal like a buzzard waiting for his meal to die.

I'm sure Hal could have shooed the pest away, but like any ancient (and patient) vampire, he chose to ignore it instead.

"This is Hal," Ilya introduced the vampire, who rose when we approached his table. He'd ordered ale, but had barely touched it.

"Want to eat here, or go back to the compound?" Darkins asked after greeting Hal.

"Whatever is most convenient," Hal replied.

"We'll eat here," Darkins jerked his head at Gubb. "It's nice to have a meal out, now and then."

"Of course." Gubb scurried away to yell at his cook and barmaid.

~

Ilya

"You don't have long to settle in," I informed Hal when Zaria transported us back to the Rock after lunch. "We're heading out tomorrow on a treasure hunt."

"You won't know what your target is until you're halfway there; Tamp likes to keep those things to himself," Darkins said. "Pleasure to meet you, Hal." Darkins walked toward the trans-vator and got on. I nodded to him as the doors closed and the 'vator moved upward.

"I understand Zaria reads people. I find nothing wrong with that one," Hal said. "Lady, what say you?"

"He's as honorable as anyone, in or out of a criminal boss' compound," she said.

"Good. I left my poison kit behind, but Rylend says he can transport it if needed. I merely want to consider anyone who could harm us in some way, or jeopardize our mission."

"We're good for now, but I'll keep you posted," Zaria said.

"I'd suggest watching out for Arna," I said. "She'll be interested in you, no doubt."

She would be—any woman would appreciate Hal's dark-blond hair and good looks. Arna had even let her eyes wander toward Turtle and Flyer, for the obvious reasons.

Neither Falchani would give her the pleasure of a raised eyebrow. I looked forward to Hal's reaction when she introduced herself the first time.

She wasn't used to being ignored by any male, including a few who didn't prefer women.

She already wanted to do away with Zaria, who outclassed her by light-years. I wondered what she wanted to do to me and the others who'd effectively spurned her advances, subtle or otherwise.

Stop worrying about it, Zaria sent. *We have bigger fish to fry.*

Fish to fry?

Honey, it's a metaphor. A colloquialism from old Earth.

I was stunned that she'd called me an endearment. *Fish to fry, eh?* I responded, as if that endearment didn't squeeze my heart. *Sounds about right,* I agreed.

Zaria

Tamp arrived with Darkins and Arna the following morning to see us off. Deen and Jin were already in our cave with their bags; this time, I was allowed to transport everyone straight to the *Hellion*.

"I am entrusting this to you—and to Zaria," Tamp handed the concealment device to Deen. It was the same one Velker used; I'd gotten it back to Tamp safely and in one piece with Velker's body.

I knew where the thing came from now, after seeing it in Tamp. That would have to be dealt with later; he was sending us after three containment spheres sold to the same ruling house on another world.

An Alliance world.

I could only imagine what plans that ruling house had for the poison; I had no idea whether they knew how dangerous it was if they merely wanted to get rid of a rival on their own world.

It no longer mattered; I and my team were determined to relieve them of their hideous treasure. I imagined more Sirenali bones waited with it.

Who had known that secret?

V'ili.

He'd known to tell someone—Vardil most likely. With all the Sirenali clones available who only lived a short while, it was easy enough to obtain the bones necessary to bury with your treasures.

At a price, I'm sure.

Vardil Cayetes was a criminal's criminal, who created a market and sold to anyone who had sufficient funds, his competitors included.

So many things required my attention, but finding containment spheres had to be first on that list. My list had a delicate balance to it; each item in its own turn, lest the entire thing turn to dust and cause millions to suffer and die.

At times, the burden of being Vhanaraszh sucked.

"Is everyone ready?" Deen took charge of our party at Tamp's nod.

"Ready," Ilya responded.

"Zaria?" Deen turned to me.

I folded our group away.

Phrinnis Tampirus

Arna was plotting. I'd seen too many humanoids during my long life to suspect anything different. She'd refused to speak and glared at Zaria the entire time we spent in the cave. Zaria had wisely ignored the insult.

I imagined Arna's plot surrounded Zaria. I waited and watched carefully as Arna laid her plans. No doubt she wanted to kill Zaria; she despised anyone whom she saw as a competitor for a desired male.

Her decisions in the matter would determine whether I had her eliminated or not. I was tired of the jealousy and the games. No sex was worth that.

It was time to speak with one of my spies and my chief assassin. They would ensure Arna's death was painless, should it become necessary.

The problem, of course, was Mayyab. He and Arna had collaborated in the past to eliminate someone they hadn't liked.

I didn't interfere, as long as the one they targeted was unimportant and easily replaced.

This time, the one she targeted was important—in ways I couldn't define as yet. Arna's actions regarding Zaria and her team would determine her future.

Or the lack of it.

~

Star Cruiser Hellion

Ilya

We're heading for Q'eefur, Zaria informed me. *Deen doesn't know yet; Tamp will let him know in two days.*

Q'eefur. A Campiian Alliance world. *A four-day trip each way,* she'd said. At least Captain Meric and his navigator knew where our destination was.

Tamp trusted those two more than he trusted his treasure hunters.

Deen and Jin have no idea what we're collecting, Zaria said. *They think the spheres are valuable artifacts that they've never heard of before.*

I don't know whether to be happy or upset about that, I said. *Not good for them if they end up touching a containment sphere that hasn't been properly shielded.*

That's why it's a good idea for me to go in ahead of the rest of you, to check the residents for poison sickness. If it's there, I'll place a containment spell of my own around those spheres. We don't need to carry leakage back with us.

Agreed. Do you think Velker provided Quin's spheres to Cayetes? I asked what had concerned me for several days.

It's possible, since he was obsessed and I couldn't read him past that. At least he's dead, so that avenue of stolen spheres is no longer available to Cayetes. My concern is the treasure hunters working on those other worlds. I hope the wards and precautions Lissa took are working to keep the other spheres safe.

As do I. Is Quin still laying spheres?

I believe so, although not in the past few days, I think. That should change soon; worlds are in need of her talents.

I have a question, I said.

What's that?

Will you bunk with the rest of us?

She and I sat at a small table in the ship's mess, drinking tea while we silently conversed.

Is that what you want? she asked.

I ducked my head and raked fingers through my hair.

I want you all to myself, but that won't happen, so I'll settle for having you close, I reluctantly admitted.

Then I'll bunk with the rest of you, she agreed.

Thank the gods, I blew out an audible breath, startling her.

"Ready to go unpack?" I asked aloud, standing and stretching.

"I suppose," she agreed. Standing, she swept out an arm and said, "Lay on, MacDuff."

I blinked at her for a moment before holding up a hand. "Don't—it's not important," I said, making her laugh.

"It's actually about a swordfight," Zaria bumped me with a shoulder as we walked out of the mess toward our berth.

"Then I may be interested," I said. "Someday."

She laughed again.

~

Queen's Palace, Le-Ath Veronis

Lissa

"We have two worlds waiting for spheres," I said. I'd invited Quin and her mates to lunch in the arboretum. Kay and Trace arrived with them. We all sat around a large table, discussing our next assignment.

"I have a team ready to go with us," I said. "Zaria is tracking more of those containment spheres—I received mindspeech from Erland this morning."

"When?" Quin asked, her fork poised halfway to her mouth.

"Is tomorrow too soon?" I asked.

"No. Will we take BlackWing VII?"

"Not this time," I said. "I'll be your transportation. We tried to lure Cayetes in that way before—with everything that happened as a result, I only see traveling aboard ship as another disaster waiting to occur."

"We can go early—before dawn," Lafe suggested.

"A good time," I agreed. "Are you up for that?" I asked Quin.

"I will be." She smiled and went back to her vegetable lasagna.

"We'll come back here and you can eat and rest afterward," I said. "We'll do the second one two days after that."

"Easy enough," she agreed. Justis, who sat next to her, reached out to massage Quin's neck. Ever since three spheres had been stolen, the idea of placing more of those precious things filled her with anxiety.

We'd taken better precautions after those thefts, but I'd seen too many times how things could go awry, even in the best of circumstances.

The thought of Quin walking into a potential trap that led through the palace on Carek Prime now worried me even more.

Yes, it had been a sound option—on the surface. Justis had already made her feel bad enough about this—I didn't need to add my worry into the mix, too.

I couldn't help thinking about Zaria, though, and those with her. I worried that the acquisition of the containment spheres was crawling along at a snail's pace. I'm sure she was frustrated as much as I was about it, too.

Ashe says to stop worrying—things will turn out or they won't, Kay sent mindspeech.

Yeah. It's just that things are becoming more complicated, I replied.

He says he understands.

I'm glad somebody does, I grumped mentally. Kay smiled and went back to her meal.

~

Star Cruiser Hellion

   Zaria

"What's this?" Bleek sat on the edge of my bunk where I sat, back against the wall, using a comp-vid to play solitaire.

"It's an old Earth game. Not easy to win," I said.

"Why play it then? Sounds frustrating." He scooted closer to watch me lay a red card on black. "I don't recognize these symbols."

"Old Earth numbers, mostly," I said. "See—this card is called a jack," I explained. "There are face cards and number cards. You have to place them in descending order. Once you no longer have a place for the remaining cards, the game is over. The goal is to play all cards."

"You're crippling yourself by pulling three cards at once," Bleek peeled me away from the wall and settled me in his arms while I continued my game.

"That's the rule. If you play the top card, you can then play the second one down and so on."

"Sounds frustrating."

"I find it relaxing," I confessed. "The cards either play or they don't. They don't change colors or loyalties on you—it's always straightforward."

"This is an analogy?" He breathed on my neck before placing a kiss there.

"Sort of."

"Can you explain it?"

"Not yet," I said, giving up on the current game and tapping the comp-vid to reshuffle the virtual deck.

"You know something, don't you?"

"Whatever makes you say that?" I turned in his arms and smiled at him. He took advantage and kissed me.

Paricos II

Phrinnis Tampirus

Arna took a shuttle, one guard and a pilot with her to Fendala before lunch. Mayyab brought the information to me not long after, while I sat in sunlight on my terrace.

I was surprised—Mayyab seldom reported on Arna's comings and goings. "Shopping?" I asked, my question noncommittal.

"What else?" Mayyab lied.

"Very well," I shrugged, as if her actions no longer concerned me. "Leave me now, I wish to enjoy the sunlight while we have it."

The moment Mayyab was gone, I tapped my communicator.

"Master Tamp?" my chief spy answered.

"Are you having Arna followed?"

"Of course, Master Tamp."

"I want a report of all her appointments in Fendala," I said.

Queen's Palace, Le-Ath Veronis

Lissa

"I haven't seen you here in ages," Merrill sat beside me atop the largest dome of my palace.

"I know. I haven't been this worried in ages," I admitted.

"About?"

"About Quin. This plan that we hatched to use her as bait. It will have to be canceled or revised."

"You said it was the best idea put forward," Merrill began.

"And that's exactly what it was a few days ago."

"Not now?"

"It's more complicated, now."

"How is it more complicated?"

"A few days ago, it was the best idea we could come up with," I said.

"What changed?"

"A few days ago, Quin wasn't pregnant," I confessed.

CHAPTER 9

*S*tar Cruiser Hellion
    Ilya

Valegar arrived, provided energy sex for Zaria, Bleek and me, then left after resting for a short time.

I admit, resting after the best sex of my life was an excellent idea. I'd forgotten how good sex was for relieving tension. I promised myself not to forget again.

Deen, Jin and the others had no idea; we'd been heavily shielded the entire time. Hal had politely excused himself and spent the time drinking tea in the ship's galley.

Bleek slept, Zaria still cuddled in his arms. Next time, I wanted that position and he could lie on his bunk.

"Are we there yet?" Zaria mumbled sleepily.

"Love, we've barely been gone a day," Bleek whispered against her hair. I muffled a laugh.

Zaria

I played a lot of solitaire during the four long days it took to get to Q'eefur. Valegar would tell me that they were the same length as any other day, but for me, they lasted so much longer than that.

I wanted to fold in, get the items and fold out again. I wanted to do the same thing a thousand more times, or as many as it took to collect all the poison Marid stole from Siriaa.

I'd never gone stir-crazy quite like that before. That's why I decided to go on a field trip the third day.

I need to visit Le-Ath Veronis, I informed Ilya and Bleek. *I'll leave a decent facsimile of myself here, and appear to be taking a nap.*

If you were going anywhere else, I'd be tempted to say no, Ilya said. *Unless I went with you. Yes, I know you can take care of yourself, but that doesn't stop my worry.*

I know. I patted his cheek and stood on tip-toe to kiss him. *I'll be back before you know it.*

Where are you going on Le-Ath Veronis? Bleek demanded.

I turned to him; he was frowning at me.

To the library, I admitted.

He lifted an eyebrow and the frown disappeared. *Fine*, he said. *Don't be gone long.*

What, and miss all the action here on this boring trip?

There's that, he admitted, rubbing his neck with one hand. *Have fun. Write when you can.*

I laughed and folded space at the same time.

~

Le-Ath Veronis
  Avii Castle
  Zaria

I never said I was going to Queen Lissa's library. The one I needed belonged to the Avii. That meant traveling back in time before the castle was moved to Avendor.

Gurnil was away, having a meal with Ordin and a few others. That left me free time to wander through the library while shielding myself. It wouldn't do if someone were to walk in and find a female Larentii wandering the stacks.

I'd only seen what I searched for in Quin, when reading her in the past. This time, I wanted to see it for myself.

Quin, Gurnil and the other Avii thought the painting a romanticized version of a saving performed by Elabeth. I stood before it for a very long time, soaking in every detail. I imagined the artist had taken many liberties to make his Queen appear beautiful in the forest setting.

As for the vision of her disappearing into the bark of a tree—perhaps some truth could be derived from this bit of whimsy after all.

~

Vardil Cayetes' Private Quarters
  V'ili

"Any word from Skyf?" Vardil asked. "We have five more requests for cleaned bones."

"I hear that the mutes aren't dying fast enough, so the sick are being tossed to the carrion worms. You'll have bones soon. As for Skyf, he's attached himself to a work crew assigned to repair the ASD facility. He's hoping to find where the attackers and their device originated."

"I hope he gets the information soon; I want that technology," Vardil muttered.

"It would be more than useful," I agreed. "My obsessions, combined with such would be formidable."

"My thoughts as well," Vardil agreed. "I'll contact the buyers and tell them we'll have bones ready soon. They can transfer half the credits now and the other half on delivery."

"Sound business decision," I said. "I'll let you know when they're ready."

~

Star Cruiser Hellion

Ilya

"What did you find?" I asked when Zaria reappeared after a brief visit to the palatial home located outside Q'eefur's capital.

"Several of the residents are sick," she said, flopping onto her bunk with a sigh and dropping her face into her hands. "So far, the poison hasn't spread beyond the perimeter of the Pre-Empsis' palace, but it won't be long before that happens."

"Did you find the spheres?" Hal asked.

"Yes. They're shielded now, but the poison has soaked into the Sirenali's bones around it. I've shielded those, too, but I worry about carrying that back to Tamp. If Nyarr or his brothers examine the spheres, they'll know somebody very strong placed those shields."

"Will they trace it back to you?" Bleek asked.

"I doubt it—they don't think I can keep a coffee cup from spilling. I'm worried Tamp will be curious enough to send someone back to look into the matter. That could be disastrous and carry the poison back to Paricos II, which I certainly don't want to happen."

"What do you think we should do, then?" Hal asked.

"I think we should inform Lissa, and ask her to carry this news to Teeg San Gerxon," Zaria said. "If a convenient explosion or some such could be arranged, after removing the entire estate and sending it elsewhere," she shrugged.

"What about the infected people?" Their bodies would serve as a conduit for the poison, too, when they died. "How are their physicians explaining the illness away?" I queried.

"They're not—they're pretending there's a cure. That's a violation of the laws in both Alliances—physicians are required to report those cases."

"And things get progressively worse," Hal muttered.

"Here's my problem," Zaria said. "I've shielded those things, because we're not carrying them away without that safeguard. If Tamp finds out later that Q'eefur is infected, he'll think one of two things—either those things were shielded after our arrival, or that there are other spheres on Q'eefur. I'm voting for the former, since the shields will have his warlocks stumped."

"He won't imagine that the poison could have arrived by other means?" Hal offered.

"Q'eefur is blocked against fallout by its sun and surrounding planets. You won't find a drop of poison on any of those. Hence, the shields and the one who placed them will be called into question first thing." Zaria's frown worried me.

"Let's hope that doesn't happen," Hal said. "Shall we proceed as planned and leave this worry for later?"

"Fine. I'll just make sure that everybody here is shielded inside the bubble that Tamp's device will create. We don't want to carry away dust on our shoes or clothes that's infected with that shit."

"I fully agree," Hal said.

~

Pre-Empsis' Palace, Q'eefur
Zaria

Deen had his map and the coordinates of the Pre-Empsis' vault. I had to transport us inside the palace; there were no conveniently open doors to slip through this time. What I hadn't told the others was that the Pre-Empsis had three wives and all three had small children.

He'd given them a terrible legacy—and a disease, because he wanted his older brother, the Empsis and first in line for the throne, to die before their father did.

Fool.

Get in, get out, Ilya sent.

Yeah.

~

Paricos II
Phrinnis Tampirus

"She's fucking Weir?" I wanted to make sure I'd heard the message clearly. Arna never had dealings with Weir. He made everyone around him nervous and uneasy.

"That's affirmative," Reykx replied. "I was sure she was on her way to meet Zarbec, as she usually does, but this time it's Weir."

"She wants something from him," I mused.

"What can he offer? He deals in smuggled goods."

"Yes, but he smuggles out as well as in," I pointed out.

"You think she wants to leave?"

"If she wanted that, I would open the door for her myself," I mocked. "I imagine she wants to smuggle something else—or someone else."

"Perhaps Mayyab," Reykx began.

"Mayyab has his nose to her posterior already. What would he tell me, were I to ask?"

"Not the truth," Reykx admitted.

"And that is why I trust your judgment," I said. "Do you have vids to share?"

"Yes. I will transmit immediately."

"Thank you, that will be all."

∾

Pre-Empsis' Palace, Q'eefur

Zaria

At least there were no archaic weapons waiting when Deen lifted the pile of bones and three spheres into a bag and shut it softly. His fingers shook as he clutched the bag to his chest and released a breath.

"Zaria," his whisper was barely audible, "please take us away from here."

Somehow, this place spooked him, just as it did me. We'd passed three children on our way to the vault's steps. All looked thin and sickly to me. Deen saw two servants who were the same.

Deen just figured out what those spheres contain, I sent to Ilya and the others before folding all of us away.

~

Star Cruiser Hellion

Ilya

"The bag is locked inside an empty berth, and Deen and Jin are locked in Deen's berth while Deen is having his fit," Hal reappeared after misting through the ship to learn what Deen and Jin were discussing.

"What are they saying?" I asked. Zaria, who sat on her bunk playing a game called solitaire, looked up at my question. Bleek, who was sharpening his blades merely for something to do, also lifted his head.

"Deen wants to unload these spheres and get the hell off Paricos II. His first stop is a physician's office somewhere, to be tested for the poison sickness. Jin says it won't be that easy to leave Master Tamp. He thinks Tamp will kill them rather than let them go, since they know what those spheres contain. They're also wondering what in the name of all gods Tamp wants with that stuff, anyway."

I'd been wondering the same thing, actually. Zaria would have said something, I figured, if Tamp intended to do evil with it right away. For now, he seemed happy enough just to collect it.

"My concern," Bleek pointed his whetstone at Hal, "is that Tamp will hire another treasure hunter like Velker—or worse if those two leave. If Velker hadn't conveniently died when he did, I may have killed him myself."

"I certainly wanted to kill him," I admitted.

"I can fix this," Zaria set her comp-vid on her bunk and rose to stretch.

"What are you going to do?" Bleek asked.

"Hal and I are going to see Deen and Jin, to convince them to stay where they are."

"With compulsion?" It was a big reason we'd brought Hal in—along with the misting trick.

"If necessary," Zaria brushed dark hair over her shoulder and walked toward the door. Hal fell in behind her.

"Think we need in on that conversation?" Bleek went back to

sharpening his blade, the stone snicking across the steel edge in a more than familiar sound.

"No. Nor do I want to be."

"I hear that."

~

Zaria

"Deen, it's Zaria," I tapped the com outside his berth.

"Zaria?"

"Yes."

"Come in. I want to talk to you," Deen said as he opened the door from the inside for me. Hal and I strode in.

"Sit down," he indicated the empty berth across from him. Jin had gone to the galley, I read that in Deen's face. "I suppose you're wondering what's going on," Deen sighed and turned his head away for a moment. "Jin and I—we signed up to hunt treasure. We didn't sign up for this."

"What are you talking about?" I asked.

"Those containment spheres—they contain the poison disease," he muttered. "I'd bet my life—or what may be left of it—on that."

"You're right," I said.

His head swiveled back quickly and he blinked at me in surprise. "You know?" His voice went up an octave.

"Yes. What you picked up today has been shielded carefully. It won't harm you. You didn't carry any poison away with you. I can't say the same thing for the Pre-Empsis and his family, however. The poison is spreading throughout his palace."

"How do you know that?" Deen had gone pale and his voice lowered to a whisper.

"I know a few things," I said. "I'm hoping you'll trust me on this. We can continue to hunt those spheres, and I will guarantee your safety from the poison every time."

"Nobody can do that," he huffed and turned away again.

"Deen, look at me," I said.

It took a few moments, but eventually he turned back to me.

He immediately dropped to his knees and his mouth formed an O of surprise and wonder.

He'd never seen a Larentii before.

~

Ilya

"They can't reveal anything about any of us, and readily agreed to the compulsion," Hal said, accepting the bottle of Karathian ale I handed to him. "Once they saw there was a Larentii on the team, they were on board in a hurry."

"Did Zaria explain that the poison will be removed eventually, and destroyed if possible?"

"She did tell them that. They were happy to hear it."

"Good. That makes this a little better, since we don't have to hide things from those two. We only have to worry about the ship's crew, now."

"If they hear or see anything they shouldn't, it's an easy fix," Hal said and tipped the bottle up to drink.

"And that's why we asked for a vampire," I said, holding my own bottle up in a salute.

"Vampires, the answer to so many household troubles," Hal grinned.

"And housewives' dreams, if the tales are true," I laughed.

~

Queen's Palace, Le-Ath Veronis

Lissa

Gavril and Tybus had both come. "You're sure of this?" My son, Gavril, who'd adopted the name Teeg San Gerxon, asked.

"Zaria says so."

"This will bear some thought," Tybus mused. "Q'eefur must be protected, but how can you go about that without panicking the entire royal family?"

"Isolate the sick ones immediately," Gavril suggested. "There's no need for others to be infected. I say hire a warlock to take out the entire infected palace and grounds and ship them to an asteroid or someplace else where they can't do more damage."

"That's just it, honey," I looked at him and shook my head. "Asteroids can fall to ground. Thieves can plunder them. We need one of Quin's spheres. For now, the smallest one will do, I think. Those who are sick —they need treatment to ease their way. They'll have to be isolated, too. I want you to charge those physicians involved with everything you can and make sure they never treat anyone again. Fucking idiots."

"How soon?" Gavril asked.

"Look, I think we can bring Quin in a few days. You may need to speak with Q'eefur's King yourself—and tell him what you know."

"What about the missing spheres?"

"Tell him they are in safe hands and quarantined, now. We don't need to produce them to point a finger at the Pre-Empsis; half his family and servants are sick already. That's evidence enough that he planned to kill his brother."

"I'll make the call," Tybus offered. Tybus was a master of diplomacy; he and Gavril were identical in many ways. I knew the difference—scent and age will always be clear to me. Both ruled the Campiaan Alliance as one; I was one of the few who knew it.

"Let me know how it turns out," I said as they rose to leave. "Just make sure Zaria's name is never connected to this in any way."

"I think I have a good plan for that," Tybus took my hand and kissed it. "Do not fear, lady, all will be well."

~

"Lissa, my love," Perdil came to sit with me in the arboretum. I found myself spending an inordinate amount of time there, lately.

"What, honey?" I asked absently as I gazed through the massive windows at the city of Lissia below my palace.

"I want to talk to you about V'ili, Cayetes, and how criminals think," he said.

I turned toward him and frowned. He wasn't the handsomest man, but his love for me consumed him. He never yelled at me for putting my life in danger; he called me his formidable Queen and laughed whenever I said something funny.

"All right, what do you have?" I blinked at him.

"V'ili escaped, right?"

"He did."

"Then he likely knows something of what precipitated the attack at the detention facility, and has determined something of what may have been involved."

"I understand that," I began.

"No, hear me out," he said, his voice gruff. "What I'm saying is this; what V'ili knows or suspects, Cayetes also knows or suspects. Imagine that Cayetes has any number of spies and willing assassins at his disposal. He will see the potential in this immediately. It's my guess that he already has a spy or spies here, looking into the matter to determine who slipped past the guards and the electronic security. If any word is spoken of Carek Prime, I'm sure you know what could happen next."

"That Carek Prime was competing for Quin, and had sufficient technology to pull it off if we hadn't been aiming for V'ili at the same time."

"Yes. Exactly. He sent Carek Prime after Quin himself; I fear for that world, my love, if Cayetes learns any of this."

"What do you think we should do?" I asked.

"Look for the spy. Have him followed. Intercept his communications. Find out if he's heard anything he shouldn't, then feed him false information, perhaps. Keep him as far away from Carek Prime as possible."

"Good idea. I'll put Rigo and his crew on this right away."

"May I work with them?"

"If Rigo says yes."

"I know how to be discreet, even if I won't blend in very well," he grinned at his own joke—the top of his head would reach the middle of Rigo's chest. That didn't mean he was weak—Perdil could hold his own in any weight-lifting contest.

"You have my confidence and permission, if Rigo agrees."

"You are perfect," he said and leaned in to kiss me.

"Even when I have tiara hair?"

"Especially then. I'll keep you apprised of the situation."

"Thank you."

Star Cruiser Hellion

Zaria

The news feeds were filled with information regarding the Pre-Empsis of Q'eefur, his purchase of three containment spheres of poison and the fact that half his family was sick with the disease.

Deen, Jin and the rest of us watched onboard the Hellion as a news conference was held on Q'eefur.

"We learned of this earlier," a representative for the Campiian Security Detail said in an interview. "We suspected, of course, and slipped in to check for sure. We found leaking spheres and took measures to seal them up. We left them where they were while continuing our investigation. Yesterday, as you know, the Pre-Empsis was arrested, along with the physicians treating his family. The physicians failed to report the illness to the proper authorities, and we only learned of this when information was provided by an anonymous source."

"Where are the poison spheres, now?" a journalist asked.

"I cannot divulge that information, for obvious reasons," the CSD rep answered.

"Is Q'eefur in danger?" another asked.

"We are taking steps to contain the Pre-Empsis' palace and surrounding property. It is my belief that we may be able to prevent the spreading of the poison by catching it so early."

"What about the affected family members and staff?"

"All quarantined, as proscribed by law," the representative explained. "We will provide further updates as information becomes available."

"One last question," someone shouted. "What will happen to the Pre-Empsis? He may have doomed the entire planet."

"He will be held accountable, according to the laws of the Campiaan Alliance. The King has already disinherited him."

"Wow," Deen breathed when Ilya shut off the broadcast. "I think we've been saved from a lot of uncomfortable questioning."

"I sure hope so," Bleek murmured. "Whoever put that together is a genius."

"I'm worried about riots on Q'eefur," I said. "People are already scared; I can feel it."

"Perhaps it's time that people learned that some of the poison was sold to others who intend to harm, like the Pre-Empsis of Q'eefur did." Hal said. "That information has been held back for many years. It is time the people knew what to look for, I think. Do you suppose the servants in that household wouldn't have said something sooner if they realized their lives were on the line?"

"There's that, of course, but on the other side of that coin is who may try to steal it for their own gain. No matter how dangerous something is, if somebody sees a profit in it, they'll take their chances. So many believe themselves invincible, when they are anything but," Ilya grumbled.

"Like we're stealing it?" Jin turned to me.

"You know why I'm taking it," I said. "As for Tamp's intentions, I can't really talk about that right now."

"I say let everyone know that the original containment spheres were faulty," Hal said. "Tell them the spheres need to be heavily shielded to remain safe."

"I'd say that's a sound idea, unless somebody wants to kill entire planets with the stuff. Then we're back to where we started," Ilya countered.

"If that were their intentions, it would have happened already," Hal argued.

"Look, both of you are right—that's not impossible, you know. We have our own set of problems. Hal, send your thoughts to your boss. Let him and the others decide," I said.

"Who's your boss?" Deen asked Hal.

"Ah, young one," Hal breathed, "someday, perhaps, I will introduce you."

~

Q'eefur

    Quin

"If this weren't such an emergency," Teeg San Gerxon grimaced when Lissa, Kay, Daragar and I arrived on the grounds surrounding the former Pre-Empsis' palace.

"I know. I can feel the poison surging," I confessed. "This was the proper thing to do, to keep the people of Q'eefur safe."

"I can't believe the asshole let it go that long. He had to know it was happening," Lissa huffed as she gazed about us. The gardens were dying; that was easy enough to see. No amount of water or a gardener's best care could cure what killed the exotic plants and trees.

"He did know. He answered that question under compulsion," Teeg said. "His excuse was that he could marry more wives and have more children."

"Is he affected by the poison?"

"Sadly, no. He spent a great deal of time away from his palace—intentionally—after he learned the poison was spreading from those spheres."

"Dearest," Daragar sighed as one of my downy feathers lifted and floated away in the breeze.

"I know," I said. Somehow, amidst all this, I was molting. It was coming at a terribly inconvenient time, too, in my opinion.

"All the Avii molt," Daragar pointed out. "It is nothing to fear. New feathers will come."

"Yes. It will merely take time," I agreed. "Shall we plant our sphere?" I held up the smallest sphere I'd found in Avii Castle's secret treasury. It would do for this.

"How deep?" Lissa asked. I told her.

"Come," I whispered to the tiny sphere and dropped it into the hole Lissa made with power.

∼

Paricos II

Ilya

"They did exceptional work; I can find no flaws in the many layers of shields surrounding the spheres and the bones," Nyarr reported to Tamp.

The bones and spheres lay on the same table as last time; Tamp was determined to ensure that the poison was no longer leaking from what we'd brought to him.

"The CSD must have a powerful warlock in their employ," Loor observed.

"Hmmph. Karathia is a part of the Campiian Alliance; don't forget that," Tamp said absently. "I find this fascinating, that the fool would allow these to sicken his household. I also find it fascinating," he lifted his head and smiled at Deen and Zaria, "that you managed to pull this away right under the CSD's nose."

"I find it amusing that those fools aren't admitting it," Nyarr said. "I've seen the vids—they say the location of the spheres is secret and can't be released."

"That is the truth," Tamp pointed out. "They have no idea who took them. I've been searching the sites on my comp-vid. Nothing. I did find," Tamp turned toward Bleek and I held my breath, "that there is a price on our Blevakian's head, here."

"I will not allow you to sell him," Zaria came to stand beside Bleek.

"My dear, I have no intention to do so. He is more valuable to me where he is. I do have a question, however," Tamp continued, leveling his gaze on Bleek again. "Tell me about the black-winged woman."

 aricos II

Zaria

"Yes, I worked with the BlackWing crew," Bleek shrugged. "As did Zaria. When the ASD began their search, we resolved to find other work."

"There is no reward offered for you, my dear," Tamp turned to me.

"Because the authorities have no knowledge of my involvement in piracy. I made a choice to go with Bleek."

"Fair enough. Thank you for these," Tamp swept a hand over the spheres and bones. "I am happy with your success in this. You'll receive a bonus for your work. Zaria, I wish you to accompany me tomorrow evening; I have a business matter to attend to."

"All right. How shall I dress?" I asked. I already knew, but it was the proper question to ask.

"Nyarr will provide for you—he and Loor will also be going. Be ready for transport at seventeen bells."

"As you say," I nodded.

He smiled.

Le-Ath Veronis

Perdil

"Where are we going?" Captain Lenk asked as he, Rigo and I climbed into the hover-van.

"To the detention facility," Rigo replied. "You've seen Cayetes and a few of his men, I believe. We will attempt to identify one of his spies, if possible. We have reason to believe that at least one has been sent to learn more about your security device, Captain."

Lenk's face paled, but he merely nodded and settled into his seat. He'd cast several questioning glances my way when Rigo and I arrived at his suite to collect him, but he never remarked on my height or any other question that crowded his mind.

I'd learned to decipher those looks long ago. Most dealt with natural curiosity. Some were downright insulting.

The curse of being different from what surrounds you, my Lissa said often enough.

Don't worry about it, Drew always said. *People will underestimate you. That's a good advantage to have in a battle of wits or steel.*

He was right. I could have someone gutted physically or mentally, if it were necessary and they weren't paying attention.

The entrance to the detention facility's parking area was well-lit, with security-cams hidden throughout to record the comings and goings of employees and visitors alike. Large, hover-trucks were parked at one end, filled with supplies and equipment waiting to be used or installed.

A few workmen were unloading a crate near the freight-vator; we walked toward them, first. Those four appeared normal enough; one was vampire and Rigo knew he wasn't involved with Cayetes.

Rigo didn't speak until we'd boarded the freight-vator and its doors closed to transport us to the detention cell levels. "All four of those have been on Le-Ath Veronis for several years; I doubt they're involved with Cayetes," he said.

I was of the same opinion, but that was only four of many. There were three shifts, working around the clock to effect repairs, strengthen damaged walls and replace prisoner cages and locks.

All four workers had stared at me as I passed.

Another gauntlet waited for me downstairs.

~

Paricos II

Ilya

"Where is he taking you?" I demanded of Zaria, once we arrived in our cave.

"The bosses are meeting—they do it once per sun-turn," Zaria sounded weary. "It's one of the few events Tamp feels obligated to attend. Normally he takes three of his warlocks, but chose to take Nyarr, Loor and me this time."

"Has he ever taken Arna?" I asked.

"No."

"She'll be pissed," I said.

"Did you notice she wasn't present when we met with Tamp, this time?" Zaria asked.

"I did. I wondered about it, too, up until Tamp made his comments about the price on Bleek's head."

"When I leave tomorrow with Tamp, I want you to place your best shield around all of you, and ask Flyer and Turtle to do the same," she said.

"You worried about something?" In my experience, if Zaria were worried about something, then I should worry, too.

"Something isn't right," she said. "I can feel it."

"How will he dress you?" I asked. I wanted to know—for personal reasons.

"Like Nyarr and Loor—in a guard's uniform," she said. "Dark blue with gold—Tamp's colors. All the bosses have their own servants' colors—it's easier to sort them at a meeting."

"I know you can take care of yourself," I admitted, "Just—be careful, all right?"

"I will. You do the same."

"I will." I leaned in to kiss her.

"Hey, now," Bleek interrupted. "I haven't gotten a kiss."

"You want one?" Zaria asked.

"Of course I do. Then I want food."

"Of course you do," she laughed.

~

Queen's Palace, Le-Ath Veronis

Quin

"Here are the images that Perdil and Rigo recorded when they walked through the detention facility," Lissa set a comp-vid on the small table beside me. I'd chosen the palace pool as a place to relax. The sound of the waterfall spilling into the indoor pool at the far end was quite soothing.

"You're worried that someone could be spying on us?" I asked, lifting the comp-vid.

"Yes. It won't take a genius to add things together and come up with the knowledge that new technology was used to get a dozen men into the facility—without anybody seeing or hearing anything," Lissa said.

"I know." I shivered at the thought of it.

"Will you be able to tell from the images whether we should investigate any of these?"

"I should," I said. "I think Zaria does this best, but I can do it, too."

"Unfortunately, Zaria is in the middle of tracking containment spheres and keeping a criminal boss happy," Lissa sighed.

"I heard Drake and Drew say the same thing," I admitted.

"Where is Justis?" she asked.

"Speaking with Wolter and Captain Ardis about the guards and others who are staying at the replacement castle. Wolter, Orik and Deeds are still running the boat tours as if nothing is different. Ardis says that they haven't seen anyone approach the castle, but there are still boat jumpers."

"It amazes me daily how stupid people can be," Lissa offered a grim smile.

"Did you wish to speak with Justis?"

"When he isn't busy," Lissa said.

"I'll let him know," I offered.

"I'll send mindspeech," Lissa waved a hand. "When you've had a chance to look at those images, let me know if anything stands out. This is the first shift only; there will be two more shifts to examine before we're done."

"I'll have it finished by tonight," I promised.

"Thank you."

Justis

"There isn't a thing out of the ordinary so far," Ardis said. "We've been watching carefully, and the soldiers and agents sent by Queen Lissa are recording everything. Nothing is amiss."

"I want it to stay that way," I grumbled. "Don't let your guard down, just because things are proceeding as normal."

"I don't intend to. Lives depend upon it," Ardis said.

"What do you want me to do about the receipts for the tours? Tomorrow, Orik is scheduled to bring the accounts to Dena, as usual," Wolter said.

"Then treat it as a normal occurrence; just make sure there are extra guards discreetly placed when the boat arrives at the cleft."

"I'll make sure of it," Ardis agreed. "I will likely be there myself."

"Very well. I expect to have regular communication, as usual," I said, rising and stretching my wings.

"How is Quin?" Wolter asked.

"Very well," I replied. "Although she is going through the molt. It is time, I suppose—it comes to all who bear wings."

"I hear from Amlis now and then," Wolter said. "He often says he wishes that Quin would visit. I know not what to tell him."

"I will pass that message to Quin. Her decision in the matter will stand."

"Of course." Wolter dipped his head. At that moment, I received mindspeech from Queen Lissa, expressing her desire to meet with me privately.

"I have to go—I have another matter to attend to," I said.

"Thank you, my King," Ardis dipped his head respectfully. Wolter followed suit.

~

Lissa

"You asked to see me?" Justis strode in after Renée, who'd brought him straight to my private study.

"I did," I said, waving Renée out of the room. She closed the door softly behind her.

"What do you have?" Justis got right to business.

"Something that involves you, I believe—and Quin. She doesn't know yet, so please behave in a circumspect manner after I tell you the news."

"Please, go on," Justis swept out a regal hand.

"Quin's pregnant," I said. "I think the baby's yours."

~

Paricos II

Zaria

At least the uniform fit well; the boots I altered to suit me better. I was expected in Tamp's suite in a few minutes as I pulled my hair back in a braided bun and secured it.

I'd look the part of a guard, whether I was one or not.

"Remember what I said," Ilya reminded me as I walked toward the trans-vator.

"You, too," I pointed a finger at him. "Your best shields. Don't forget." Something wasn't right and it troubled me. Perhaps too many were in danger at the same time, which didn't allow me to focus on one as opposed to many.

The crowding spirits and my feeling of uneasiness had only grown as the last day passed, until it was time for me to join Tamp, Nyarr and Loor upstairs.

Squaring my shoulders, I gave Ilya a nod and walked into the trans-vator when it opened. Good or bad, I had my guard up and prayed that all would be safe.

∽

"Right on time," Tamp said with a smile as I walked into his suite. Nyarr and Loor had arrived ahead of me and flanked Tamp, who was dressed formally.

It was a meeting disguised as a dinner party, looked like. "Nyarr, will you do us the honor?" Tamp turned to the eldest of his warlocks.

"It will be my pleasure," Nyarr agreed. "Zaria, if you will stand beside Loor, we will arrive properly at the venue."

"Of course," I said and took my position next to Loor. Nyarr folded us away.

∽

The Rock

Chief Darkins

"Chief," Reyks walked into my office.

"Reyks?" I wasn't visited often by Tamp's chief of spies.

"I felt I should inform you, since Tamp has left already," Reyks said.

"Of what?" He wouldn't be here unless it were important.

"Arna went to Gubb's bar earlier. At first, I believed it another dalliance, but she received a small package from one of Weir's guards. Afterward, she left and went to a dress shop. I had someone watching all exits, Chief. She went in and never came out again. I had the shop carefully searched. Arna has disappeared."

"She didn't return here?" I rose from my chair, ready to search the Rock for her presence.

"Not that anyone has seen," Reyks said. "Nobody knows where she is, including that fool, Mayyab."

"Or so he says," I snapped. "Come, shall we call the warlocks who are here and question Mayyab together?"

"Most certainly."

~

Zarbec's Compound

Zaria

Zarbec hid his insecurities behind a simpering façade. While pleasantly chatting with other bosses, he was busy mentally calculating their worth and determining ways to ingratiate himself.

A few bought into that image; he stood to profit from their gullibility.

Tamp could read the fool like a book and gave noncommittal answers to Zarbec's seemingly inane questions regarding recent business successes.

Most of the bosses were men; three were women. Nyarr, Loor and I followed Tamp, just as other bodyguards followed their boss. All of them were wary and watchful. A handful had warlocks like Tamp; most had humans or humanoids who were armed to the hairline—secretly, of course.

"Weir is noticeably late," Tamp murmured to Nyarr.

I went still. Just the mention of that name sent a shiver through me. Terrible thoughts crowded my mind.

"Get us out of here," I snapped at Nyarr. Zarbec's compound exploded in a series of detonations less than a blink after Nyarr folded us away.

~

Ilya

The five of us sat at the table in our small kitchen inside the cave, having some of the best Falchani noodles with chicken that I'd ever tasted.

Flyer was a genius with rice noodles. I hadn't forgotten what Zaria told me, either—Flyer, Turtle and I had our strongest shields in place surrounding the cave.

Those shields stopped just short of the trans-vator door; if anyone dropped in to visit, they'd at least be able to step out, giving us time to alter the shields well enough to allow them in—depending on who it was.

"I can teach you how to make these," Flyer offered with a grin as I dipped more noodles into my bowl.

"I think I'll continue to appreciate them like this," I said and employed my chopsticks to lift noodles to my mouth.

That's when the trans-vator doors opened—to reveal a blank space. I blinked, as did the others.

Ilya, Zaria's voice shouted into my mind. *We're under attack.*

That's when we felt the rumble and shudder of the rock above our heads—the entire thing was collapsing around us.

~

Le-Ath Veronis
Tourist Vessel Whimsy
Orik

A small part of my brain told me to weep. His words kept me from it. "Tell me about the black-winged woman," he'd demanded. I couldn't hold the words back. Information regarding Quin tumbled unwillingly from my lips.

"She has white wings," I'd confessed. "Her name is Quin. The black wings were a disguise."

"Where is she?" he asked.

"The Queen has her," I said. I wasn't sure where she was; I only knew that Queen Lissa was keeping her safe.

"Tell me how to convince the Queen to give the winged woman to me."

"I don't know," I whimpered. "The Queen is very strong. I have no influence upon her."

"What about the Avii King? Might he have influence with her?"

"She will listen to him," I nodded.

"Good. Perhaps a few shots at his castle with a small, ranos cannon will garner his attention, then. Come, you say you have accounts to deliver. I will travel with you. We will command the Avii King's attention, never fear. Board your boat, captain. We go now."

That is how I found myself guiding the tourist vessel toward the cleft in the glass castle.

My kidnapper hadn't asked about the castle; I didn't tell him it wasn't the real thing. King Justis wasn't in residence. Guards and soldiers inhabited the structure, along with a few wives and children.

The original castle was impervious to bullets, bombs and missiles. I could only hope this one was the same as I cut the engine and drifted the boat closer to the cleft.

"Drop anchor," my captor demanded.

I did as I was told and watched in horror as he pulled a device from the large bag he carried. I'd never seen such before; it looked like a large pipe, the circumference the same as my forearm.

Setting the device on his shoulder, he took aim at the crevice.

"No," I whispered.

Dena would be waiting there.

Her child could be with her.

"No," I whispered again, before he told me to shut up and fired.

Queen's Palace, Le-Ath Veronis
Quin

Get out! My mental shout must have echoed in every mind across the planet, I was suddenly so terrified.

Lissa's mental sending echoed mine a fraction of a second later.

In my mind, I saw the horror of it; the replacement castle blasted, cracked and disintegrating, with only a few Black Wings flying to safety. I saw it as if in slow motion, falling into the sea with a terrible roar and the sounds of grinding glass.

Huge waves poured toward the shore, causing me to send another message to anyone there.

Get out, I whimpered. *Higher ground.*

Please.

Lissa

More than half of Justis' Black Wing army was dead, along with many wives and a few of their children.

Dena, Ardis and their child were among the victims.

V'ili had folded away when the castle started to fall, leaving Orik behind to wash ashore and die when his boat crashed into a pier on the beach.

I knew this because Bree arrived to read Orik afterward. I wanted to ask her about *Changing What Was.* She answered my question before I could ask it.

"This has to proceed as is," she sighed. "Changing these things will interrupt the future."

"Things?"

"This isn't the only fortress to fall," she replied. "We are at a delicate balance. I shouldn't have to fix everything, you know." She'd left me then to ponder her words.

Justis was devastated by the events, yet still had a terrible duty to perform; Trace took him and Quin to Avendor, so they could tell the Avii of the attack and arrange for a mourning period.

"It could have been worse," Winkler sat beside me atop the main dome of my palace.

"People always say that," I snapped. "As if what happened wasn't bad enough already."

"I know." He settled an arm around my shoulders and pulled me close. "We can't change everything," he whispered against my hair before placing a kiss there. "Terrible things happen all the time. I used to tell myself that it taught us strength. How many scars can be cut into our hearts before there is no room left for new ones?"

That's when I buried my face against his shoulder and wept.

~

Paricos II

Ilya

Tamp stood at the edge of the mainland cliff, staring out at what remained of his compound.

The Rock was nothing more than a pile of rubble, now. The number of survivors was relatively small, but those of us who remained stood at Tamp's back, studying the devastation with him.

I had an idea that Zaria had pulled several away the moment she knew the Rock was targeted. Deen, Jin, Chief Darkins, Tamp's chief spy and the three remaining warlocks were among those rescued.

Turtle, Flyer and I made sure that our shields held up long enough to get Hal, Bleek and our belongings out before allowing the cave to collapse behind us.

Zaria stepped forward and placed her hand inside mine—she was chilled to the bone and wore no coat. *Weir and Arna are behind this,* she said. *They killed everybody at the meeting last night except us.*

Weir wants Paricos II? I asked. *Baby, you're freezing.*

He and Arna want Paricos II, she said. *Gubb's in on it, too, I think.*

I'll take care of that, I began.

Hold on; let's plan this carefully, she cautioned. *There's something else you don't know, too. V'ili fired a ranos rocket at the replacement castle on Le-Ath Veronis. Most of the people inside it died when the whole thing shattered and came down.*

Fuck, I said. *What about?* I'd been about to say Ardis and his wife.

Dead, Zaria sighed. *Their baby, too. Quin is devastated.*

Understandable, Hal said. Zaria had included all our group in her sending. *I sincerely hope that we are there when Cayetes and his pet Sirenali die,* Hal added.

It would be a true pleasure, Turtle agreed.

At that moment, Tamp turned and his gaze settled on Zaria.

"Whose compound shall we take? There are many available after last night," he said.

"You must realize," Zaria said, "that many out of work employees have run to Weir after last night's events. He is adding them to his army. Weir thinks we are weak and intends to take us, too. He has no idea what he will truly face, should he challenge us."

"Where shall we go to rebuild my army?" Tamp asked her.

"Come. We won't need to rebuild, although if you wish to add more employees, we will do so."

"Where are we going, lady?" Nyarr asked.

"Revis' compound. There are a few left who do not wish to serve Weir. We will offer jobs to those deserving. There, too, we will have the sea at our backs."

"We can place floating bombs about Revis' harbor," Nyarr agreed. "It will be difficult to bring anything past those."

"That compound has a thick wall surrounding it," Darkins agreed. "With shielding spells placed by the warlocks, it will be next to impossible to breach."

"Good," Tamp agreed. "Chief Darkins, place a reward on those sites," he said. "For Arna, Weir and anyone else in league with them."

"I'll do it right away, Master Tamp."

"Good. Who wishes to visit Gubb's bar with me, to watch him die?"

"I've imagined his death many times," I let go of Zaria's hand and stepped forward.

"Smith, I will allow your steel to dispose of that traitor."

"I will come," Zaria said. "I want to see his face before he dies."

∽

Avii Castle, Avendor

Quin

I watched as three of my feathers floated away in the breeze on Gurnil's terrace. Ordin had already been to check on me—at Justis' insistence. I'd read in him what Lissa had already known by scent; I was pregnant with Justis' child.

I should have felt joy at that revelation. Instead, it only brought home the sharp pain of Dena's loss, with that of Ardis and their child.

Grinding glass had killed them and destroyed their bodies. Somewhere on the light half of Le-Ath Veronis, bits of feathers were washing ashore.

It was all that was left of those who'd died, which hadn't already sunk to the floor of the sea.

The remainder of the Black Wing army had come to Avendor with Justis and me; in time, Justis would be forced to choose a new commander.

For now, they were leaderless and in mourning, many bearing guilt because they survived while others didn't.

"Here." Gurnil laid a light blanket about my shoulders as I stared, unseeing, at the groves of gishi trees south of his terrace. Even in the warmth of Avendor's sun I felt chilled.

"When Elabeth and Camryn died," Gurnil sat beside me on the bench I occupied, "We didn't know what to do. We walked about in a daze, I think, because we were so numb. There was no sleep, few felt hungry—I thought we were done as a race."

"Why them?" I asked. He knew I meant Dena and her small family, not Elabeth and Camryn.

"That question is asked whenever someone is taken before their time," Gurnil said softly. "Why not another? Someone deserving of death. I cannot tell you how many times I asked myself that when Elabeth died."

"How do you get through it?" I wiped tears away.

"You don't. Eventually, you are reminded that your purpose—and your time—is still functional. If there is anyone who can stop time, they are far more powerful than any I've met. Dena and Ardis—they served until the end. Just as we must serve until the end. If death had taken you, instead, would you want Dena to collapse and die, too?"

"No, she had so many things to live for," I mumbled, wiping more tears.

"As do you. Never forget that, dear one." Gurnil rose and stretched his wings. "If you need something, ask Ordin or me. We will do anything in our power for you."

"Thank you." I clamped my wings tighter to my back beneath the blanket before wrapping the warmth of it better around me. Perhaps I should go to Justis—he suffered just as I did in this terrible, terrible loss.

❧

Paricos II

Ilya

"Somebody beat us to it," Nyarr muttered as we stared at Gubb's body. We'd found the bar gutted by looters, the employees scattered and Gubb's body lying half in and half out the doorway into the kitchen.

"Weir's men," Zaria grumbled. "To prevent him from talking or taking money to reveal Weir's many betrayals."

Tamp's lips tightened but he made no comment and refrained from asking Zaria how she knew or suspected those things. I imagined he thought the same; Zaria was merely voicing his own opinions.

"Shall we move what little we have into Revis' compound?" Nyarr toed Gubb's body before turning to Tamp.

"It is now Tamp's compound," I said. "Revis no longer cares, as he's dead."

"True enough," Tamp agreed. "Nyarr, take us, if you please."

❧

Zaria

"Just as I was getting the hang of working metal, too," Turtle grumbled as we walked through the massive kitchen in the new compound. Much of the compound had been looted by escaping employees, but the kitchen remained intact for the most part.

"We have barely fifty here with us," Loor said as he walked in to find us taking stock of the food and supplies. "Tamp asks if you can cook for that many. He knows you cooked for yourselves at the Rock."

"I can cook for that many, and we have enough food here to do for a few days," Turtle agreed. "With Flyer's and Zaria's help, we can feed the crew until a suitable kitchen staff is hired."

"My brothers and I can arrange for supplies to be brought in," Loor said.

"We'll need fresh milk, eggs, that sort of thing soonest," Turtle said. "Zaria can do the same, if Tamp allows."

"Master Tamp wants Zaria beside him most of the time, I think," Loor said after a brief hesitation. "He is grateful for her warning at Zarbec's compound, you understand."

"I do," Turtle agreed amiably. "Nevertheless, she is also a fine cook."

"Noted," Loor grinned. "Zaria, after you freshen up, Tamp would like to see you."

"I'll be there soon," I said.

"I'll inform him."

~

Queen's Palace, Le-Ath Veronis
Lissa

Lenk wasn't expecting me—he hid his surprise well when I knocked on his door, but he was still surprised—and curious.

He was under house arrest and knew it—vampire guards were posted outside his door at all times and went with him if he walked through the palace for any reason. I was there for a different reason.

"Captain Lenk, it has occurred to me that you suffered losses, too," I said before he could form words.

"You knew those who perished in the destruction—the winged ones," he said.

"Yes. That's why I'm here—I want to take you to the light half of my planet today. We'll visit an old friend of mine."

"What about?" he blinked at me in confusion. Vampires—in his knowledge, anyway—couldn't survive in the sun.

"I'm special, as are a few others," I said. "Come, I'll take you."

It was obvious that Captain Lenk had never been with anyone who could fold space, before. We stood in Corent's apple orchard in a blink, while the winds whispered through the leaves and the trees pushed out buds to tempt honey bees.

"Lissa?" Corent appeared as if called, walking from between trees to greet us. If he'd materialized from a tree trunk, Lenk would have been less amazed.

"Corent, Lenk and I have deaths to mourn," I explained.

"Ah." Corent's hair, a sky-blue when we arrived, darkened. "The winged ones. Such a terrible loss."

"Lenk also lost eleven of his men—who'd stood beside him for years," I said.

Corent's stormy eyes studied me for a moment. "I see," he nodded. "Come. Please," he motioned us forward.

Without a word, and with wonder still on his face, Lenk followed Corent and me. Eventually, Corent stopped beside a gnarled, bent apple tree. Those around it stood straighter. Taller. Bore more buds.

"This is Angeline, my favorite tree," Corent turned and smiled at us. "She has lived long, and I have treated her carefully all these years. As you can see, however, she is failing. Another year, perhaps before she gives up her life in this spot."

"Corent brought Angeline with him from another world—his people were under attack and forced to leave," I said. "She is all he has left of them, now."

"All are dead?" Lenk whispered.

"Except one other, and he lives elsewhere," Corent said.

"I've baked pies from Angeline's apples," I said, brushing a tear away. "Many times. Corent always brought her apples to me."

"What will you do? When she is no more?" Lenk's voice roughened with emotion.

"I will miss her," Corent said. "And I will speak to her children about her. And we will share memories."

"Her children?"

"This grove surrounding us—they are all Angeline's children. From seed and cuttings, she created everything around you."

"You will bear the news of your loss to the families those men left behind," I said, placing an arm around Lenk's waist. "Share your words and memories, Captain. Understand that what they did and how they lived is important to those who loved them."

Corent left us after a while; Lenk and I wept together for those lost—and those who remained.

CHAPTER 11

aricos II
Revis' Rock

Zaria

"You wished to see me?" I asked when Tamp invited me into his new suite.

"I did. Still do." Tamp said as he piled comp-vids and other things onto a massive desk. He was clearing away what was left of Revis' belongings.

Someone had already cleared away debris and damaged furniture left behind—probably one or more of Tamp's warlocks had relocated all of it.

I could easily read in Tamp how angry he was that his library and artifacts collection had been destroyed when the Rock came down. He held that anger in check as he continued clearing out Revis' desk.

"How many compounds did Weir seize?" Tamp asked. He knew; he merely wanted to see whether I knew, too.

"Thirty-seven, although many were small and not worth noting. Of the ones that matter, twenty-three. It would have been twenty-four, had he been successful in taking you down."

"Are you always so thorough?" He looked up from his work to gaze at me.

"I've learned that things go smoother and more people live if I am."

"I wonder if Weir would have made this move so soon had Arna not whispered in his ear."

"I wonder that, too," I agreed. Tamp had already suspected Weir of duplicity. "Did Mayyab tell you of it?"

"He said that Weir should be watched, but I suspected for years that Weir wanted all of Paricos II. He wishes to be feared. He wishes to compete with the biggest and the worst, I think. His nervousness—that comes from his fear that his ambition would be discovered. Arna has shored up his desires and cleared the way for his takeover, no doubt."

"Does he have any idea who the biggest and worst are?"

"I believe he knows of some," Tamp shrugged. "Perhaps not all. That could change quickly."

"I agree," I said.

"Tell me what you're thinking—and please do not filter your words to keep from offending me."

"I think," I said, "That Weir of Paricos II, even with the assets he now has, is headed for the biggest war ever if he wants to get into a fight with Vardil Cayetes."

Tamp went still for a moment. "I shouldn't be surprised that you know of Cayetes. He dropped out of sight for a while, but now is back and as strong as ever."

"I know," I said. "I also know that several here had dealings with Cayetes, in one way or another. Weir may be calling for the heavens to fall if he wants a fight with Cayetes."

"And those heavens will fall on Paricos II."

"Yes."

~

Vardil Cayetes' Private Study
  V'ili

"I had no idea the entire thing would fall," I snapped. "I merely wanted to get the attention of the winged king."

"That isn't all our troubles," Vardil growled. "There was a coup on Paricos II. I've already received a message from the new —*management*."

"We'll get our clones and bones from him, then," I huffed. "Simple."

"Not so simple. He is refusing to do business with me. Says he has other buyers—*our* buyers—and will sell directly to them. At a lower price."

Anger burned through my mind at Vardil's words. "He wishes to start a war with us?"

"He wants what we have. I want the winged woman and that security device before we fire the first shot," Vardil hissed. He wanted assurance that he'd be kept healthy while he waged war, and the device would get us in and out of Paricos II without anyone the wiser.

"Who is it?" I asked. "Who wants war with us?"

"Weir, that sniveling bastard," Vardil replied. "I want to watch while he is cut into strips in front of me."

"That can be arranged. What does he have in the way of an army and ships?"

"He's taken everything on Paricos II—according to his messages. That gives him a substantial fleet and more than enough resources."

"How long will it take to gather an army and send them to Paricos II? I think we should teach him a lesson. We had a contract in place for those bones and clones—as the sole purchaser."

"The contract requires courts to enforce," Vardil's laugh contained no humor. "Even the legislative system, such as it was on Paricos II, was destroyed when Weir killed his fellow bosses."

"What about Skyf? Has he heard anything on the device?"

"Nothing yet, but it takes time to build trust—or so he says. He does not have your talents for forcing information from those who have it. Until that happens, I want you to assess all my superior officers. We will choose one to lead our army against Paricos II."

"I'll do that immediately."

~

Paricos II

Ilya

Zaria says that a war is brewing, I sent to King Rylend. *One of the bosses killed the others—except for Tamp—and she says the new megaboss now wants Vardil's empire.*

Just what we need—two assholes instead of one to worry about, Ry's sending was grim.

Those two will leave the Alliances covered in their excrement, if something isn't done, I said.

You and Zaria could likely handle the situation on Paricos II, Rylend began.

She says we have to hold back for now; I think she hopes that Weir's gamble for power will draw Cayetes' attention away from other things—like stealing the saving spheres.

True enough, Rylend appeared thoughtful. *Although I doubt he'll let his desire for Quin go.*

He may be more than obsessed with his health and continued existence, since someone is blatantly threatening him now, I observed.

Yes—that would make sense. Quin is safe on Avendor for the moment—all the Avii are in mourning after so many of theirs were killed.

I'd like it if she stayed there, I confessed. *Keep her as far away from this mess as possible. I'm hoping Zaria will find a solution to all this; I'm out of ideas after Tamp's compound was destroyed around us.*

What about the containment spheres Tamp collected?

Zaria says she sent them to Nefrigar in the archives. He will make sure they are kept safe, there.

Good. I'm having breakfast with my mother tomorrow, Rylend said. *I'm hoping she knows something, or has some advice to offer after I give her this information. A war between two master criminals could destroy many innocents caught between them.*

Any suggestions or advice from your mother will be most welcome, I assure you.

~

Avii Castle, Avendor
  Quin

Justis stood on the wide edge of the glass castle, at the very top. I stood beside him. Guild Masters spread out on either side, followed by multitudes of family members, friends and others as we said goodbye to those we'd lost.

It was tradition to pluck a feather and place it with the body.

There were no bodies.

Therefore, Justis decreed that we would loose our feathers onto the winds surrounding Avii Castle, to fly where they would in remembrance of those who'd perished.

Those among us without wings stood on the narrow strip of sand at the base of the castle below us, to cast flowers and wreaths into the waters on Justis' command.

"We will remember," Justis spoke and lifted the red feather he held. "Always," he added, and released the feather.

Hundreds of feathers followed his as the wind carried them away. Those below us released their flowers and wreaths.

And that's when the petals flew past us. I watched them while blinking tears from my eyes; there were black rose petals. Yellow rose petals. Blue. Green. Brown. Gray. All the colors of the Avii wings flew past us, leaving their sweet scent behind as they flurried and swept in eddies to follow our feathers.

The Mighty were grieving with us. I knew it as surely as I knew anything. I turned to Justis and buried my head against his shoulder to weep. He wrapped his arms and wings about me as the petals continued to pass us, their journey continuing and leaving us behind.

~

Paricos II
  Revis' Rock
  Zaria

"Do you know others who might join us? Tamp thinks we're in a war with Weir, now," Nyarr said as we sat at a table in the kitchen, having dinner.

"Weir thinks we're vulnerable, I can guarantee it," Bleek pointed his fork at Nyarr. "He imagines he can come in and take us whenever he wants, although he worries that you five," he grinned at Nyarr and his brothers, "are still alive."

"There are at least thirty other warlocks on this planet—provided they didn't abandon it the moment Weir seized power," Loor said.

"Yes, but do they have the power you do?" Ilya asked.

"There are at least three Fourth-levels—that we know of," Nyarr said. "Besides, Weir now has the combined wealth of all the bosses except one. That gives him unlimited buying power, if he's in the market for power wielders or weapons."

"My worry is what Arna may be telling him," Kear, one of the warlock brothers, observed. "She knows too much about us—Tamp included."

"I hope Weir is good in bed," Loor huffed.

"Oh, his money makes him attractive," I said. "For now, he holds enough power and wealth to keep her happy. If I were him, I'd watch his supply of sharp knives. She intended to kill all of us. What's to keep her from doing the same to him?"

"The answer, of course, is nothing," Tamp walked into the kitchen and pulled out a chair at the table. "I thought I'd have dinner with my friends tonight," he said.

I floated a plate and utensils to the table and let them settle in front of him. He chuckled and accepted the glass of wine I floated to him next.

Turtle placed a bowl of noodles in front of him as the first course and Tamp began to eat and listen as the rest of us talked.

"Master Smith," Tamp said when Flyer placed a sizzling filet in front of him.

"Yes?" Ilya asked.

"Might you know more suitable employees to hire? It seems our numbers are small and not enough to worry Weir—or Arna."

"I may be able to find a few," Ilya shrugged. "Give me time to make connections. Perhaps I'll have an answer in a few days."

"This is very good," Tamp said after tasting the filet. "I should have hired Falchani cooks long ago."

~

Carek Prime

Arna

Weir and I wanted more devices. I'd learned from Mayyab where Tamp had gotten his.

Hulce, Carek Prime's chief scientist and inventor, had secretly sold one to Tamp.

With Weir's warlock at my back, we'd convinced Hulce to sell us another—after we'd threatened to reveal his duplicity to his king.

Weir now wanted more. He and I had plans to take over Cayetes' empire, just as we'd taken Paricos II.

It didn't concern me that Tamp still lived; Mayyab and most of those he'd employed died when the Rock came down. Tamp was weak and inconsequential, now. Weir and I planned to allow him to feel safe —before we destroyed him and what little he had left.

"You will do this, or you face the consequences," Laan, Weir's Fourth-level warlock, warned as he turned up the heating spell surrounding Hulce.

"All right, all right," Hulce held up a hand before wiping sweat from his face with a sleeve. "I'll have them ready in an eight-day."

"See that you do," Laan snapped. "We will return. Here are funds for supplies," he tossed a bag at Hulce, who missed catching it before it dropped to the floor with a chink of metal. Laan zapped him with a needling spell when Hulce bent to lift the bag.

"I swear, I will have them ready," Hulce was close to tears as he straightened up.

I laughed at his discomfort. Cayetes' empire would be mine —and soon.

Paricos II

Revis' Rock

Zaria

"What are you doing?" Bleek settled beside me on the bed and wrapped all four arms about me.

I'd been staring into space—at least that's what he thought.

"Recalling everything from those last few moments at Zarbec's compound," I said. "Going over every inch of everything and everybody."

"Sounds tiring," he dropped his head and kissed my shoulder.

"Somebody blew the place apart—from the inside and right in the middle of it," I said. "I can see through a warlock's shields, so it wasn't that."

"My love, you look tired," he said.

"I am, but this is bothering me."

"What do you think it was?" Bleek asked.

"I think they sent out hidden bombing squads, which included at least one warlock or witch, to get them out after the explosives were delivered," I said. "Was there anything unusual happening just before the Rock came down?"

"The trans-vator doors opened, but nobody was there," Bleek said.

"Let me guess—Tamp no longer has his device, does he?"

"Not sure—you could ask Nyarr."

"Want to come with me?"

"Sure. And then I want to bring you back here and go to bed. I think I can tire you out enough that you can sleep."

"Really?"

"I do."

"Let's go find Nyarr."

"Want a glass?" We found Nyarr at one end of the new compound, in what should have been a library and wasn't. He and his brothers were sharing a bottle of Revis' wine that someone had forgotten—probably because their arms were full of other loot.

"No, although it looks good," I said. "I have a question. Did Tamp's device survive the destruction?"

"No," Nyarr said.

"I think it did," I said. "I think Mayyab and Arna handed it to some traitors, and that's how the Rock was destroyed."

"Come with me," Nyarr set his glass down and strode toward Bleek and me. "Tamp will want this information right away."

He did want the information.

"You think Weir has two devices, now?" Tamp paced inside his suite while Bleek, Nyarr and I watched.

"Yes, and I think Arna knows where to get them," I said. "She stole yours and acquired another. That means Weir now has that knowledge. I imagine that someone, somewhere, has been threatened if they don't produce a lot more for those two."

"This is untenable," Tamp hissed. "I should have known not to trust Mayyab."

"Too bad Arna let him die with everybody else," Nyarr grumbled. "Still doesn't discharge his debt for this betrayal."

"Gubb paid the same price," I said. "Neither understood the depths of her ambition, I think."

"I have a question," Bleek said.

"Go on," Tamp nodded to him.

"How do we circumvent these devices? If we can't, what's to keep the enemy from showing up at our door and killing everyone here?"

"Here's the problem," I said. I was tired, but the device and its abilities had bothered me for a while. After all, we'd walked through some of the best security systems money could buy in two places, to get containment spheres for Tamp.

The device could get past anything, including a warlock's shields, if my estimations were correct. That's why the Rock fell, even with five Fifth-level warlocks' shields around it.

"How does it work?" I said, naming my main concern. "How does it get past all these things without anybody knowing? I think this is more dangerous than anybody thought up until now."

"We need one, to study it," Hal offered.

"I don't want to play our hand with the one who makes them, if I can help it," I said. "That's why I want to get one of Weir's."

"Get the one Arna stole from Tamp. It wasn't hers to take," Nyarr suggested.

"Sounds reasonable to me, but how do we do it?" Bleek asked.

"Maybe somebody who can get past anything by natural means should go in and look for it," Hal said.

Ilya lifted an eyebrow. That would take either my ability or Hal's and he knew that. "What are you talking about?" Loor asked.

"I'm a misting vampire," Hal said calmly, as if he were talking about the weather. "I can get in and out without causing a stir."

"A vampire in daylight?" Nyarr blinked at Hal.

"A few have the talent and the ability," Hal said.

"The Vampire Queen," Tamp walked through the door, shaking raindrops off his shoulders. He was naked from the waist up; he'd been standing outside in the rain as a tree for a while.

"I'm surprised you know that," Hal said.

"It is evident at times; I've watched her since she took the throne on Le-Ath Veronis. Are you truly a vampire? No wonder our Bladesmith was anxious to hire you."

"I think we work well together," Ilya said.

"Then bring me more wonders, Bladesmith, and you will be rewarded for your efforts."

～

Ilya

I'm looking for a small army of volunteers, I sent to King Rylend. *I believe the situation here places us in a strategic position—one that could enable us to take down two criminals at the same time.*

You think to get rid of Cayetes, V'ili and Weir, don't you?

And Arna—don't forget her. She's the one who instigated Weir's rush for power. I think he'd have waited another year or two before making his move if she hadn't defected.

Do you think she's the one who's most power hungry?

I do. I've met her—she's used to getting her own way.

I'll discuss this with my mother, and see what she suggests, Rylend replied.

I appreciate that.

How soon?

I'd say an eight-day or less.

Done.

～

Queen's Palace, Le-Ath Veronis

Lissa

Ry and I were having breakfast when Trajan appeared inside the arboretum. "Quin sends this," he said, setting a comp-vid beside my place at the table.

"She took time to make notes?" I blinked up at Trajan.

"Yes. She thinks this is important, as do I. She went through all three shifts for you."

"Send her my thanks and my love," I said.

"Bel Erland is still with her," Trajan said. "I imagine he is relaying both those sentiments." The tall werewolf grinned at me, making me smile in return. Ry snickered his response; I kicked him under the table.

"Want to sit down?" Ry asked, ignoring the contact between my shoe and his shin. "I think we have enough food here—even for a werewolf."

"Don't mind if I do," Trajan laughed and took a seat.

"So, what's up with Ilya and Zaria?" I asked. Ry had been updating me on current events surrounding Paricos II when Trajan arrived.

"Ilya thinks that being with Tamp places him and the others in a unique position—between two criminal factions about to go to war. On one hand, we have Weir of Paricos II and his newly-formed alliance with Arna, who is more than power hungry. On the other side, we have Vardil Cayetes and V'ili, who won't take kindly to someone invading their turf."

"So, when those two start lobbing bombs and armies at one another, Tamp and his bunch of volunteers can drive a wedge in and take both sides down?" Trajan asked.

"That's the idea."

"Sounds interesting. How many is he asking for?"

"Not more than fifty, I think."

"Small but effective, huh?"

"Something like that. He's asking for cooks and a kitchen staff, too."

"Armies do have a tendency to look forward to a good meal," Trajan agreed.

"I'll put the word out, to see if anybody's interested," I said.

"Ashe says that he gives his permission, if somebody's worried about the interference rules."

"Wisdom gives his permission," Charles appeared from nothing and took the fourth chair at the table.

"Well, look who we have here," I said. "What does my sister say?"

"She's commandeering a few that she wants to put in this fight," Charles shrugged. "I take that as confirmation."

"Are we leaving Ilya in charge?" I asked Charles.

"I believe Zaria is in charge," Charles grinned. "As it should be."

~

Paricos II
  Ilya

When the Mighty Heart sends a message—even while you are in deep sleep—you sit up and listen carefully.

"We have four who have agreed to come," I informed Tamp and the others at breakfast.

"When will they arrive?" Tamp asked. He was happy with what he'd been served for breakfast and was eating with good appetite.

"In a day or two. I'm still waiting for answers to other messages."

"How many do you think will come? As an estimate," Tamp used his knife to coax more sauce and eggs onto his fork.

"I'd say perhaps thirty or forty," I said. "I think that will be enough," I held up a hand.

"We're a talented bunch," Zaria smiled at Tamp. He blinked at her, placed food in his mouth and nodded as he chewed.

"Are the shops still open for business in Fendala?" Turtle asked as he and Flyer took seats at the table to eat. "We need eggs, cheese, meats—that sort of thing."

"They are—Loor and I went in this morning to get a few things. I feel Weir has his spies in place, but I doubt he's ready for a direct confrontation yet."

"He wants to size us up to see what it will take to destroy us," Tamp agreed. "It's what I would do."

"So the smugglers are still in business—they just have new management," Zaria observed.

"I would offer a slight increase, to buy their loyalty," Tamp said. "After all, Weir can afford it, now."

"And they don't have to search for new territory or risk getting arrested if they take off with Weir's new fleet of ships," Hal said.

"Wise words," Tamp said.

"Want to go grocery shopping?" Flyer grinned at Zaria.

"Sure," she said.

"Don't be gone long; I dislike worry," Tamp said.

～

Zaria

Who is coming tomorrow? I asked Ilya. He, Bleek and Hal insisted on coming with Turtle, Flyer and me to buy groceries. The shopping trip was a ruse, mostly, to size up our competition and see how widespread Weir's spy network ran.

Although we did need eggs and cheese.

Two High Demons and two others—she said we'd see who they were when they arrived, Ilya answered my question.

High Demons are a good choice, I agreed. *Weir's warlocks won't be able to get past them—they'll nullify their power.*

Do you think Cayetes has hired anyone to replace Deris and Daris? Bleek asked. *Or does he intend to get his army here by conventional means?*

Good question, I said. *I don't have an answer. He's probably waiting for Weir's first move, and Weir may be hesitating while he gets his army in shape and ready to work together. Remember, he's got tons of draftees who used to work for somebody else.*

True. Plus, hesitation is good—it gives us time to pull more in and get ready, Ilya said.

We no longer have Zarbec's ship or crew at our disposal, Flyer pointed out. *Perhaps we need ships of our own.*

"You know, I didn't have a problem with those guys," I said aloud. "Maybe we should send them an invitation."

We walked through the aisles of what Paricos II called a grocer's market, setting things in a hovercart as we went along.

"You think they'll want to join us?" Turtle's voice was soft. "We have nothing to offer them."

"Except free will and friends to stand beside them," I said.

"Try. Don't expect anything," Ilya muttered.

"Are these things for Weir?" the cashier asked when we arrived at the door to pay.

"No," I answered right away. "These things are for Master Tamp."

"We were instructed to tell Weir's guards if any of you showed up. My boss has chosen to ignore that warning, as some of his friends who were Zarbec's servants died when Weir took over."

"I think I'd like to speak with him—to thank him," I said. "And to offer him and all of you who wish to come a place with Master Tamp."

≈

"Well, Neren and all his employees wished to come, so we brought them and emptied his store at the same time," I grinned at Tamp.

Turtle, Flyer, Neren and all sixteen of his employees were now filling cabinets, freezers and refrigerators with food from Neren's store.

"Nyarr and his brothers can place stasis spells on the perishables—to keep them fresh until needed."

"Can any of them cook?" Tamp tried to hide his smile behind gruff words.

"I believe Turtle and Flyer can supervise well enough," I said.

"Good. Do you think anyone else may be interested in wiggling away from Weir's heavy hand?"

"Perhaps. I'll look into it," I said.

"Very well. You trust these?" Tamp asked.

"Yes."

"Good."

≈

Star Cruiser Hellion

Captain Meric

If I'd been shot, I'd have been less surprised. The envelope materialized between my skin and shirt, lodging near where my heart now beat at an increased rhythm.

Bray, my navigator, looked up from his station, fear and wonder on his face. The same thing had happened to him

"I'll go first," I held up a hand. Opening the fastenings, I found the paper envelope resting against my chest. Lifting it carefully away, as I had no idea what it could be, I opened it with unsteady hands.

Greetings from Zaria Keppler to Captain Meric, it read. *I wish to extend an invitation to you and all who have received an envelope from me. Master Tamp has taken Revis' old compound to regroup. Should you wish to leave your new employer, I'd like to offer you a place with us. We are small, yes;*

many of ours died in the coup. However, if you desire the freedom to make your own choices, and friends who will stand beside you in the coming war, then write yes on this note. I will come for you in two days.

Be warned, however. Only the recipients of these notes will be able to read or write upon them. Any other will only see blank paper. Therefore, do not attempt to take this to Weir or any of his loyal employees. It will not go well.

Z.

I cursed under my breath before reading the note again. Bray pulled out his note and began to read as well. We had a choice to make, it appeared. I already had my mind made up after reading it the second time.

CHAPTER 12

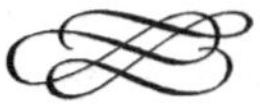

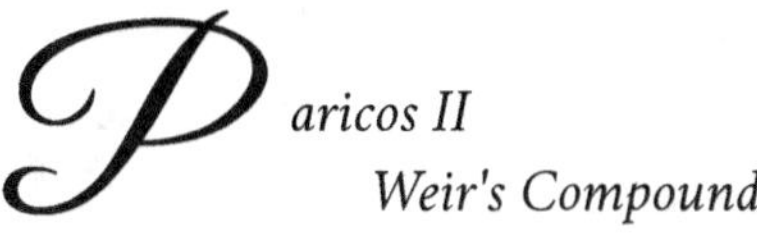

aricos II
   Weir's Compound

Arna

"What do you mean, they kidnapped everyone in the store?" Weir demanded. If he hadn't been speaking on a communicator, Weir would probably have shot the spy reporting to him now.

"It's that bitch—I'd lay money on it," I interrupted after a moment. "She's good at transporting people around, but that's about it."

Weir turned to frown at me briefly before going back to his conversation. "Was there a woman with them?" He demanded.

"Yes," came the answer. "Had dark hair. Pretty."

"Don't ever call her that again," I hissed under my breath.

"How many did they take?" Weir demanded.

"Seventeen, I believe. Neren and his employees."

"Is that all? What do you think grocery store employees can do against me? He probably wanted a cook," Weir snapped. "Unless it's more important than that, don't bother reporting next time."

"Yes, Master Weir."

~

Ilya

"You sent out invitations? Real invitations?" I frowned at Zaria.

"Yes. But they're spelled invitations," she said. "Only the recipient can read or reply. Anybody else will only see blank paper."

"What happens when they tell Weir?"

"Oh, that won't happen."

"Zaria?" I narrowed my eyes at her while my fists settled on my hips.

"No. Honest," she said, holding up a hand to stave off my pretended anger.

"I'm teasing," I grinned at her. "Who did you send them to?"

"The people who want to get away from Weir, and deserve to get away from him."

"I love you," I said, stepping forward to place my hands on her face before kissing her.

"I love you, too," she said when I pulled back. "You just choose to ignore it most of the time."

Her words caused me to turn away. *I don't deserve you*, I admitted and stalked off.

~

Queen's Palace, Le-Ath Veronis

Lissa

"I thought I'd bring a few visitors before taking them to Paricos II," Breanne arrived just as my bunch was sitting down for lunch.

The sight of those she'd brought had me standing quickly and opening my arms. Lexsi skipped into my embrace while Kordevik stood behind her, grinning like a fool. Behind those two stood Kell and Opal.

My sister had brought formidable reinforcements for our small group on Paricos II. "I missed you, baby girl," I whispered against Lexsi's ear.

"I missed you, too, Gran," she breathed.

"They can arrive with the other volunteers," Bree took an offered seat at the table shortly after Kooper arrived to kiss her. "Things could get hairy fast," she said as more plates were brought.

~

Avii Castle, Avendor
   Quin

"I know you want to help," Ashe held up a hand. The Mighty Hand had arrived to speak with Justis and me.

I knew about the call for volunteers. I wanted to go more than anything to help Zaria and the others.

It wasn't only my life I would be risking for now, and I knew that.

It made me want to weep.

"I can't go," I hung my head and admitted to Ashe what he knew already.

"You don't have to go—you can help from here," he said, causing me to jerk my head up quickly. "You're still needed to place spheres, too, but those trips can be carefully spaced out so you won't deplete your energy too much."

"How can I help them defeat V'ili and Cayetes? I want to make them pay for the lives they've taken," I whispered. It was a plea—to one of the Mighty from a small soldier.

"Zaria will see to it that you have plenty to do, and I will have other healers here to help you, so you won't weary yourself."

"Who will need healing?" I asked. "Will ours suffer?"

"Some, possibly," he agreed, his eyes going dark as midnight, while stars fell through their depths. "Most of those who need your help will be broken in body and spirit. You'll see soon enough."

Ashe disappeared, leaving me to ponder his words.

~

Paricos II
   Revis' Rock
   Zaria

"Are you ready?" Ilya asked Hal. The vampire was ready to mist into Weir's compound to look for Tamp's device.

"I am."

"Send mindspeech if you run into difficulty," I said. "Take this," I handed him a button.

"What's that?" Hal blinked at me.

"A way for me to find you," I said. "Just in case. Also, take this," I handed him something else. It was a duplicate of Tamp's device, although it held nothing more than a jumbled bit of circuitry inside it.

"Nice work," Hal breathed after examining the device. "I didn't want to call the hounds after us immediately when one of those things disappeared."

"Neither do I," I admitted. "I have too much work to do before Weir and Cayetes are at each other's throats."

"I'll go now," Hal nodded to Ilya and me.

"Be careful. I'd rather have you return empty-handed than not return at all," I said.

"I understand, Lady." With that, Hal was gone. I released a sigh.

~

Queen's Palace, Le-Ath Veronis

Lissa

"How many ground troops?" I pointed my question at Dragon, who'd taken charge of the volunteers. I wasn't surprised at all by that.

"With the four Bree added, thirty-seven."

"I think that'll be enough," I nodded. Turtle and Flyer were already on Paricos II. Most of the Falchani belonging to the Saa Thalarr had volunteered, too, including my twins and our sons, Travis and Trent. Only Caylon wasn't going, although he wanted to.

I'd already had a stern word with my sons and their fathers, telling them this wasn't a pretend fight—this was real and people could die. I was also sending all the BlackWing ships, including the newest, BlackWing VIII, at Zaria's request.

We'll need ships of our own, she'd sent, and I agreed with her.

The army we'd gathered was small.

And deadly.

Vampires, werewolves and shifters, including the two black lions the Saa Thalarr boasted—Rush and Rachel, wanted to go.

With Lexsi and Kory representing the High Demons, they were formidable enough. I worried that Cayetes, who was known for such things, would attempt to blast Paricos II to bits beneath their feet.

"You have three more," a man shouldered his way through the crowd toward Dragon and me.

They weren't really men.

They were Black Ra'Ak.

"I hope you're hungry," I said, smiling at them.

"I think we'll have sufficient appetite," the first one grinned.

"That makes an even number," Dragon approved of the new recruits. "Are your duffels packed and ready?" he asked the crowd.

"Ready, Warlord," they responded.

"Good. We go." Dragon offered a grin and disappeared with his army.

~

BlackWing I

Bear Wright

"We'll fold space after we pass this point," I indicated the spot on the three-dimensional star map. The captains of all the other BlackWing ships were connected with BlackWing I through our closed communication system. They were seeing what I was seeing.

"That should put us in orbit around Paricos II in three days," Marco DeLuca, Captain of BlackWing III, observed.

"We'll be shielded heavily once we fold space," Winkler said. He was riding along on BlackWing VII, to provide assistance as needed.

"BlackWing IV is ready," Captain Dori Anderson announced.

"Are you ready, Amos?" I asked Amos Thompson, who'd transferred to captain BlackWing V.

"Just like old times, buddy," he laughed.

"Then let's make like bullshit and hit the trail," I said.

~

Paricos II

Weir's Compound

Arna

"They're not bothering us," Weir snapped at me. "We'll take care of them later, when we have this thing with Cayetes settled."

I'd complained that the bitch was still alive, and probably transporting Tamp wherever he wanted to go. Weir wasn't listening to me. I was beginning to regret that Mayyab was dead; he'd agree with me that Tamp and his people who'd survived should be eliminated. Especially that bitch.

Now.

"They could get away," I pointed out.

"Even better," Weir said. "Get them off Paricos II, by all means. It doesn't matter how it's done, just that it happens."

"You're not listening to me," I wailed before running from the room.

~

Weir's Compound

Hal

My mist hovered in a corner of Weir's private office as the conversation between Arna and Weir took place.

Arna was so jealous of Zaria, she wanted her and the rest of us dead. As a result, she was doing her best to convince Weir that Zaria was dangerous.

While Arna didn't really believe that, she was right. I was grateful Weir discounted Arna's words, or we'd be defending ourselves already.

Now it was time to resume my hunt for the device. As yet, I'd failed to find its hiding place. Weir hadn't locked it in his office safe;

I'd made sure of that already. My visit had included stopping to listen to Weir and Arna's disagreement.

Many more rooms and hidden spaces awaited; I continued my search.

~

Revis' Rock

Ilya

"They're on the way," I informed Tamp. "They'll be here before dinner."

"Do any have special talents, such as our vampire does?" Tamp asked.

"Several. I think you'll be pleased, Master Tamp."

"Are they trustworthy?"

"I trust them with my life," I said.

"Can I trust them with my life?" he asked, his eyes narrowing at me.

"Zaria will make sure of that, I think."

His eyes widened as he studied me for a moment. "Zaria I trust," he said. "I cannot say why, but I do."

"She believes in you, otherwise we'd have left when the Rock came down." I handed him truth for truth.

"I wondered why you didn't anyway," he sighed. "Most of those who died would have deserted, I think."

"They failed to see the whole of the image," I said. "Weir has no business being a criminal kingpin. Cayetes has no business being one, either."

"So, a little crime upon occasion is all right?" Tamp lifted an eyebrow.

"If it's for a good cause," I grinned.

His guffaw surprised me.

~

Zaria

Hal was gone three hours before he returned empty-handed.

My shoulders sagged when he shook his head at me after materializing. I'd hoped Weir and his cronies wouldn't be so smart.

That hope was now crushed.

They'd left one of the devices on, to hide both—probably in plain sight.

"Thank you for the attempt," I said. "Dinner will be ready in half an hour, but I think they can find something for you if you're hungry or thirsty."

"I'll go to the kitchen," Hal said.

"The others will arrive in a few minutes, I think."

"Good." He waved an arm and left my suite.

~

Ilya

Tamp had dressed carefully for the occasion, in a dark suit he'd acquired from somewhere.

We stood in the grand hall of Revis' former compound, waiting as our army was ushered in by Nyarr and his brothers.

The Dragon Warlord marched at the head of that small army, his brother and former General, Crane, at his side.

They were identical, except for the tattoos decorating bare arms and chests. They'd worn the traditional leather vests, sleeveless and open to reveal their full sets of tattoos.

"Welcome, Dragon," I bowed before the former Warlord of Falchan.

"Well met, Bladesmith," Dragon nodded in return.

"This is outstanding," Tamp moved to my side to examine the army. Most were male, but sprinkled throughout, I saw the women.

Kay and Jana. Others I didn't recognize, although they'd likely come with their mates and stood beside them.

All were armed, except Kay.

Devin and Grace are here with Dragon, Crane and Radomir, Zaria supplied. *Kyler is here with Flavio. Kiarra is here with Adam and Merrill.* My heart almost stopped when I heard Kiarra's name. Real power had come to help us. It made me think we might need it.

You have real power here already, a beautiful voice whispered in my mind.

Kiarra reminded me that Zaria was with us.

Thank you, Lady, I responded.

Just a friendly reminder. Men's heads are often thicker than necessary, her mental laugh tickled my brain.

Guilty, I admitted.

"I trust you'll be in charge of the army?" Tamp held out a hand to Dragon, who took it.

"Yes," Dragon agreed. "I'll start putting our defenses together after dinner."

~

Zaria

"You're telling me that the experienced treasure hunter wasn't expecting an ancient method of protection, and died because of it?" Dragon asked me as he buttered bread at dinner.

"Yes. He expected the latest in electronic surveillance and protection, only to be killed by a mundane bullet to the forehead."

"Fascinating," Dragon mused. "Shall we resort to a few old-fashioned defenses—just in case?" He turned to Crane, who would be serving as his General, just as he'd done far in the past.

"I have a few things we can put in place," Crane grinned.

"I'll have Adam and Merrill look into the defenses employed by the former owner of this compound, to see what's intact and what needs repairs." Dragon bit into the bread and nodded—Flyer and his new kitchen staff made excellent bread.

"My brothers and I can put up spelled defenses," Nyarr offered. "We're just not used to that sort of thing."

"Then ask the Bladesmith," Dragon pointed at Ilya. "He knows about such."

"Is there something I don't know?" Tamp asked, as he looked from Nyarr to Ilya.

"Hmmph," Dragon chuckled. "Too bad you've never heard of Ilya Ironsmith."

Tamp went still while he studied Ilya. Ilya ignored his gaze and kept eating.

"I have heard of him—the warlock who went to war for the Falchani and seldom used his power."

"You're looking at him now," Dragon pointed his fork in Ilya's direction.

"I heard you dropped out of sight for a while," Tamp mused. "I see the reason, now. Fell in with pirates and then came here, to Paricos II."

"Nailed it," Ilya shrugged.

"What level?" Nyarr asked.

"Fifth." Ilya's answer was barely a grunt.

"Well, fuck me," Loor laughed. "All this time, too."

~

Ilya

"We'll have more new recruits outside the gates tonight at midnight," Zaria interrupted my meeting with Nyarr and his brothers. We'd gathered to discuss what sorts of defenses we could set up using our power.

"How many?" I asked.

"Oh, around two hundred, I think."

"How? The perimeter alarms will go off," Nyarr said.

"No," Zaria shook her head. "I'm bringing them in."

"That many?" Loor asked. "At once?"

"Maybe," Zaria smiled. "We'll see who shows up."

~

Zaria

"I can't believe she asked us to help you," Lexsi was almost bouncing with joy.

"I can't believe how happy I am that you said yes," I countered. Opal and Kell stood nearby with Kory, who was smiling as Lexsi and I had our moment.

"What do you think they're going to do?" Lexsi asked. The bounce hadn't gone away.

"Well, according to Hal, Arna, who is public enemy number two at this stage of the game, wants me dead. Weir thinks Tamp and the rest of us will be an easy afterthought when he gets rid of Cayetes. Arna may have other ideas."

"You mean she may attack on her own?"

Lexsi is a smart woman.

"Oh, it won't be all alone—she couldn't find her way out of a potato sack without directions," I said. "But I figure it won't be long before she has Weir's warlocks following her around like starved dogs. That's when we need to worry."

"How long do you think that will take?" Opal asked.

"A day or two. What we need to do is make sure our water supply is guarded. We'll be drinking poisoned sea water if they manage to tamper with our inflow and desalination pumps."

"That doesn't sound good," Kell said.

"It won't be. We have humanoids showing up tonight—by my invitation. We don't need them dying right after I promised their freedom."

"What will you do with them?" Kory asked.

"Some will want to stay and fight. They don't like the thought of Weir taking over Paricos II because this is their home. Others will want to leave. Lissa has already offered to sort those out. We'll send those to Le-Ath Veronis, first, and she'll decide where to send them from there."

"What should we do about the water system, then?" Opal asked.

"We ought to work on that first," I said.

❧

Ilya

"They'll have to get close enough to place a spell," I said when Zaria and a few others came to me with their warlock/water system questions. "Too bad we don't have sharks we can command. They won't expect to be attacked from below; I'd bet money on it."

Zaria turned to Opal and twisted her mouth in thought. "Dinosaur Boy?" she asked Opal.

"You think he'd cooperate?"

"With a few of his best friends, and if I set an invisible barrier around the area so they couldn't escape," Zaria suggested.

"I wonder what warlocks taste like?" Opal asked.

"Chicken?" Zaria grinned.

"Yeah."

"If we're lucky, Arna will come with them," Zaria said.

"What the hell are you talking about?" I demanded. Both laughed.

~

Phrinnis Tampirus

Nyarr and his brothers surrounded me when people began to appear in the wide entry of the compound.

Zaria and several others were nearby, waiting.

"How did she accomplish this?" I said softly.

"A Third-level doesn't have this kind of power," Nyarr echoed my thoughts. Somehow, our witch had magically pulled nearly two hundred away from Weir, including the pilot, navigator and some of the crew from the Hellion.

Those I could trust, but the others? I had no idea who any of them were.

Please, trust me, Zaria's voice filtered into my mind. I blinked—even my own warlocks couldn't send mindspeech to me, as I didn't have the talent for it.

"What is she?" I rephrased my question in a whisper of fear and awe.

All in good time, my dearest pod'l-morph, she replied.

~

Ilya

I and several others, including Lexsi and Opal, watched as Zaria sorted out more than eighty to transport to Queen Lissa. They were frightened servants for the most part, who only wanted to get away from the coming war.

"I'll take them," Radomir stepped forward to offer his services. "Do not fear," he told the frightened people. "You will be transported to a safe place."

Tamp watched as Radomir and his charges disappeared. I will give him credit—he barely blinked.

I had a feeling that Zaria would have explaining to do afterward, however. Drake and Drew, Dragon's sons, took charge of our new trainees; they'd evaluate them and determine where they fit in our small but growing army.

Outside that crowd stood Meric, Bray and the crew invited from the Hellion. Zaria strode toward them as Drake and Drew herded their charges toward the compound's barracks.

I decided to join her—to hear what she had to say to them. On the way, Deen and Jin pulled into my wake. They were familiar enough with the Hellion's crew and might make them feel more comfortable in their new surroundings.

"Captain Meric," Zaria smiled at him. "Navigator Bray," she nodded at Bray. "I'm glad you came. We'll have a new ship for you in less than three days."

"What ship would that be, lady?" Meric asked. He hid his surprise well, I'll give him that, as he studied his surroundings.

"The newest ship in the BlackWing fleet," she said. "BlackWing VIII."

Eyes widening at her words, Meric drew in a breath. The BlackWing ships had a reputation among all fleets, now. They were fast. Sleek. With the best of cutting edge technology. Meric was already in love with a ship he'd never seen, I think.

"What's this?" Tamp walked up, followed and shielded by his warlocks. "You're bringing a BlackWing ship here?"

"Honey," Zaria brushed his cheek with gentle fingers, "All eight of them are coming. You'll need a fleet of ships, don't you think?"

"May I have a word with you? In private?" Tamp's left eyebrow lifted as he gazed at Zaria. I couldn't tell whether he wanted to yell or kiss her at that point. Zaria, on the other hand, would know exactly what he intended.

"If that's what you want," Zaria dipped her chin in a slight nod.

"Good. Follow me." He stalked toward the wide hall that led to his new quarters.

~

Zaria

"Please, sit," Tamp gestured toward one of two chairs beside a fireplace in Revis' old study. At least it was clean and cleared of debris, now. The last time I'd seen it, Tamp was sorting through loose papers and stray comp-vids.

The Blackmantle brothers, Nyarr, Loor, Kear, Grear and Moor, stood by the closed door, guarding Tamp while he weighed his words before speaking.

Tamp poured a drink for himself, offered the same to me, which I waved off, then settled in the chair opposite mine.

I watched him drink while he considered things. Mostly, he considered me; who and what I was and why I was where I was.

"I knew Mayyab was a charlatan—most of the time," Tamp began. "Yes, he had talent, but he often withheld what he knew, or twisted it to suit his purposes."

I knew all those things, so I didn't speak.

"He said I should watch you," Tamp said. "He didn't trust you at all."

"I know," I shrugged.

"Tell me why I should trust you," Tamp said. "I've seen you do things I can no longer explain. You've taken over this compound in all but name. Why should I continue to believe anything about you?"

I studied him for a moment while crafting my reply. "Mayyab had moments when he couldn't help but speak what he knew—as if it took hold of him and forced the words past his teeth. Is that not so?" I asked.

"That is so. It's one of the reasons I kept him with me."

"Did he not tell you, in one of those moments, that your salvation would come when you least expected it, and in the strangest way possible?"

"Did he tell you that?" Tamp's fingers gripped the arms of his chair, and I saw that he wanted to grow roots from those fingers.

Roots that would then grind the chair to dust and floating bits of fluff.

Yes, pod'l-morphs were more than dangerous if they were angry or attacked in some way.

He imagined that I was something bent on his destruction. That was the farthest thing from the truth.

I knew why he searched for the containment spheres.

Pod'l-morphs are immortal, unless they are killed.

He was the last.

He'd been searching for a way to die.

"I want you to see something," I said, and rose from my chair.

"I'd prefer that you keep your distance," Tamp growled.

"Oh, if you want to stand ten feet away from me—as if that would save you—then by all means," I waved a hand.

Nyarr took a step forward, to protect Tamp.

From me.

I wanted to laugh.

"Stand down, cousin," I turned to him. "Tampirus and I will be back in a few."

I'll give Nyarr credit—he was quick.

He merely didn't have the power to hold me back.

Tamp and I landed in a small valley that could only be reached if one could fly. Trees and vegetation grew and flourished everywhere, between steep, sharp cliffs.

"Where are we?" Tamp demanded to know.

"We are on a planet called Siriaa—fifty years in the past," I told him. "On a continent known as Fyris to its inhabitants. You are standing in a place only a few of them knew about."

"I fail to see the point. If you wish to harm me, get it over with." His voice was sullen. Angry. I didn't point out that Weir's attack against him had given him new purpose and a reason to live. He wanted vengeance. I wanted him to have it.

"I will never harm you, unless you harm me first," I said.

"How can I trust that?" He snapped at me.

"You don't trust this," I swept a hand down my body. "Mayyab said your salvation would come in the strangest way possible. Phrinnis Tampirus, perhaps you will trust this." I drew myself up to my full Larentii height, my hair turning to blonde, my sky-blue skin soaking in the sunlight of a bright morning in Fyris.

It felt good. Wonderful, even, to drink in the light and allow it to feed me.

After a while, I turned to see that Tamp had fallen to his knees, his mouth open and an expression of wonder on his face.

"Get up, honey," I said to him. "We're going to visit your relatives."

CHAPTER 13

vii Castle, Avendor
   Quin

I allowed my wings to draggle behind me. With the molting in progress, they looked half-naked and forlorn.

Morning sickness had come to call, too, and Justis had Ordin hovering about me every morning.

"Are your wings sore?" Ordin asked as I dutifully ate the thin crackers he'd given me to stave off the vomiting.

"Not much," I said. "After the sickness goes away in the mornings, I feel fine." I didn't add that I wondered when those who'd need my healing would arrive, but it was never a good idea to question one of the Mighty, I think. The spheres, too, needed placing. Perhaps Lissa would come when the time was right for that.

"You're molting faster than normal, but then I really don't know what normal for you is," he smiled at me. "You grew your wings faster than normal, too, as I recall. At this rate, we'll be seeing the new pinfeathers very soon."

"Good. I feel naked without my feathers," I grumbled.

"Most of us do," he chuckled. "I hate molting. I have to walk when it's at its worst."

"Poor you," I couldn't help smiling.

"At least you're here to soothe sore wings when I molt again," he said. "That is the greatest blessing of all, I think. I hear that the young ones are fighting over your feathers—they all want to add a white one to their collection."

"I still have one of Justis' black ones," I sighed.

"I have red ones from Camryn and Elabeth," Ordin nodded and turned away. His words reminded me of our recent loss and I bowed my head as tears threatened.

"My love?" Justis walked into Ordin's study; he'd come to check on me, to see if I wanted breakfast with him.

"Justis," I stood and wrapped my arms about his waist.

"How is she?" Justis asked Ordin over my head.

"You could ask me," I leaned away and wrinkled my nose at him.

"I've heard healers make the worst patients," he grinned at me. He was attempting to cheer me up.

It was working.

"I think I can eat breakfast this morning," I said.

"Then come with me; Ordin will join us and we will discuss our future."

"Our future?"

"Yes. Some wish to return to Le-Ath Veronis when this crisis is over. Others wish to stay here. We must study this and make a decision eventually."

"Oh. All right." I didn't say it, but I wanted the baby to be born in the safety Avendor offered. *If Dena had only stayed here with her child,* my thoughts made my chest tighten with fresh grief.

"It's fine," Justis lifted my hand and kissed it. "I said eventually. Not right now."

~

Siriaa

Zaria

"How?" Tamp gazed up at the mighty tree we stood beside.

"A rogue god," I said. "I realize that doesn't make sense to you, but that's who did this."

"They're stuck like this?" Tamp touched the bark of the tree. The small valley held hundreds of similar trees; all pod'l-morphs in stasis.

"For now," I said.

"Why? Why would anyone do this?"

"It has to do with a terrible plot, and the poison you were collecting," I said. "The poison was created and grew inside the core of this world. As you would expect, some of it leached out to infect the planet itself. Halfway across the sea surrounding Fyris, the Avii Castle stood. The Queen who lived there was charged with periodically saving the planet from the leaching poison."

"But why did they need pod'l-morphs?" Tamp asked. "It makes no sense."

"Except that it does," I said. "The spheres used to call the poison and collect it inside them have to be buried deep. On Fyris, there were no power wielders or devices that could accomplish that."

"So a pod'l-morph tree was needed to dig deep." Tamp's forehead now rested against the tree, as if he could communicate with it that way.

"Yes. This was the one spot Liron's Orb could appear. It was here that he forced a pod'l-morph out of its stasis and instructed it to dig deep. The winged Queen then walked into the cleft in the tree and it carried her to the bottom, so the sphere could be planted."

"Liron's Orb?"

"Nothing to be concerned about now," I said. "I killed him."

"Where is this planet now? I know the winged ones live elsewhere."

"Blown to bits, by Vardil Cayetes," I said. "He was angry with Marid of Belancour, who sold him some of the poison he stole from here. His containment spheres leaked, giving Cayetes the poison disease. Instead of taking his revenge against Marid only, Cayetes destroyed an entire world and effectively spread the poison across the universes."

"This is why you came to me, isn't it? You felt the war coming." Tamp pulled away from the tree to gaze evenly at me.

"Yes. There is a delicate balance to it, too. One wrong step and it could disintegrate, leaving us right where we were in the beginning."

"Is Cayetes still sick?"

"No, sadly enough. The black-winged woman, who is actually a white-winged woman, has a great talent for healing. Inadvertently, she healed him after too many transfers to count. He is now healthy and searching for her, to keep that precious health."

"Where is she? Aboard one of those BlackWing ships?"

"Not now. She is safe elsewhere. Cayetes doesn't want to move until he has her, but that is not going to happen. Therefore, we will urge Weir to fire the first shot—or so it will seem."

"What are you planning to do, Zaria?" Tamp asked.

"That will be revealed later," I said. "Before we go back, I have somewhere else to take you."

"Nothing will compare to this," Tamp touched the tree again in reverence.

"Don't say that just yet," I said and folded him away.

∾

Paricos II

Weir's Compound

Arna

"I'm telling you she took them," I wanted to scream at Weir, but held my temper. He had no idea how much strength that took. I couldn't believe he wouldn't take the bait and send someone to kill the bitch witch on suspicion alone.

"Less than two hundred? Out of thousands?" Weir dismissed the disappearances with a wave of his hand. "Deserters, nothing more. What if they did go to Tamp? What is he going to do with only that many? We live in a fortress, here, which is heavily armed. I have the entire military force on Paricos II under my command. Never forget that. Those deserters—my reports list them as servants, mostly, who only want to run away."

"What about the crew of the Hellion, then?" I said.

"The ship is still there; it merely waits for another crew. If they'd taken the ship itself, I may have gone after it. As it is, only the crew deserted. They were always sympathetic to Tamp and his treasure hunts. I imagine they'll die with the rest of them when we attack later. Tamp has no ships; that's why he hired mine. You're reading far too much into these isolated incidents, my dear."

"Ugggh," I voiced my wordless frustration at Weir and stalked out of his study.

~

Larentii Archives

Zaria

I will never forget the wonder on Tamp's face when I set him down in the Larentii Archives. Everything he ever wanted to know or was curious about was there. Lost books and other treasures lay on shelves and tables, an enticement to one who'd only recently decided there was nothing left to live for.

"Zaria," Nefrigar appeared in front of us and leaned in to kiss my cheek. "How are you, my daughter?"

"Who?" Tamp was only able to speak the single word.

"I am Nefrigar, Chief Archivist for the Larentii," Nefrigar smiled at him. "I have never welcomed a pod'l-morph into the Archives before; you are the first."

"May I stay?" Tamp breathed as he turned to look about him.

"Not now—perhaps if all goes well, Zaria will bring you again. You will be welcome to browse and read as much as you like, then."

"We have work to do," I reminded Tamp. "I merely brought you with me on these two journeys to show you I might still be trusted."

"When you became Larentii, I knew that," Tamp sighed. "I had never seen one of the blue giants before. Now I have seen two."

"We only have to convince my long-lost relatives, now," I said.

"Relatives?"

"The Blackmantle brothers," Nefrigar said. "They and Zaria are related from long ago."

"But," Tamp began.

"It's a long story. I'll tell you someday," I said. "When we have time, as Nefrigar says. For now, we have to put our army together and be ready when Weir and Cayetes go after each other."

"I can't help but feel excited," he said. "I have a purpose again."

"Then let's go."

~

Avii Castle, Avendor

Bel Erland

"Your wings would be red," Gurnil informed me as he ate dinner with Berel, Lafe, Terrett and me in the Library. "You're royalty. I imagine Lafe's would be black or brown, depending upon his artistry and warrior's skills."

"Justis already said mine would be blue," Berel grinned. "I'd love to have wings."

"Wings might make things a little strange on Karathia," I said. "Although the red would be nice."

"I'm probably better off without, although flight intrigues me," Lafe said.

"A winged Sirenali?" Terrett spoke aloud. "That sounds like a dream coming true."

"What color?" I asked Terrett.

"Black. I am formidable when I turn," he smiled.

~

Paricos II

Revis' Rock

Zaria

"What's our plan?" Tamp asked the moment I set him down inside his study.

"You weren't gone for more than a few seconds," Nyarr accused.

"Because Larentii can bend time," I said.

"Don't," Tamp held up a hand. "We have work to do."

"The first thing, I think, is for me to go to Weir's compound and take one of those devices," I said. "Hal couldn't find either because they had one turned on. That means I have to go in, read Weir or Arna to see where they're hidden, exchange one for the dummy we have and get out."

"I don't understand why you're not able to just locate one," Tamp pointed out. "With your ability."

He meant as a Larentii.

"The Larentii can't find anything hidden by Sirenali, either," I pointed out. "It's the way they were made," I said before stopping.

"Holy honking cow horns," I said. "I think I know how those things work. I'll be back." I heard shouting as I disappeared, but that could wait.

~

Queen's Palace, Le-Ath Veronis

Lissa

"I've gone over this scene so many times," Zaria explained as she presented a three-dimensional image of the last minutes of Zarbec's compound before it was destroyed.

"We've gone over our images here, too," Kooper agreed. "We still haven't seen or heard anything, other than the trans-vator door popping open when one of those men bumped it."

"I think that whoever made these devices has finally solved the mystery of the Sirenali," Zaria said.

My breath stopped when she said that.

"Have you looked at the images from inside the trans-vator?" Zaria asked.

"Yes. We see nothing," I replied.

"Exactly. Because for that brief period of time, V'ili was included in the device's perimeter. They let him get off first, so he's the first one you see when he exits the trans-vator on the cellblock. Is that right?"

Kooper was silent for a moment. "We never went back to the

images from the 'vator before Captain Lenk and his men boarded—we saw V'ili get on from the outside, so we only loaded images after the door was bumped."

"Can you bring up those images?" Zaria asked.

"Absolutely." Kooper tapped his comp-vid and retrieved the information, before telling his comp-vid to project them.

We watched from above as V'ili boarded the trans-vator. We saw the door bump and V'ili's disappearance, which appeared to happen simultaneously.

"And I thought it would only conceal those Captain Lenk brought with him," Kooper breathed.

"Now, watch my images again," Zaria said. We went back to her projection. It was difficult to see because in her memory, it happened far across the room from where she stood. It was easy, after that; the occasional visitor would disappear and then reappear as the device and those it cloaked made their way toward the center of Zarbec's massive ballroom.

"Fuck," Kooper sighed.

"How do you think this works?" I turned to Zaria. "Are you sure it's the same thing as what a Sirenali can do?"

"I think it is," she said. "We didn't create the Sirenali. They were a dark race, as you recall. I don't think Kifirin created them, either. I think his creator did this and never explained the logistics to anybody. Therefore, the Sirenali have been able to conceal who knows what, place obsessions that nobody except the one who placed them could remove, and were the only race able to get past the Larentii's shields around their homeworld."

"An abomination," Kooper said.

"Some of them," Zaria turned bright-blue eyes in his direction. "Not all. They were created by Acrimus as his ace in the hole—that and the poison hidden on Siriaa. He is still attempting to destroy everything—from the grave, so to speak."

"How does that device work?" I asked.

"It's actually simple and not anything anyone would suspect," Zaria said. "Everything vibrates at a certain frequency—you know that. I believe the device causes those it cloaks to vibrate with the same frequency as their surroundings, making it appear as if nothing is amiss. Fundamentally, it makes the users appear to be what they're passing—floors, walls, air or whatever. Then, take the new technology that renders things nearly two-dimensional and you can fit thirteen men on a trans-vator that should only hold eight or nine. Combine that with sound-dampening technology, and those things can get you past any security device on the market."

"Effectively rendering them invisible in sight and sound," I tossed up a hand. "Is that how the Sirenali work, too?"

"The devices ramp up the same effect the Sirenali produce—to a level of ten or so. The Sirenali can't hide something from sight with what they have, like the devices can. And they certainly can't dampen sound. What they have is in their bones, I think," Zaria said. "We've recently learned that a Sirenali's bones continues to hide people and objects from those powerful enough to find them otherwise. A secret long kept by the Sirenali, because it kept them alive."

"Jeez Louise," I muttered.

"All this time, we've been examining the flesh and brains of dead Sirenali, hoping to find their secret," Kooper said. "Bones. Huh."

"We still need one of those devices to study it," I said.

"I'm working on that. I believe that Weir and his new lapbitch, Arna, have blackmailed the maker to give them more. I'm working on a way to sense one of those things, but I haven't come up with anything, yet. I've also sent what I have to Nefrigar and Valegar. They're working on this, too."

"I hope you haven't forgotten that Cayetes may have access to a ranos cannon or some such," Kooper pointed out. "If he fires at Paricos II, you may be left floating on a small piece of rock—provided you can shield Tamp's compound well enough."

"I know. Arna wants to have me killed, so that's another problem I have to deal with," Zaria said. "I think it's only a matter of time before Weir lets her have her way and sends someone over, or attempts to blast Tamp's new quarters to destroy all of us. When we don't fall, he'll know something's up. I really need him to engage with Cayetes, first, and forget about us."

"Use some of those vampires," I said. "They all know how to place compulsion."

"What if there's a delicate balance that can't be interrupted?" she asked. "Nobody expects Arna to give up on her campaign to destroy me. I need enough time to get some very important things done, and that will require a great deal of stealth, not to mention permission from the Mighty."

"That may be easier than you think," I began.

"You don't know what it is, yet," she said.

~

Avii Castle, Avendor

Quin

I saw it in Justis' face the moment the council meeting was over. I'd begged off, because I felt ill from morning sickness.

I should have known better. The Avii can't help but gossip, if there is any information to be had.

A few Yellow Wings knew I was pregnant—how could they not after cleaning up vomit and witnessing my regular visits with Master Ordin? That information was now spread all through Avii Castle, and the usual suspicions and doubts had cropped up.

I had white wings. Justis' child with me would never be recognized as royal without red wings.

Where would a white-winged child fit in? He or she would have no place with any of the others. He would always be different.

My child was doomed if he were born with my white as his wing color. The thought of my past troubling my child's future made me feel ill again.

Justis knew almost immediately.

"It's not their fault," I held up a hand before doubling over and losing what I'd managed to eat for breakfast.

Justis shouted for a guard to fetch Ordin and strode toward me.

~

"Prejudices can't be overcome in a single generation, or so it has been in my experience," Trajan informed me. He and Trace had brought a friend to see me.

Kevis, the healer, smiled at me as I told them how the Avii reacted to news of my pregnancy.

"They have been mostly isolated throughout the centuries—there are no other races like theirs," Kevis said, placing hands on my abdomen. "That doesn't excuse the prejudice, it merely explains parts of it."

"Justis will suffer, just as our child will suffer, if it has white wings," I said.

"I say this," Kevis pulled his hands away. "You won't know what color wings the child will have until he begins to grow them, unless one of the powerful reads it in you beforehand."

"If white wings were forecast, I'd leave Avii Castle—for the sake of the child," I muttered. "I won't have their ridicule placed upon an innocent."

"I hope that will not be the case," Kevis said. "And it is still too early to determine the sex of the child. We will wait this out, eh? Stop troubling yourself over it. Ashe says you may stay at the big house if things become unbearable here."

"Justis won't like it," I hung my head.

"I know. You have to protect yourself, young one," he said. "Surely Justis will see the reason in that."

"If it gets worse, I'll speak to him about it."

"Good. In the meantime, I suggest plenty of rest, good food and reading."

"If Dena were here, she'd make sure of it," I picked at the coverlet on my bed.

"Ah. Another loss to trouble you. Call for me if you wish to talk about all this," Kevis said. "It's my specialty."

"All right."

"Send mindspeech if you want me to come for you; you really are welcome at the big house," Trajan grinned before my three visitors disappeared.

~

Paricos II
Revis' Rock
Zaria

Tamp found me pacing in my suite. It wasn't half the size of his, but I didn't care about that—except for the fact that I had to make frequent turns as I paced.

"You think these devices employ the same properties as a Sirenali's bones?" he asked after watching me for a minute or two.

"Except the effect is multiplied. Combine that with the new technology that makes people almost two-dimensional, and you have a way past anything."

"Two-dimensional?"

"It works like a miniature black hole," I said. "Pulling you in upon yourself. It's strange, yes, but effective in this case."

"Is this what's worrying you?"

"Yes and no."

"So it isn't all that's worrying you, then."

"Yes."

"What must be done?" he asked.

"I think—to prevent a greater catastrophe, you understand, I'll have to let Arna kill me."

I hadn't realized until that moment how effectively Tamp could curse. He said some things about Arna that almost made me blush, they were so graphic and filled with anger.

"She'll only think she's gotten rid of me. I'll look different afterward, that's all, and she'll happily go back to Weir and fuck his brains out," I explained when Tamp paused for breath. His head jerked toward me and narrowed eyes studied me as I stood my ground.

"I dislike this. What will happen if we do not do it?"

"The unthinkable may happen, and things will be much, much worse."

"I still dislike this. Very much. I say we discuss this with the others and take a vote."

"Honey," I shook my head at him.

"Do not call me honey, now. I am angry with you."

"Are you telling me to never call you honey?"

"No. When you call me that, my insides melt. I am angry. Allow me my snit."

"Well, what about when I'm angry with you?"

"You may call me honey as much as you like, then."

"This sounds so one-sided," I pointed out. "Either way, you come out ahead."

"I do, don't I?" A devilish smile appeared. "I must have some advantage, you know. Otherwise, I will be intimidated by what you are."

"Oh, please. I can't see you being intimidated by anything."

I'd never been kissed by a pod'l-morph before.

It was nice.

～

Ilya

"I don't like this." All of Bleek's arms were crossed tightly over his chest.

"It'll be completely fake from the beginning," Zaria pleaded. Tamp had pulled her into a meeting with our original group, to tell us what Zaria had already told him.

That she wanted to allow Arna to appear to kill her. I didn't want to give the bitch the satisfaction of even thinking she could kill Zaria.

Tamp didn't like it at all, and frowned deeply whenever Zaria attempted to convince all of us. Bleek was just as angry as Tamp; Hal, Turtle and Flyer just shook their heads at the suggestion.

"I think we should kill Arna instead," Bleek argued.

"If we do, we draw Weir's attention to us, taking his aim away from Cayetes," Zaria pointed out. "For now, Arna has to stay alive."

"I refuse to give Weir or Arna any satisfaction in this," Tamp said. "They have killed enough already, and have gone unpunished for their misdeeds. I wish to see both dead."

"I'd say take out Weir and all his army, but that eliminates the feud between him and Cayetes, leaving us no better off in our hunt for Cayetes. We need him to come here, so we can see that bastard with our own eyes," Zaria countered. "I want to make damn sure he's dead, and V'ili with him. We have to stand apart and appear uninvolved in this, or Cayetes may target us, too."

"I must admit, I hadn't considered that," Tamp sighed.

"There are too many possibilities in this, and all of them rest on the width of a hair," Zaria shook her head. "Please—stand with me in this. For the greater good."

"When and how do you think she'll arrive?" I asked.

"I'd say in the next day and a half. She has access to those devices, you know. She and the warlocks she has wrapped around her fingers will walk right in here."

"Zaria, we don't have a method of detection for those devices," Tamp warned.

"Yeah. Tell me something I don't know," she said.

∼

Avii Castle, Avendor
    Quin

"Quinnie Bee, I know you can find just about anything." Queen Lissa had come to see me, and asked me to provide spheres for needy planets. I'd argued that I needed to go myself, to determine where the spheres should be planted and how deep.

"Here," she said, creating a three-dimensional image of the first world in need of a saving sphere. "Find the place where we should put it, honey."

I blinked at the image—it seemed so real, floating in Gurnil's

Library. It even rotated slowly as I watched it; Lissa was providing the image in real time, I realized. "Here," I pointed to one of the larger continents.

Lissa enlarged that continent and allowed the rest of the image to dissipate. "Find me a closer target," she breathed.

Using the gift I'd had as long as I could remember, I pointed out a country on that continent. Again, that portion was enlarged while the rest disappeared.

"Here," I pointed again. The area was at the center of a dying forest. It was easy enough to tell why it was dying—the poison was killing it.

"There is an underground river here," Ashe appeared as if called as we studied a close image of the area I'd chosen. "That means you should plant the sphere deep here," he pointed to another area roughly half a mile from the underground water. "This way, it won't get washed away if the river erodes the underground caverns."

"How deep?" Lissa asked me.

"Five hundred feet, or thereabouts, I think," I said. "My senses say the worst of it is at that level."

"I agree," Ashe nodded.

"Can you do the same thing for seven more? All are in dire need," Lissa said.

"Yes. This wearies me much less than the actual doing."

"Let us take care of it, then," Lissa smiled. "I and my Larentii will accomplish that part of it, at least."

"Thank you," I said. "I have been so worried about leaving Avendor, lately." My hand brushed my belly unconsciously. There was no outward indication, yet, but soon, I hoped, there would be.

"I know. That's why I came to you," Lissa said. She understood my reluctance, as any mother would.

"Will you let me know when these spheres have been placed?" I asked.

"I will. I'll send images, so you can see for yourself."

"That sounds wonderful," I breathed. "Let's work on the next seven, then I will choose spheres for each and place my call inside them."

CHAPTER 14

*L*e-Ath Veronis
Perdil

Rigo and I watched the vid-screens as our target worked with the others in the evening crew. Quin had given information to Lissa on this one, saying that his purpose was to provide information to Cayetes.

We'd found a spy, just as I'd expected. Rigo and two of his underlings had already gone through this one's quarters, finding nothing incriminating there—not even a comp-vid.

That meant he had such things hidden elsewhere. Rigo and I were determined to discover that hiding place, although in my experience, it was likely protected by security devices set to explode if someone were to tamper with it.

"It's too bad Quin couldn't tell us where his hiding place is," Rigo said. "Can't really fault his work, either."

"He has a stake in keeping his employment, never forget that," I said.

"True enough," Rigo agreed.

"I think he won't go back to his hiding place unless he actually has something to report," I mused.

"You're right. Let me communicate with Lissa. Perhaps she'll agree to feed him false information, now."

"I'd like to grab him and let you place compulsion," I said.

"Yes, but Quin says he's obsessed. Compulsion won't compete with that."

"Well, that sucks, as Lissa says."

"I'd bet everything I have that he knows where those kidnap victims are, or what happened to them, if they're no longer alive."

"I imagine it would be a coup if we could bring them or their remains home," I observed.

"We're back to feeding him false information, then following him to a stashed comp-vid somewhere."

"I say we contact Lissa now."

"Agreed."

~

Le-Ath Veronis

Skyf

Nobody knew anything, and I found that more than strange. People always gossip. I'd worked with the crew long enough that I'd become one of them, even going out for drinks after a shift.

Alcohol loosens tongues well enough, in most cases.

Those I worked with really didn't know anything, or they'd had compulsion placed by one of the Queen's fucking vampires. That I could believe easily enough.

That's why I shoveled concrete debris from a cell as if I were happy enough to do it. Dark stains covered some of the debris; the pirates seeking the black-winged woman had died near this cell.

I recalled that had V'ili not gotten away so quickly when the guns began firing, it would be his blood I was scooping up in a shovel.

"What's this?" Something chinked when I scooted the shovel beneath another load. Bending down, I searched through the rust-colored concrete to see what made the unfamiliar sound.

A chain—or so I though when I lifted it up. Instead, I found it was a bracelet, the type some men wore. The initials on the top of the name plate meant nothing to me. On the underside of the nameplate, however, was pure gold.

Made in Bastell was stamped there.

Bastell.

A large city on Carek Prime.

One of our pirates had forgotten to remove the bracelet his sweetheart had given him.

They weren't pirates, I realized then. Cayetes had offered the King of Carek Prime a refund if he could bring the black-winged woman to him.

Devarr had sent some of his, to do that very thing.

They had the technology Cayetes sought.

It would be up to him whether he dealt directly with Carek Prime to buy the technology, or merely went in to take it for his own. Either way, I doubted it would go well for Devarr.

∾

Queen's Palace

Lissa

"Sure—give the bastard false information," I waved a hand. Connegar, Reemagar and I had been out all day, placing spheres. I was tired and ready for food and bed when Rigo and Perdil showed up at my door.

"Tiessa, I know you are tired," Rigo dipped his head. "I will have something sent from the kitchen. Perdil and I will deal with this."

"Thank you," I sighed and rubbed my forehead. "It's—so nerve-wracking to place those spheres, honey."

"My love, stop fretting and get in bed," Perdil coaxed. "You can have your meal there."

"That sounds like heaven," I dropped my hand and gazed at Perdil. "Thanks for the suggestion."

They left shortly afterward, allowing me to climb into bed and wait for my dinner to arrive.

~

Perdil

"What do you mean, he walked off the job?" Rigo's hand gripped the foreman's shirt. The man was terrified of what an angry vampire might do to him.

"He did. The two he was working with said he dropped his shovel and walked out. They thought at first he was headed for the toilet, but when he didn't return after two hours, they came to me." His voice quavered as he spoke, but Rigo and I knew he spoke the truth.

"How long ago?" The evening shift was about to end; we'd sought the foreman to deliver Rigo's false information.

Had our spy learned he was being watched?

Or was it something else?

"Four hours." The foreman rubbed his throat when Rigo let him go. He understood the dangers of a vampire's claws, it seems.

"Damnation," Rigo muttered. "Tell no one of this. I want any vid-images available, before and after he left. Immediately."

"Right away." The foreman almost stumbled, he turned so quickly to do Rigo's bidding.

He's probably off the planet already, Rigo sent mindspeech.

I didn't reply—it was exactly what I was thinking.

~

Lissa

I'd been asleep for almost an hour.

Almost.

Gavin was at the door this time, with Rigo and Perdil.

"What in the name of the zucchini god do you want now?" I asked. I had bed head, on top of being tired and cranky.

"Our spy escaped before we could give him false information," Perdil began.

"He found out we knew about him?" I asked, rubbing sleep out of my eyes.

"I don't think that's it, Tiessa," Rigo said. "We have images from security cameras. You need to see this."

I was ushered into my office, where Kooper waited. He looked almost as cranky as I was, which meant he'd been dragged from his sleep, too.

"He found something," Kooper said and ran the footage on his comp-vid for me to see.

The spy had found something, all right. "Get Lenk," I snapped. "I want him to explain this. If what I'm thinking is correct, we need to put an envoy together and get to Carek Prime now."

~

"Noris," Lenk sighed after seeing close-ups of the bracelet the spy had uncovered. "Newly-engaged. I told all of them to leave their personal items behind."

"This will send Cayetes straight to Carek Prime," I said. Adrenalin had kicked in and I was almost vibrating from it.

"Devarr will refuse," Lenk said.

"Devarr has no defense against the likes of Vardil Cayetes," I hissed. "Get dressed. You're going back to Carek Prime. Pray that you get there before Vardil and V'ili do."

~

"Edden, this requires the best diplomacy ever," I said. I'd sent mindspeech to Trajan the moment Captain Lenk left my office. Trajan managed to get Edden and Berel Charkisul into my office in record time.

"Pap, Devarr is an isolationist," Berel said. "Even with the threat of Cayetes showing up on his doorstep, he may still refuse to listen to us."

"That's why I want Rigo to go with you," I said. "If compulsion is necessary, well, Devarr attacked us, remember? We're still rebuilding the detention facility because he sent a dozen of his men here. You can pick the rest of your envoy."

"I'd like a warlock to be with us," Edden confessed. "I'd choose Ilya, but he is needed elsewhere."

I studied Edden for several seconds, while names ran through my mind.

Until it settled on two.

They were more than well-versed on diplomacy.

Their credentials were practically flawless.

Somewhere, far in the past, we were related.

"I'll ask Wellend and Warlend," I said. "With those two, you'll have power and diplomacy skills."

"I ask for two or three of Director Griff's agents," Berel added after agreeing on my choice of warlocks.

"I'll send that message along. You need to be ready to go in half an hour."

"Lady, we are ready now," Edden replied.

~

King's Palace, Carek Prime

Devarr

I will remember this night as long as my life lasts.

It began as any other recent night—up late enough, working through budget cuts to ensure the planet could get by on what we now had to support ourselves. I cursed the poison that afflicted our world; many had died from it and more were sick.

While the small sphere appeared to be working, it occurred to Hulce and some of my other scientists that perhaps we hadn't buried it deeply enough. We'd imagined that the depth of a grave would be sufficient.

In other words, the sphere was effectively drawing the poison toward the surface instead of away from it. That, in turn was killing trees and vegetation as the poison traveled toward the sphere.

A meeting was scheduled in the morning, to determine whether

215

we should stay the course or dig deeper. The necessity of moving everything away from the burial spot was moot.

The booming noise that woke me was only the beginning, although I and my guards didn't realize it at the time.

The palace was under attack.

Sixteen of my guards and servants died, I was quick to learn, their bodies either hacked or blown apart by rifles or small explosives. The ones who'd attacked us disappeared quickly, once my remaining guards began to fire back.

We'd thought we'd successfully defended ourselves, and the new captain of the guard was pulling in troops to guard against further attacks upon my palace.

Until we began to count the dead.

Three of ours were missing. I ordered that my advisors be called after that, to alert them to potential danger.

That's when the full extent of our troubles became clear.

Hulce and half his laboratory had been taken away; the rest of his quarters was reduced to shambles after a swift, merciless search.

My advisors arrived quickly, rubbing sleep from their eyes and asking servants for tea to widen their eyes and wake their minds. I had no idea who'd arrived to kidnap my chief scientist, but it terrified me that he'd been the apparent target.

When Captain Lenk, whom we'd presumed dead, arrived with an envoy from the Reth Alliance, he brought with him the worst news of all.

~

King's Palace, Carek Prime
Berel

Devarr, King of Carek Prime, listened to Rigo's explanation, his eyes red from lack of sleep and unshed tears.

Many of his palace guards were dead, their blood spattered across the wide, marble foyer leading into the throne room.

Bodies had been removed, but it would take time and much work to eradicate the blood.

The evil the universes held had come knocking at Devarr's door, leaving its bloody handprints behind. What was worse, however, was the kidnapping of the scientist who'd invented the security devices.

Vardil Cayetes now held one of the deadliest weapons I'd ever seen.

"This is the image we had of Cayetes' spy, when he found the bracelet belonging to one of yours."

"I imagine it was stamped with the place it was made," Devarr's Chief Counsel muttered.

"All my men were instructed to leave such behind," Lenk said. "All followed my instructions, except Noris. That bracelet was his—a gift from his intended."

"You are sure Hulce is in Cayetes' hands?" Devarr locked gazes with Rigo.

"Most assuredly," Rigo replied. "I will allow Captain Lenk to describe to you the events that led up to the deaths of his men, and the involvement of V'ili, Vardil Cayetes' right hand, who invaded the ASD Criminal Detention Facility to take the same thing—the black-winged woman."

Paricos II

Revis' Rock

Ilya

King Rylend relayed the information to me regarding Cayetes' attack on Carek Prime and the abduction of the one who'd designed the security devices.

Until then, I hadn't known the true origin of those devices.

Zaria did.

"It was to keep him as safe as she could," Kay said, setting a cup of tea in front of me.

"All it took was one small thing to betray Carek Prime," I said.

"Rylend says it was a bloodbath when Devarr's guards attempted to fight off Cayetes' men."

"No doubt they were in and out quickly," Dragon set his own cup of Falchani black on the table beside me and took a seat. "I received mindspeech from Lissa," he said. "Saying much the same, I imagine."

"Can things get any worse?" Bleek arrived at the breakfast table, a cup of tea in one hand, a plate covered by an enormous omelet in another. "Zaria is locked up in her room and refuses to come out."

"This is a terrible setback," Hal joined us. "Rigo is on Carek Prime with Edden and Berel Charkisul and a few others, explaining things to Devarr."

"Zaria keeps saying there is a delicate balance to all this," Kay pointed out. "I believe her. This may have upset too many things."

"All we need is for that bastard Cayetes to be able to fly in while concealed by those devices, to kill us all," Bleek grumbled as he cut into his omelet.

~

Carek Prime

 Wellend

Father and I took precautions with Hulce's lab, placing spells about it so it would be protected inside and out—against any power wielder who didn't have permission to be there.

He and I stayed close, too. Zaria had contacted us. *Someone else is blackmailing Hulce,* she'd said. *I expect them to show up eventually, and figure out what happened.*

 Will it not mean that they merely won't get what they want? Father sent.

 It may escalate the war, she replied.

Father and I exchanged glances. *Do you need more time?* I asked.

 I won't get it, no matter how this plays out.

~

Weir's Compound

218

Arna

"I had my strongest shields up, and they still fired on me for asking questions," Laan explained to Weir. "Hulce's laboratory is destroyed and the rumor is that Cayetes has kidnapped him and stolen his work. I barely escaped with my life."

Weir's jaw worked; I'd never seen him so angry before. I was angry, too; this was a terrible setback. We were counting on those devices; they gave us a great advantage against Cayetes.

The devices we'd ordered Hulce to make were now in the hands of the enemy. "This is unacceptable," I huffed.

"There's something else Cayetes wants," Weir snarled as I turned to leave. "He's not known for letting grudges go, either. Laan, we have preparations to make."

"What do you intend to do?" I narrowed my eyes at Weir.

"You told me yourself he wants the black-winged woman. We're about to show him we have her."

"But," I said.

"A bargain, to even the odds?" Laan asked.

"Sure. Or to lure Cayetes in so we can destroy him."

"Why does he want that woman? The bitch and that four-armed behemoth never explained that," I pointed out.

"Likely because she runs those pirate ships and has something he wants back," Weir said. "He wants her quite badly, if he's offering that much for her. The reward specifically says he wants her alive."

"I'll leave you to it," I said and started for the door.

"Perhaps it wasn't such a bad idea after all—to go after the black-haired bitch," Weir spoke to my back. "She has information we need on the black-winged woman; I'd bet on it. You have permission to take one of our devices and two warlocks. Laan stays here and works on our decoy," he was quick to add. "Make sure she's alive when you bring her back."

I stiffened and stopped walking for a moment.

Alive?

We'd see about that.

~

Zaria

"I think things just went from bad to worse," I said.

"They're coming?" Ilya asked. He and I stood on a rampart of Tamp's new stronghold and watched the sea wash Jagged Bay to the south.

"Because of what happened on Carek Prime, Weir wants to play an ace he's holding against Cayetes. He wants me alive. Arna still wants me dead. There's no reason both objectives can't be satisfied—with a bit of cooperation."

"You are not going to Weir," Ilya snapped.

"I don't intend to go to Weir. Arna doesn't want me to go to Weir, either. She wants me dead."

"Why does Weir want you alive?"

"Because he wants to know why Cayetes is looking for Quin. He plans to have one of his warlocks do a disguise on a servant and present her to Cayetes as Quin. No doubt he plans to threaten her life in the message he sends."

"What does he hope to gain?"

"A trade, maybe?" I turned to Ilya. "Cayetes has the inventor of the security devices and the batch he manufactured for Weir. Perhaps a few of those devices could be offered in exchange for the black-winged woman?"

Ilya's dark hair was windblown in the constant breeze this close to the bay. Dark eyes, filled with concern, watched me carefully. He disliked this plan I'd concocted.

I disliked it, too.

Nevertheless, I had to play this out until the end. Too many things —and lives—depended on it. Even outside on the ramparts, ghosts crowded about us. Some had never heard of Paricos II during their lifetime. Here they were anyway, hovering about me as if I could answer the riddle of their deaths.

~

Avii Castle, Avendor

Quin

I was beginning to see the supply of saving spheres inside the hidden room as more than a finite source.

They could become the most precious of finite sources.

What would happen when we ran out? Would we run out of worlds that needed them, too? Zaria and I imagined we'd have enough.

That was before some were stolen, and even more worlds became poisoned through Marid and Vardil's greed and treachery.

How many more would learn that poison spheres had been sold upon their world, and then allowed to leak? I wanted to curse Marid's lack of skill as a wizard, but that would be a useless endeavor.

I stood on the terrace outside the library; it was a sanctuary from the looks and furtive whisperings going on inside the rest of it. Justis found me there, flying up from below and settling nearby before folding his wings and walking toward me.

"You should have come to the meeting earlier," he said, wrapping his arms about me from behind and settling his chin on my shoulder. "The glassmakers wish to sell what they make, as they usually do. For now, those sales are suspended, since everyone believes the Avii perished on Le-Ath Veronis. They also need more sand; there isn't enough silica sand surrounding the castle here to fill their needs. The metalworkers, too, don't have a ready supply of iron ore available."

"So those two factions are fueling the desire to return to Le-Ath Veronis?" I asked.

"Among them, yes. I promised I would visit their workshops this afternoon. I'd like you to be with me. I need my best advisor by my side, to tell me what their true motives are."

I wanted to shrink away from that veiled command. Their distrust of my white wings would be paramount in their gazes and I was ill-prepared for such. "You can't hide from them forever, love," Justis said gently. "Come, we will have lunch together, and visit the workshops at the far end of the bowl afterward."

~

My stomach threatened to turn on me as Justis and I walked into the metalworkers' massive shop. Yes, they'd upgraded their equipment and their furnace after their arrival on Le-Ath Veronis.

I understood their desire to be nearer to the latest technology and sufficient supplies. All I could see when I considered a return to Le-Ath Veronis was Dena dying with little Dara in her arms.

She'd shortened Daragar's name and gave it to her child. Daragar had smiled broadly when he heard of it.

Now both were dead, and Ardis with them.

"My King," Farisa greeted Justis. Her mouth clenched shut when she gazed at me.

I knew Lissa had placed compulsion for her not to harm me with words or deeds. Therefore, she couldn't give me her greeting gloved in an insult as she wished to do.

I read it in her anyway.

She hated me. She hated my white wings. She hated that I stood beside Justis instead of any other, but she especially wanted Wimla, young Liron's mother, at Justis' side. Farisa was sure that if given time, Wimla would produce a red-winged heir—if Liron didn't bear red wings.

As it was, Wimla still brought honor to the Brown Wings, as a former King's mate and mother to his child.

Liron would not bear red wings—I knew that already. Justis merely frowned at Farisa's apparent refusal to greet me and followed her into the shop. It was perched on the highest level at the opposite end of the bowl from the library and King's quarters.

Huge smokestacks constructed of the impervious glass that made up the castle interrupted the top of the bowl above the workshop, although the massive chimneys no longer emitted dark, polluting clouds. Filters on the furnace prevented anything other than heat escaping—another thing living on Le-Ath Veronis had afforded us.

It was understandable that they wanted to go back. I had no

argument on that quarter. I wanted to stay on Avendor—at least until my child was born.

I worried that the Brown Wings wanted to break from the rest of us. Many of the others were satisfied with Avendor. They could fly wherever they wanted without worry. They'd made friends with some of the residents.

New fears were holding me back.

How could they not?

I didn't have answers for the new problems that Justis faced—the potential for a breaking away of factions from the Avii.

They'd always lived and worked together. The castle protected them from harm. I knew it was my fault so many had died. They'd moved the castle because Vardil Cayetes hunted a winged woman.

If this castle had been left on Le-Ath Veronis, I imagined it would have withstood the weapon leveled against it. Perhaps it would have enabled us to kill V'ili instead, when his weapon held no power against Liron's creation.

That stopped me for a moment.

Liron created this behemoth. He'd also created the saving spheres —and others that were capable of holding powerful beings.

Something teased my mind about all of it, but eluded me the moment Farisa began her whining that they were running out of iron ore and silica sand.

∼

Vardil Cayetes' Private Quarters

 V'ili

"I have a demand here," Vardil waved his comp-vid at Hulce. "From your former king. He wants you back. Not only that, he's calling me a —let's see," Vardil turned the comp-vid around to read Devarr's private message, "An excrement-covered piece of reptagator bait."

"He is not my former king," Hulce muttered. "He is still my king."

"Except that by your own admission, you were going against his commands and selling your devices to others."

I'd placed an obsession on Hulce, who hadn't wanted to cooperate at first. He was more than cooperative, now.

"I've never heard of Devarr reacting so strongly before," Vardil baited Hulce. "Even when his men died on Le-Ath Veronis, attempting to bring me the winged woman."

Hulce went quiet immediately. It raised my suspicions that he was holding something back—there was a question I hadn't asked, yet.

"What is your relationship with Devarr?" I demanded. "Besides being his chief scientist?"

Hulce began to weep. My question was answered.

"Well, well," Vardil set the comp-vid on his desk while a gleeful light appeared in his eyes. "Hulce loves his king—in every way. V'ili," Vardil turned toward me. "I think it's time we tested the ranos cannon, don't you? Let's send a message to that filth on Paricos II—that I hold the upper hand in this and always will. The ship isn't far from Carek Prime."

My smile was slow and genuine. Vardil was more than furious that Weir imagined he had the winged woman we sought. Vardil and I knew she had white wings instead of black—the fool on Le-Ath Veronis had told me that much. Weir had shown us a black-winged fake in his message.

Weir needed a lesson for his deceit.

Carek Prime was about to pay the price for that lesson.

"I'll speak with the captain and the technicians immediately," I said and turned to leave.

"Tell them to fire the moment they're in range." Vardil laughed as Hulce dropped to his knees and keened.

～

Paricos II
Revis' Rock
Zaria

Arna was on her way with two of Weir's Third-level warlocks. In fact, they'd already made their way through the front gates of the compound. Something was off—I knew it the moment Arna's warlocks sent blasting spells toward me.

$$\approx$$

Avii Castle, Avendor
Justis

We were studying the problem of slag glass—the natural leftovers from smelting iron ore, when Quin shrieked Berel's name and dropped to the stone floor before I could reach her.

Something had gone wrong.

I didn't learn for several hours just how badly it had gone wrong.

CHAPTER 15

*P**aricos II*
     Revis' Rock

Ilya

"It is a decoy," Valegar arrived to examine the crumpled body on the floor. It was such an exact replica of Zaria, I felt it should breathe and talk—except for the bloody hole in her head.

The sight of it made me ill.

What made it worse was Dragon's news from Lissa.

Carek Prime had been blasted to bits by a ranos cannon, likely fired by Cayetes' minions at his command.

Rigo had gotten some away, but Berel and Edden Charkisul, who'd gone into the city to speak with the common people, had been too far away for him to save.

Not only that, but Carek Prime still bore poison. While it wouldn't be as severe a dusting as Siriaa had been, once again Cayetes was responsible for spreading the poison to other worlds.

For what?

Was he angry that Devarr kept the secret of the devices from him? Whatever it was, I'd wager that it was petty revenge that played a part in this.

While Zaria's copy lay on the floor, Zaria herself had disappeared.

She had something with her, however, that she hadn't had before; she'd taken the device from Arna, who, along with two Third-level warlocks, cooled their heels in a powerlight cage I'd constructed myself.

Tamp, Dragon and Crane were holding a meeting in Tamp's quarters, to decide what to do with those three.

I wanted to kill them—in the most painful way possible.

Yes, I wanted revenge, too. Revenge for Carek Prime and the two who'd died that I cared for. Cayetes was behind this—there was no question. Perhaps it was a message to Weir, although I couldn't imagine what kept Cayetes from destroying Paricos II instead.

"Zaria is likely elsewhere, mourning her mate Edden and his child, Berel," Valegar sighed. "I will send this to Father; he will know what to do with it." Valegar held a hand over Zaria's bloody copy, causing it to disappear.

"What are we to do? Berel's death will destroy Barc," Bleek sighed as he walked into the room.

"Berel's death will destroy Quin," I whispered.

"I know."

I'd never been hugged or held by a Blevakian before. I didn't mind it and appreciated the warmth of Bleek's embrace.

Queen's Palace, Le-Ath Veronis

Lissa

"This is my fault."

Devarr of Carek Prime stood in my study, his expression one of loss and bewilderment. Rigo had managed to save most of our envoy, plus Devarr, Lenk and a few others. Wellend and Warlend had done the same.

Berel and Edden—they'd been outside the palace and too far away for Rigo or the warlocks to pull away when forced to fold space.

Those two died with the rest of Carek Prime.

"How is this your fault?" I said. "Please, sit. You're making me nervous."

"I sent a message to the contact number Cayetes gave me," Devarr chose one of my guest chairs and sat. "I called him names for taking Hulce."

"You what?" I was standing, now.

"Hulce and I," he didn't finish. He didn't have to. Devarr and Hulce were together. Or had been, anyway.

"I had no idea this would be the result," Devarr wiped tears away. "I thought to call Cayetes out. To make him reveal himself."

"He revealed himself, all right," I snapped. "Fuck. Fuck to the ten-thousandth power."

"I cannot say how sorry I am," Devarr continued.

"Yeah? Tell that to all the people Cayetes is going to kill with the technology Hulce handed to him. I have a suite for you that connects to Captain Lenk's. We'll discuss this later; I have another meeting to attend."

❧

My meeting was with Dragon, Merrill and a few others who'd come from Paricos II. Zaria had disappeared—I would have, too, if one of my mates had died on Carek Prime. She needed time to mourn; I understood that.

"I know how I'd like to proceed," Dragon said, lifting his cup of Falchani black tea and drinking. We'd met in the library to discuss Zaria's absence and what should be done during that time.

"Call Weir out," Breanne said. She and Charles had appeared at our meeting together. "Bait him. Tell him that he killed Zaria. Yes, I know you can't lie," Bree held up a hand before Dragon could speak. "Let Tamp do the talking. He can lie as much as he wants."

"But Cayetes doesn't have an argument with us," Merrill pointed out. He had coffee in his cup—no surprise; I'd never seen anyone who loved coffee more than he did.

"Yet," a slight smile curved Charles' lips. "I suggest this, once you have Weir in hand." A photograph appeared in Charles' hands. He handed it to Merrill, who blinked when he saw it.

"You're saying that we pull Cayetes in with the promise that we have her?"

I knew then whose image was on that photograph.

Quin. As she really was. Yes, Orik had been questioned by V'ili before his death. He'd likely told V'ili everything he knew about Quin, which was a lot. Cayetes knew Quin didn't have black wings—she had white feathers, except for the metallic-colored bands at the ends of her primary feathers.

"I'm still trying to determine why Cayetes went after Carek Prime instead of going straight to Paricos II to destroy Weir," I said.

"I think the truth of that will come out," Bree said. "Eventually."

~

Avii Castle, Avendor

Justis

Barc was inconsolable; Quin was still unconscious. I felt ill at the news of Berel's death—and that of his father. This was a terrible blow, and caused concern for Ordin and me for Quin's health and that of our child.

I sat beside my bed where Quin lay unconscious, my head in my hands. Already, too many had died at Cayetes' and V'ili's hands.

"Kevis placed Barc in a healing sleep," Master Morwin sighed as he and Kevis walked into my suite. Ordin straightened from examining Quin on the other side of the bed and blinked at the two who'd arrived.

Morwin's bushy red eyebrows were drawn in a frown as he studied Quin; Kevis went straight to her and placed a hand on her forehead.

Kevis didn't speak for several moments; he merely allowed his hand to rest on Quin's forehead during that time.

"She's now in a healing sleep, too," Kevis said as he drew his hand away. "I had to call her back from the dark place she'd retreated to in her mind."

I drew in a breath as Kevis' eyes locked with mine. I'd forced Quin to accompany me to Farisa's environment, to show Farisa that Quin was my mate and it mattered not what the brown-winged guild master thought regarding Wimla or the color of my child's wings.

Instead, Quin had fainted the moment she felt Berel die, and tongues were wagging all through the castle as a result.

None of them sympathetic, most likely.

Dena's death meant that Quin no longer had a female friend inside Avii Castle to turn to for support. Berel was dead, too, and that was another level of support that had crumbled.

Lafe and Terrett were outside in my sitting room, waiting to hear from Kevis and Morwin, no doubt. Word had it that Kaldill would arrive soon. Finally, I considered a move to the big house, as they called it. I wasn't willing to allow Quin to go alone. I could fly to Avii Castle whenever it suited me or I had a meeting to attend.

I no longer had the stomach for gossipmongers and those who wished ill on my love. She and I had suffered too many recent losses for me to have patience for such.

"Can she be moved?" I asked while standing and shaking out my wings. "I wish to relocate to the big house and take her with me."

Siriaa, Twenty-five Years in the Past
Zaria

I walked through the wide grove of sleeping pod'l-morph trees, Arna's device rolling in my fingers as I lost myself in the last memories I had of Edden Charkisul.

I'd chosen this time on Siriaa; it was just before Camryn and Elabeth's deaths. I knew there would be no further visits to this grove to save Fyris or Siriaa.

Far to the south, Tandelis still held the throne, although Yevil and Tamblin plotted against him and the Avii royalty.

Far to the north, Avii Castle stood, a bulwark against all who thought to attack it.

East of there, Edden served as a member of the Council. He hadn't yet made a bid for the High Presidency.

My neck ached with tension.

My heart ached with loss.

So many things came back to Liron—and other rogue gods. They'd traveled back in time to rescue V'ili and others of his kind, just before the Larentii destroyed Sirena. Those gods had given the Sirenali they'd rescued a purpose—and likely an obsession—for revenge.

Otherwise, it made no sense for V'ili to serve criminal after criminal, whose goals were to destroy as much as possible.

In V'ili's mind, it was a form of displacement. He couldn't destroy the Larentii directly in retribution. He'd been pointed toward replacement targets instead, to suit those who'd saved him from intended death.

How many rogue gods had it taken to place those obsessions on rescued Sirenali?

How many angels could dance on the head of a pin?

Perhaps it was time to learn those answers for myself.

~

Paricos II
Revis' Rock
Phrinnis Tampirus

"We have this," I moved my comp-vid so Weir couldn't help but see Arna and his two warlocks inside the powerlight cage. "My witch is dead—Arna never intended to bring her back to you as instructed," I turned the comp-vid toward my face so Weir could see how angry I was.

I was angry, but it was because Zaria had fled when Carek Prime was destroyed and one of her mates with it.

Yes, perhaps I felt some responsibility—but Hulce had

approached me and not the other way around. My mistake was in allowing Arna to discover where the device came from—probably through Mayyab.

I'd paid Hulce a great deal of money for the thing, after all. Not surprising, actually; Devarr wouldn't allow trade with outside worlds. Hulce's inventions would prove more than lucrative if that law weren't in place on Carek Prime.

Regardless, Carek Prime was nothing more than blasted dust flying through space at this point, and poisoned dust at that.

"Do what you want with Arna and the other two," Weir hissed. "I only want the device she carried."

"You mean the device she stole from me?" I lifted the decoy Zaria created and dangled it in front of Weir's image. It looked exactly like the real thing.

Weir almost whimpered when I showed it to him.

"I'll pay," he mumbled. "I'll give you Arna, both warlocks and twice what you paid for it in the beginning."

"But I already have all four of those things," I reminded Weir. "I don't need or want your money."

"I can send an army against you," Weir snapped. "And take everything you have, including your sorry life."

"Try." Dragon had stood nearby while I spoke with Weir. All eight of the BlackWing ships had arrived and now orbited Paricos II behind a strong shield. In fact, Captain Meric and his crew had already taken over BlackWing VIII and were quite happy with it.

"Who are you?" Weir demanded of Dragon.

He knew Dragon was Falchani. Weir and I both received a surprise when Dragon introduced himself.

"I'm the Dragon Warlord," Dragon grinned. "And I'm far older than you will ever be. Send your army. You can't hide all of them behind a single device. I and mine will be waiting."

⁓

Ilya

"Tell me this," I said, pointing my cup of tea at Bleek. "Why wouldn't Cayetes just come to blast Paricos II to bits?"

"He may still do it," Bleek pointed out.

"True, but it seems to me he'd do this one first and leave Carek Prime for later."

"Cayetes has never been accused of acting logically where his temper is concerned," Bleek pointed out. "Maybe Carek Prime pissed him off, as Zaria is so fond of saying."

"Do you think it's a good idea to call Weir out now?" I went to my second question. "Zaria wanted to wait until Weir and Cayetes went after each other."

"That was before Carek Prime died," Bleek said. "Plus, this is the Dragon Warlord we're talking about. He's seen a war or two in his time."

"He has," I agreed. I didn't add that I'd gone against Zaria's wishes before, and ended up regretting it.

"Besides, Dragon conferred with Queen Lissa. With Zaria absent, this was the best plan they could come up with. Call out Weir, see if there's a reason Cayetes hasn't attacked Paricos II yet and have enough reserve power here to get all of us away if Cayetes and his ranos cannon come to call."

"It sounds so simple when you put it that way," I said.

"Let's hope it stays that way, and that Zaria comes back to us soon."

～

Ranos, Distant Past

Zaria

What was happening on Ranos made World War II on Earth look like a child's game.

Ranos technology. These people had created those weapons, and then pointed them at each other. Smoke drifted past me as I walked invisibly across a battlefield. Blasted machinery, vehicles and rotting corpses were everywhere.

This is where they came from—the people of Fyris and the Avii, I reminded myself. How had Liron chosen those to save? At this time, none of them had wings.

Liron had wings.

He'd given some of those he'd rescued feathers, and charged them with watching over the wingless ones.

There was no poison here.

Siriaa, in the distant past, had already been visited by Acrimus and the seeds of that disease planted in its core.

Liron was charged with the safety of that world, until Acrimus called for the poison to be extracted and used.

Neither had any care for the original inhabitants of Siriaa.

Edden and Berel had come from them. Their race had evolved on its own and stood on its own, while two rogue gods had done all in their power to destroy them.

Vardil Cayetes, with Liron and Acrimus' tool, V'ili, had killed two from that race whom I cared about most.

"Where are you, Liron?" I breathed softly before engaging the device I held.

∽

The Big House, Avendor

Quin

The last thing I remembered was feeling Berel die. I woke in a strange bed, with Justis leaning over me.

Berel was truly dead. I hadn't dreamed or imagined it. I could see the concern in Justis' eyes as he brushed fingers across my forehead.

"Edden is dead, too, isn't he?" I felt hot tears behind my eyelids as I shut out the pain in Justis' face.

"You and I will be staying here for a while," Justis whispered as he moved to lie down beside me. "Kevis says the baby is fine, my love. We will mourn Berel and Edden, as is proper, in a few days."

I buried my head against Justis' shoulder and allowed the tears to spill from my eyes. At that moment, I silently begged any deity listening to keep the rest of those I loved safe.

~

Ranos, Distant Past

Zaria

It looked like a giant beehive.

Liron flashed in and out while I watched; he was making the beehive larger. Already it stood the height of a fifteen-story building, and was growing by the second.

I knew what it was. When the sun broke through the cloudy sky over this part of Ranos, I could see the colors and patterns swirling in the slag glass Liron collected.

Far away, on battlefields too distant to see, Ranos was still at war with itself. Soon—very soon—it would die.

Liron had created Ranos; Acrimus had handed it the technology to design the weapons named after it.

Against Liron's wishes.

Liron wanted another world to suffer the atrocities of such creations. For Ranos, it had been placing a grenade in the hands of an infant, who couldn't help but pull the pin out of curiosity.

Like the N'il Mo'erti on Tiralia, Acrimus wanted to watch the chaos such technology would produce, as a microcosmic example of what the universes might do with it afterward.

Just as dangerous, I reminded myself, *as the technology produced on Carek Prime*. Not only had it played a part in the destruction of that planet, the technology hid me, even now, from a god's gaze.

~

Paricos II

Revis' Rock

Phrinnis Tampirus

Two days had passed since Zaria's disappearance, and there had been no word from her. I was learning how many of those who'd come at Ilya's call had mindspeech. Many of them had sent messages to her, with no reply to any.

"We have no power over her," Dragon informed me, when I asked if there were someone who could order her to return. Until then, I'd have said Dragon could order anyone or anything about, and they would be too terrified not to obey.

Zaria appeared to be in a league of her own making, with none who held sway over her decisions. Ilya was decidedly closed-mouthed about it all, and wore an expression of chagrin mixed with guilt whenever someone spoke of Zaria's absence.

There was history there; I merely didn't know what it was.

Too, Weir was gathering his army and making final preparations to strike at me and what looked like a much smaller army. In all this, I wondered what Cayetes was planning and how Dragon and his troops intended to deal with him when he came calling—as he surely would, when Dragon played the card he held.

I'd been shown the images not long ago—of the white-winged woman, who looked exactly like the black-winged one, except for the color of hair, wings and eyes.

Someone had done a very good job of disguising her. I didn't ask—I could disguise myself as anything, by becoming anything. Perhaps she could do the same.

What I knew for sure is that I missed Zaria, and wanted more than anything for her to come back to me.

To us.

Bleek wore a frown all the time as he, Dragon and Crane drilled troops. Ilya worked with my warlocks on how to lay spells against an invading army. The first time I saw the two High Demons in their other form, I was terrified.

I knew they existed, but information and images are difficult to find. The actuality was much more frightening—and impressive—than I'd ever imagined.

The vampires (and I learned there were several) held meetings, over which Merrill, Kell and Rigo presided. They were working on a stealth mission, but as yet hadn't given me the particulars.

In my long life, I'd never seen a group so focused on their task and willing to work together. If Weir could be defeated by determination alone, he'd already be dead.

Therefore, I chose to visit Arna and her warlocks in their cage.

I'd never seen a powerlight cage before; it took a great deal of power from a Fifth-level to create, and Ilya had made this one large enough for all to lie down comfortably if they wanted.

Just as well, I didn't intend to offer comforts of any kind; Ilya saw to it that food could be passed through the glowing bars, but no respect for privacy had been given to Arna, who cursed us long and often.

"You placed yourself where you are," I said as she hurled an insult at me when I walked in. The warlocks remained sullen and silent; Arna had gotten them into this mess, too.

"At least we killed your witch," Arna hissed at me.

I laughed.

~

Siriaa, Distant Past

Zaria

The Avii tales say that Liron created their glass castle in a day.

That much was true.

What they didn't know was that Liron spent the better part of a week reinforcing it with power, so it would be impenetrable.

Acrimus' instructions to Liron had been clear, too; Liron could only visit those he placed in this castle, and wasn't to interfere with the rest of Siriaa's development. Only the poison could be siphoned off at intervals, during which Liron could help those he'd created for that purpose.

That's why the Orb only appeared in the pod'l-morph groves when it was time for a saving.

Liron couldn't go anywhere else on Siriaa and risk interference.

Therefore, he'd hired Marid of Belancour to place a shield around Fyris, when the rest of Siriaa was advanced enough to discover that continent. He'd given a ring to the Avii King, then, to hand to the

Prince of Fyris at the time, so that the shield would be maintained so long as the ring remained in Fyris.

I stood on the small strip of sand outside the newly-built castle, while waves lapped the sand at my back and Liron sat in what would become the King's throne room far above my head, writing the words that would become the First Ordinance.

The first rule was this; No winged Avii may harm in any way those pureblood inhabitants of the continent of Fyris.

The second rule was that the Avii were charged with protecting those same purebloods. Anyone with less than pure blood fell outside their protection.

I imagine Liron's words meant that if any from Fyris sailed past the boundaries and mated with the natives of Siriaa, that the protection rule didn't apply to their offspring. Liron wanted to preserve the race he'd created, without dilution.

The Avii had interpreted that to mean the half Avii, half Fyrisian children. Both the winged and non-winged had come to see those mixed children as aberrations deserving of death.

What a nasty, fucked up way to interpret the blasted book.

Liron would eventually kidnap pod'l-morphs, force them into their tree shapes and plant them in the Saving Grove.

It angered me greatly that he'd worked out this kink in his and Acrimus' plan by effectively destroying their population. There were thousands in that grove, all forced into stasis as trees.

When Siriaa was destroyed, they died with it.

Liron.

Marid.

Cayetes.

I wanted to destroy all of them. Two would die in the future, Liron by my own hand, with borrowed power.

Cayetes—well, I was aiming for him, now, but there were places I needed to visit first.

◦

The Big House, Avendor

Quin

"The original has rum in it, but this one is non-alcoholic, has plenty of juices and is just as good," Bill Jennings placed a glass in my hand.

I sat by the pool on a wide patio outside the house, half in and half out of shade and hoped the sun would warm what felt frozen inside me. Kaldill sat with me, one of my hands enclosed in his, offering silent comfort as I considered my future without Berel.

"Try it, my love—it really is good, and good for you," Kaldill coaxed. "You barely ate any breakfast."

I sipped—it was good but cold, and I already felt cold. It made me want to crawl out of my skin and leave the chilling pain behind; to feel half normal instead of drowning in grief.

Kaldill and I watched as two of my feathers dropped to the flagstones beneath our chaise—my suffering only caused the molting to accelerate.

"You should be seeing replacement feathers soon," Bill said. He took a nearby chair, sat and leaned back, crossing his legs and closing his eyes as he turned his face toward Avendor's sun.

Justis had flown to Avii Castle after breakfast; he wanted to meet with his council again, then confer with Ordin and Gurnil.

I'm sure he'd be talking to the healer and the librarian about me and what to do about my unrelenting sorrow.

As if words could fix this, somehow.

I set my glass on the table next to my seat and watched as Bill appeared to fall asleep. My eyes were still on him when his mouth curled into a smile and *she* arrived.

The Mighty Heart.

I stared into cobalt-blue eyes as she pulled me to my feet and into her embrace.

So often, joy is tinged with sadness. She understood that as well as anyone. What she gave me I cannot describe, except to say it was love that infused every cell of my body.

Don't give up, she sent and kissed my cheek before stepping away.

Kaldill was already up and supporting me, or I may have fallen when she let me go. Bill was on his feet and kissing her shortly after.

I turned my head and blinked at Kaldill, who smiled. "Not all is lost," he whispered before his lips met mine.

~

Paricos II

Revis' Rock

Ilya

Weir attacked us on the third day after Zaria's disappearance. He imagined that a small portion of his army, equipped with lesser weapons, was enough to deal with Tamp and his rabble army, even if it were led by someone claiming to be the Dragon Warlord.

I warned Nyarr and his brothers to stay out of range of Kordevik, who turned Thifilathi, lifted the warlock-spelled, armored vehicle at the front of Weir's army and flung it toward the rest of his troops.

Those troops screamed and scattered as the tank exploded when it crashed among them.

Lexsi, Kordevik's mate, had another nasty surprise in store for the vanguard who still marched toward us.

I'd wondered at first why she wanted us to build a fire outside the compound. I'd wondered, too, as her silver Thifilatha appeared to absorb all of it.

Weir's warlocks were learning that their spells didn't hold against any High Demon, who could nullify anything within a certain radius.

Lexsi released her fire, and the resulting screams were probably heard by Weir, who was miles away.

Lexsi wasn't the only one who could send fire against the enemy. Dragon's sons and grandsons, Drake, Drew, Travis and Trent, morphed into dragons and blew fire at an advancing line of vehicles.

Enemy soldiers scrambled out of those vehicles, running away as the metal heated up around them.

Shots fired bounced off shields Nyarr, his brothers and I placed around the two youngest dragons.

Tamp, who stood with me on the parapet overlooking the battle, blinked once or twice but never spoke or indicated his surprise at the army defending him.

"Now," I said, turning to Nyarr and the others, who flanked Tamp.

We'd planned this carefully; all six of us lobbed blasting spells at what remained of Weir's troops and machines.

The resulting damage was massive, leaving craters and blasted remains behind. Anyone who lived past that was already running back to Weir.

The whole encounter took less than half an hour.

"I'll send our demands to Weir," Tamp turned with a flourish and stalked toward the stairs. He was pleased; he merely didn't say it aloud.

~

Sirena, Distant Past

Zaria

"This is madness, brother."

This woman would call herself Anita in the future. She'd been born with a different name and was a princess—she and her sisters, who were also her cousins, as their mother had married two royal brothers.

She spoke to V'ili, who was a half-brother and crown prince of the Sirenali.

He'd convinced his father, the King, to attack the Larentii homeworld. If Larentii could be ordered to do Sirenali bidding, all the universes would be theirs for the taking.

Or so he thought.

The majority of Sirena backed his plan, sadly enough.

Only a few disagreed; fewer still said it was wrong. They knew through experience that those who disagreed with the crown prince often disappeared and were never found.

Anita and her sisters disagreed with V'ili.

Strongly.

"You cannot force your will on another like that; it's wrong," Anita snapped as V'ili crossed arms over his chest and glared at her. "We have laws against it. The King enforces those laws."

"The laws apply to Sirenali. Not to anyone else," V'ili dismissed Anita's words.

"We don't know that obsession will work on the Larentii," another sister said. "You are making a terrible mistake in this."

"It's useless to argue," V'ili dropped his arms to his sides. "We go tomorrow. And, as I can't have any detractors when we return with the blue giants," he studied his shoes for a moment. "Now," he snapped.

Six Sirenali entered the room and fired their weapons on V'ili's unarmed sisters. All but one died instantly.

V'ili nodded to his assassins and stalked from the room. His men fell in behind him. Anita's final breaths gurgled in her throat as she lay dying on the floor.

I made myself visible to her, as the Larentii I was.

"All is not lost," I reached out to touch her face gently, alleviating the pain she felt. "Someone will come for you."

Her eyes glazed in death.

CHAPTER 16

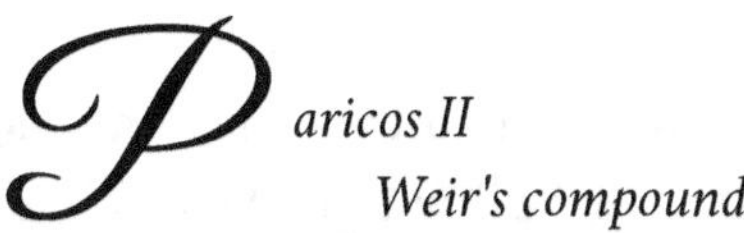

aricos II
Weir's compound

Ilya

Kell carried me inside his mist as he ghosted through Weir's compound. He desired to gauge Weir's response to his initial loss and report his findings to Dragon, who would plan accordingly for the next onslaught.

Weir was angry; his private study was in disarray and electronic equipment had been tossed against the wall, leaving dents and tiny, scattered chips behind.

"Where did they find those creatures?" he snapped at the warlock who struggled against a desire to fold space and leave Paricos II behind. "What were those creatures?"

"The dragons you already know," the warlock snarled. "I never counted on losing my associates to—to High Demons."

"What are you babbling about?" Weir hissed through clenched teeth. "There are no High Demons."

"They reside on the planet Kifirin," the warlock said. "The most powerful warlocks cannot go against them—they nullify our power."

"Why was I never told about this?" More equipment was hurled against the wall. I didn't fail to notice it wasn't lobbed at the warlock; he still held power enough to reduce Weir to a pile of ash, and there were no High Demons present to nullify that act.

"They keep to themselves," the warlock said.

"Except these didn't," Weir shouted.

"That's it—I'm done. Deal with this on your own." The warlock disappeared.

If my hands had been corporeal, I'd have slapped them over my ears, Weir's scream was so loud. I imagined that Rigo's ears—even as mist—were ringing. *We'll go now*, he sent to me. *I imagine Weir will offer us a deal soon.*

~

Phrinnis Tampirus

Rigo was adept at reading situations, I learned quickly. He and Ilya returned from their visit to Weir's compound, saying that Weir's chief warlock had left the planet, and that most of his remaining warlocks would probably follow suit.

Rigo also said Weir would attempt to bargain with us as a result, thinking we wouldn't know of his power-wielders' defection.

Weir contacted me that evening, after dinner. I imagine it had taken him that long to contain his anger and present a civil face to me.

"We are strong, but have a common enemy," he began, his voice both fawning and persuasive. "Vardil Cayetes is on his way to take this world. If we stand together, we can easily take him down. This will leave Paricos II in our hands, to be divided as we see fit."

"Why didn't you offer this as an option before you killed all the other bosses and attempted to kill me?" I asked. "Or was that merely a miscalculation on your part? You thought to get rid of all of us, then command what you'd taken from us to fight Cayetes. You want Paricos II and what Cayetes commands. Are you willing to share that, too?"

A bit of Weir's genial façade slipped and brief anger shone in his eyes. He was willing to share Paricos II, but Cayetes' empire he wanted for himself. What would Paricos II matter in the face of such wealth as Cayetes held?

It wasn't difficult to parse his thoughts on this; allow my army to do the heavy lifting against Cayetes, while he plotted ways to get rid of me and take the army I apparently held.

I wanted to laugh in his face and tell him the army acted on their own in this matter, and I had no say in any of it. In fact, I imagined that if Weir could manage to kill Cayetes, the army residing in my compound would turn their sights on him afterward.

It was as if they'd been waiting patiently for this opportunity to destroy his empire, and they'd suddenly been given permission to act on that desire.

Dragon and Crane, with Dragon's sons and grandsons, wore determined expressions constantly and refused to accept anything other than the best from those around them, whether it was training, cleaning their weapons or maintaining armor.

I could see some of those who'd abandoned Weir taking to Dragon's command like a reptagator to a swamp. Perhaps they'd never had the opportunity to follow anyone who acted honorably, before.

Dragon kept strict discipline among the troops, whether powerful or not. Even the lowest among them could expect to be treated fairly. No wonder the tales of the Dragon Warlord survived thousands of years; he was worthy.

"I said, what's your answer?" Weir snapped. He'd already asked the question while my mind wandered.

"The answer, now and always, will be no. If you wish to engage Cayetes, then keep your army where it is. I imagine it won't make a difference in the end. Send them against me now, they die. Fight Cayetes, they die later. The choice is yours."

Weir shouted curses at me before ending the transmission. I smiled at his tantrum. Like a spider in a sealed jar, he was caught and helpless—and he knew it.

❧

Cayetes' Compound

    Hulce

At first, I created devices for Cayetes that wouldn't work, or would short out if used more than once.

V'ili came after that, and ordered me to only make the best quality devices.

I was forced to obey. With tears leaking from my eyes more often than not, I made device after device for Cayetes, who intended harm against others with each one. I wept for them—those nameless, faceless souls who'd die.

I wept most of all for Devarr, who'd died with Carek Prime. I could never love anyone as much as I loved him. I'd sold a device after he emptied the treasury to save Carek Prime. I'd been paid a great deal; I felt sure Tamp would keep the device safe, and Carek Prime would be saved from destitution.

As it turned out, that was impossible.

Devarr and I—we'd both made mistakes with those devices. I wished that I'd never designed them to start with.

I'd attempted to create a shield to contain the areas where the poison spread on Carek Prime.

Instead, I'd created an unspeakable horror. Devarr had paid the ultimate price for the horror I'd built.

I was still paying my price, and, with V'ili's commands, would continue to do so as long as I lived.

I prayed to anyone listening for help, but there was no response. Perhaps it was a punishment for my treachery. Therefore, I changed my prayer to this; *destroy Cayetes and his minion, V'ili, before they destroy everything else.*

~

Zaria

I knew where and when Cayetes' pirates had attacked the passenger ship and kidnapped the wealthy aboard it.

That was my next stop.

I didn't intend to interfere with the kidnapping, or anything else. I merely intended to follow those victims in the moves Cayetes forced upon them, until they arrived in the present day.

Then I would act.

The die had been cast on Paricos II. Soon enough, those gathered at Tamp's compound would wave their bait in front of Cayetes' nose.

I was about to confuse Cayetes further.

After that, I only had a few other things to take care of.

Those things would require my utmost care, so as not to disturb the timelines.

I wanted to shiver at the worst-case scenario, but shoved it out of my mind instead. I refused to sow the seeds of failure into any part of this.

≈

Queen's Palace, Le-Ath Veronis

Wellend

"I feel guilt that we didn't think to follow Edden and Berel," Warlend, my father, sighed.

"They said they wanted to listen to the people, without interference," I reminded him.

"I know. We could have followed at a distance, though—close enough to pull them away when the moment came."

"Yes." I allowed my shoulders to droop and struggled to work tension kinks from both. "I sometimes feel the same. You have no idea how many times I've argued with myself about it, too."

"Survivor's guilt." Devarr of Carek Prime walked into the library where father and I sat, having our discussion. "I got this from the kitchen staff," he held up a bottle of bourbon. "Sometimes, this helps— even if it's only a little. Want to join me? I understand you can employ power to bring your own glass."

He set his borrowed glass on a low table with a thump before pulling the cork from the bottle and pouring a generous portion for himself.

"I'll have some," Father *Pulled* in two glasses—in case I wanted some, too.

"I'll join you," I agreed. "Let's hope it helps."

"I can't help thinking of what I did to cause this," Devarr swallowed half his bourbon. "And of what else I might have done to save my planet and its people."

"We only managed to get a few of your people away," I admitted. "We were near the kitchen at the time, so those were the ones we could save with the time we had."

"I am grateful," Devarr sighed and sipped more bourbon. "For what you and Master Rigo managed to accomplish on my behalf."

"You know Rigo's a vampire, don't you?" I asked.

"I learned that, yes."

"Did you know he was also Rigovarnus I, from Hraede? He was King long ago on that world."

"Then I will be more careful with my titles where he is concerned." Devarr emptied his glass and poured more bourbon.

"Don't worry about that—he left that behind long ago, as did we," Father admitted.

"Who?" Devarr asked.

"We were once Kings of Karathia." Father's half smile was tempered with bitterness. Without Zaria's help, we would have died long ago in the coup staged against us. "Nowadays," Father continued, "we no longer recognize that title, or who we were at that time, so many things have come to pass since."

"Who was at fault in this coup you speak of? Was it you?"

"No, unless you consider it our fault that we were born with a lower level of power than some of our murderous relatives," I said. I didn't add that people looked at us differently, now—as if we'd been afflicted with skin-rot or something. For us, the world we'd known had changed dramatically and would never be the same.

"Then let us make a toast to bitterness, and how it scrapes wounds across your soul," Devarr held up his glass.

"To bitterness," I said and raised my glass. Father's glass chinked against mine, and then against Devarr's. "May our scars fade, some day."

～

Siriaa, Distant Past

   Zaria

I watched from a distance as Liron stood in the massive glass bowl of Avii Castle. It was uninhabited, still, but he was preparing for their arrival.

Soil and grass had been brought in for animals to graze and trees and gardens to grow. What fascinated me was what Liron was doing after that.

He'd brought another huge mound of slag glass from Ranos, and now was fashioning spheres from it—large and small.

I knew what he planned to do with some of the larger ones. Those would be dealt with in the future.

The smaller ones he made, however; I watched the pile of those build with a feeling akin to greed.

Was he counting them? I only needed him to turn my way so I could read it in his face.

I waited.

And waited. His back was turned to me as he focused on the task of creating the spheres. The Orb would supply a saving sphere each time to the Avii Queen in the future, and those red-winged queens would never see the secret room Liron built near the base of the castle.

Only Quin, Lissa and I had seen the inside of it later.

Time passed; I had no idea how long I stood there, hidden behind a shield I'd created, and another created by the device I held. Far to the south, thunder rumbled. Liron turned sharply at the noise.

He wasn't counting small spheres, and an approaching storm meant nothing to him. He went back to his work.

I waited again, until he was lost in what he was doing. Cautiously, I approached. The piles of spheres were now so large that they'd started rolling off the top and scattering across the grass.

I calculated how many I would need, and ended up taking twice that number as Liron worked on the pile of slag glass that remained in front of him.

Thunder rumbled again and I froze where I was, hoping he wouldn't notice the spheres I'd pulled away.

$\approx$

Paricos II

Revis' Rock

Ilya

"Weir's army is on the way, and it's raining," Halimel walked into the kitchen where Bleek and I sat, having a late lunch after drilling troops in blade practice.

"He's going against us, because we'll be more lenient than Cayetes, no doubt," Bleek wadded his napkin and tossed it onto the table with a grimace.

"Better to die a quick death than a drawn out, painful one," Halimel agreed. "Cayetes isn't known for being kind to those who've crossed him."

"He's the example for all in carrying a grudge," Bleek acknowledged. "Shall we, brothers?" He rose from his seat and stretched all four arms.

"With pleasure, brother," Halimel nodded.

$\approx$

Queen's Palace, Le-Ath Veronis

Lissa

"Weir's army is attacking Tamp's compound," I informed Perdil. "I just heard from Dragon. He's arranging his army for effectiveness against what Weir is bringing with him."

"Will there be problems?" Perdil asked.

"There shouldn't be—Dragon has more than enough to take out a huge army, tanks and weapons included."

"Are you forgetting Liffel's Proverb?" he asked.

"Liffel's Proverb?"

"What can go awry usually does," Perdil quoted.

"Oh. We call that Murphy's law, where I'm from."

"Who's Murphy?"

"No idea."

"Then yours is invalid. Everyone knows Liffel is the father of the Liffelithi Dwarves."

"Whether he's real or not, he's dead," I pointed out. "Murphy's law in action."

"He died in battle," Perdil countered.

"My case in point," I said.

"He was four hundred eighty-five years old. Not as spry as he once was."

"Now, that's just making excuses."

"It was logical that he wouldn't live through the battle, yet he went anyway. Very brave, in my opinion."

"That has nothing to do with Murphy's law, which can apply to any situation."

"This is like sorting sand by size," he tossed up a hand.

"Is that another Liffel proverb?"

"Maybe. I refuse to say for certain." Perdil walked toward my study door.

"Want to go to Niff's with me?"

He turned back swiftly, a wide grin on his face. "I thought you'd never ask," he said.

～

Cayetes' Private Quarters

   V'ili

"You're sure the larger devices will conceal an entire fleet of ships?" Vardil asked.

"We've tested them—they work magnificently," I said. "Those replication bots we stole have been worth the effort," I added. "They were given the specifications provided by Hulce, and then created larger versions in a fraction of the time."

"Good. Will you transport me to my command ship, then?" Vardil asked. "These devices will keep me safe enough, I think. It's time we paid Weir a visit. The best part is that he'll never see us coming."

The Big House, Avendor
Quin

"Master Morwin, how are you?" I asked. "Barc my love, I've missed you." Both had come to the solarium where I'd chosen to sit and watch the exotic birds that flitted past the wide windows.

"I miss Berel," Barc came to me immediately and wrapped his arms about me.

"I miss Berel, too," I whispered against his hair as I hugged him close.

"Can I sit with you for a while? Master Morwin said no lessons for two more days."

"Of course. I was watching the birds fly past," I said. "And was trying to name the different kinds."

"I studied that with Master Morwin," Barc pulled away and blinked at me with misty, dark eyes.

So much like his father, was Barc.

"Then why don't you tell me what kind of bird it is, when one flies past," I pulled him toward my seat. Morwin nodded to me and left the solarium as Barc and I settled on the wide sofa.

"Your feathers," Barc pointed to a bare patch on one of my wings.

"They'll grow back," I said. "The pin feathers are beginning to itch, though."

"No, Quinnie," he said. "I can see a new feather poking out here," he touched my wing with two hands. "Where you can't see," he added. "It looks dark."

"What?" I stood again and struggled to pull my wing around.

"Here," Barc pointed to the pin feather in question.

It looked quite dark against the white feathers that hadn't dropped.

Soon, it would be time for Ordin to roll pin feathers. What would he say if my wings were truly turning black—or brown?

What did this mean?

I wanted to wail for Justis, but he was tending to business at Avii Castle. With my hands and body shaking, I sat beside Barc again and wrapped my arms about him, the exotic birds of Avendor forgotten as I held him close.

~

Queen's Palace, Le-Ath Veronis

Lissa

Perdil and I had just returned from Niff's, and both of us held half-eaten treats in our hands as I folded us into my study.

I should be used to seeing envelopes dropping onto my desk from nothing, but it startled me anyway and I jumped.

I went still when I saw my name spelled out in that particular handwriting. I'd only seen it once before, and that was when Zaria, who'd once been known as Corinne on Earth, had sent me a time-traveling message, designed to be delivered at a specific place and time.

Right after she'd separated her own particles.

Setting my cup of ice cream on my desk with a shaking hand, I lifted the envelope and opened it.

Lissa, the message read, *You will find the kidnapped victims at these coordinates. Take Wellend and Warlend with you, and Perdil if he wishes to go. The time to rescue them is now.*

~

Wellend

"I don't know why Zaria wants you to go," Lissa said as she handed me a ranos pistol. Father, who'd folded into my suite the moment Lissa screamed our names, took his pistol with a nod.

Behind Lissa stood Perdil, who had a short blade strapped to his back and a pistol in a holster at his hip. His height didn't compare to his determination, and any who thought to engage him could die swiftly.

"I'm ready," Father said.

"I, too," I nodded.

"Good. Let's get the hell out of Dodge," Lissa breathed and folded us away.

~

Paricos II

Revis' Rock

Ilya

"What in the name of the bloody god are they waiting for?" Bleek asked. He stood beside me on the parapet overlooking the outer wall of Revis' former compound.

Weir's army had come to us, but stopped marching forward roughly half a mile away. Bleek and I watched as tents were put up and soldiers in the distance checked vehicles and war machines.

Dragon held our army back; it wasn't his intention to start this war. He merely waited for Weir to make the first move.

Once Weir arrived, making a move looked to be an afterthought.

"What is he waiting for?" Tamp joined us at our lookout.

"No idea. You'd think he was on a picnic instead of starting a war he can't win."

"He's negotiating with three replacement warlocks, that's what," Halimel materialized next to Tamp.

"Nice to have a mister on board," Tamp grinned at Hal.

"It makes espionage so much simpler," Hal chuckled.

"How long do you think this will take?"

"No idea. I had to hover over Weir's shoulder as he communicated with the warlocks on his comp-vid—they can sense his desperation and are holding out for more money."

"Always the same," Bleek shook his head.

"It's expected," I shrugged. "I held out for more money."

"He did," Tamp agreed. "Velker was hot over it."

"Fuck Velker," I said.

"Velker is fucked—and dead," Bleek reminded me.

"I wish I'd been there to see the look on his face as he died," I said. "Zaria wouldn't give me the images—she said it was gross. Satisfying, but gross."

"Gross?" Tamp didn't understand the term. To him, it meant something else.

"Unsavory," Halimel replied. "I've heard Lissa say it."

Tamp's head swiveled in Hal's direction. Hal patted Tamp's shoulder. "I work for the Queen of Le-Ath Veronis," he said. "Many are here at her —and Zaria's—behest. How does it feel to turn to legitimate enterprises?"

"The BlackWing ships?" Tamp breathed after pondering Hal's words for a moment.

"Are operated under her guidance and are funded by the crowns of Le-Ath Veronis and Karathia, where her son sits the throne. Those ships were her grandson's idea."

"So Cayetes has been chasing the tails of both Alliances in this?" Tamp asked.

"Yes. Ildevar Wyyld and Teeg San Gerxon are aware and have given the operation their blessing."

"Well." Tamp mused for a moment. "Well. And I thought most humanoids were as dumb as dirt. I shall have to reconsider my opinions."

"Did you tell him?" Kooper Griff appeared at my side and studied the army in the distance.

"We did," Hal nodded to Kooper. Tamp drew in a breath.

He recognized the Director of the ASD, all right.

"Under most circumstances, I'd insist I was asleep and dreaming," Tamp mumbled. Kooper laughed.

∽

Siriaa, Distant Past

Zaria

Liron was halfway in the turn toward me. He was bound to notice the spheres I'd removed. If I folded space, he'd still know someone had stolen from him.

Someone who had to know *what* they were stealing.

The spheres were unattractive and useless looking, after all.

The breath caught in my throat as I watched him turn, seemingly in slow motion.

The enormous crack and subsequent booming noise made both of us jump.

Hail the size of grapefruit (and larger) began to fall, striking the piles of spheres and sending the smaller ones exploding in all directions.

Only the personal shield I held around myself prevent me from getting killed, the hail began to fall so hard.

The noise of it was deafening, too. Liron cursed; the cacophony of falling hail drowned out his words.

Move! A voice in my head shouted.

I folded space immediately.

∽

Paricos I

Lissa

It was genius—I realized it immediately.

Paricos I was little more than an uninhabited chunk of rock and dirt, with no water or atmosphere. It was larger than Paricos II, and none of us had thought to look there for Cayetes.

He'd built himself a stronghold beneath the surface, sealed it off, provided it with its own air and power, and had enough Sirenali bones hanging on its walls that the powerful would never find it.

At times, entire skeletons graced the walls, like macabre art.

Misting my companions through the compound, we took stock of what Cayetes had built. He'd spared no expense; that was evident. This—even Bleek hadn't known about this.

Look, Warlend sent.

We'd come to a door that was heavily guarded. Two armed men stood outside it, while tiny, electronic sensors and locks blinked on the wall behind them.

Inside that room was something Cayetes didn't want anybody to have.

Let's check it out, I replied and misted through the door.

Sirena, Distant Past

Zaria

What I'd come to see would be difficult to watch. I stood, shielded, in the throne room and watched when V'ili appeared before his father, the king.

The terror on his face was real.

"They're coming," V'ili wailed.

He meant the Larentii.

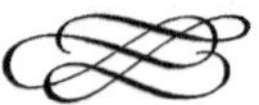

CHAPTER 17

*P*aricos II
      Revis' Rock

Lexsi

"Are you sure you want to stay?" I asked Kay.

Opal, who stood nearby in the dining hall, nodded her approval of my question.

"I'll stay," she said, determination in her voice.

"Battles are never pretty," Opal reminded her.

"I know. I have something to do," she said.

"What's that?" I asked.

"I got this—from Zaria." An envelope appeared in Kay's hand.

"Oh, lord," Opal breathed. "Can I see?"

"The message mentions you—and Lexsi," Kay said. "I just—didn't want to go by myself."

"Go where?" Opal took the envelope and lifted the flap. I walked over to stand next to Opal, so we could both read the message.

Kay, it began, *I know you can change aura lines. I need a really big favor from you—if you feel comfortable doing it. Take Opal and Lexsi with you, if that will help. Fifty miles west of Fendala, where there is nothing more than rock and desert, lies the facility where the Sirenali clones are made. I beg you to go help those poor souls before any more of them die.*

Z.

At the bottom of the note were exact coordinates. Opal already had a comp-vid in her hands and was tapping the numbers in as quickly as she could.

"I want to go," Kay said. "And put an end to this outrage."

"We're with you," I said.

~

Sirena, Distant Past

Zaria

I was nearly a million miles away and watching from a small, uninhabited moon when the Larentii destroyed Sirena.

I watched it die, the planet and its inhabitants blown to atoms by the anger of the Larentii.

No time before, and no time since, had that race ever done such.

If V'ili and his army hadn't attempted to take Larentii children at the last, Sirena may have survived.

That mistake was his, and his planet paid the price.

I folded space before the first of Sirena's particles reached my lookout.

I had things to do.

~

Paricos I

Lissa

What are you saying? I sent to Wellend.

There's a trigger spell here, he said. *If any of these people are removed, the whole room explodes. You can't pick them up one by one; the rest will die.*

Can things get any suckier? I asked.

If you mean worse, I doubt it, Warlend's sending was dry.

Is there any way to deactivate it? I asked.

Father and I may be able to hold it at bay while you collect these kidnap victims, Wellend said.

I looked around the room; it was easy to see that most of Cayetes' victims had given up on the idea of a rescue. Not only were the ones there that I expected to find, but many others, who'd likely crossed Cayetes in some way or another.

In all, there were more than fifty men and six women held captive. Some looked gaunt and in desperate need of medical care.

Cayetes didn't care or hadn't noticed.

All right, but the moment I gather them up, I'll be gone. Can you fold yourselves out of here?

Of course, Warlend said.

Perhaps I should have questioned him further, but my mind was set on this task and I was ready to get these victims away.

Ready for company, Perdil? I asked my dwarf mate.

I am.

Good. Wellend, Warlend, I'm dropping you now. Ready?

Ready.

I let those two go and moved swiftly to gather the victims in my mist. Whatever Wellend and Warlend did to temporarily hold off the spell worked; Perdil and I were already on Le-Ath Veronis when Paricos I exploded behind us.

Paricos I

Wellend

Father nodded to me as he and I stood inside that prison, holding off the trigger spell.

Yes, we could have folded away immediately.

We'd chosen not to.

It's easy enough to employ power to magnify an explosion, but we had to release the trigger spell to do it.

It was time.

We'd served our purpose.

This would be our final deed as Karathian warlocks.

I nodded to Father.

To bitterness, he sent.

To bitterness, I agreed.

We released the trigger spell together, and blasted every bit of our power outward as the room detonated.

~

Le-Ath Veronis, Recent Past

Zaria

There were no trees, gardens or sheep inside the bowl of the replacement Avii Castle. A few Black Wing troops flew in formation overhead, watching for attackers.

The attacker was even now approaching in a boat the Black Wings recognized and therefore, they paid it no mind.

No, I couldn't attack V'ili now.

The timeline would shatter, and too many important things rode on that knife's edge. I'd done what I came to do already; I folded space and bent time as the castle exploded behind me.

~

Paricos II

Lexsi

Conditions at the facility were deplorable—for the Sirenali.

All of them were young. Most were ill. The process for cloning was seriously flawed and none cared that these wouldn't live long anyway.

In fact, the employees there, under the direction of a sadist named Grast, was ordering the very ill Sirenali young to be fed to the flesh-eating worms hidden in a wide patch of contained, dark soil.

Once the bones were cleaned, they would be sold.

Vardil Cayetes was the only buyer—until recently, when Weir thought to take over.

Like Grast, Weir didn't care for the lives here, he merely wanted the money and power they would command.

It made me more than angry.

Kay, however—had begun to glow with power.

I can't hide you if you do that, Opal reminded Kay gently.

I no longer wish to be hidden, Kay said. Power boomed through my mind with her words.

This was the Mighty Hand's mate. It didn't surprise me that she could do this.

Kay walked out of Opal's shield and into the cloning room, where employees collected the ill to feed to the worms.

I blinked when the first of them dropped dead where he stood.

Kay was changing aura lines to black, killing those who deserved to die for their torture and abuse.

~

Siriaa, Thirty Years in the Past
   Zaria

I'd returned shortly after the time I'd brought Tamp here. The pod'l-morph grove slept peacefully in stasis, just as commanded by Liron.

I imagined that if removed, those trees would continue to sleep.

Unless.

This was the only thing I'd asked the Mighty for, and they'd agreed. The rest—I'd gone outlaw to do those things—for the second time in my remembered lives.

With a sigh of hope that these trees would become sentient once more, I began.

~

The Big House, Avendor
   Quin

"The time has come for your healing skills," Ashe appeared.

"Others are arriving to help, including Master Ordin. Come with me." He held out a hand.

"I want to come," Barc said. He'd been with me most of the day already, and didn't wish to remain behind.

"Then come," Ashe lifted Barc easily in his arms and folded both of us away.

∼

"Where is this place?" Barc asked when Ashe set us down. It was a wide, tent-like structure, surrounded by trees. Hundreds of cots with white sheets, pillows and blankets were lined neatly in rows.

"This is a temporary hospital, young one," Ashe smiled at Barc.

"Where are the patients?"

"They are here." Ashe waved an arm and hundreds of cloned Sirenali appeared, some so weak they couldn't move.

Kay arrived with them, but I didn't recognize the two other women with her.

"That is Opal," Ashe pointed out the dark-haired woman, "and that is Lexsi," he indicated the fair-haired woman.

At that moment, dozens of others appeared, Master Ordin among them.

The healers.

"Barc, will you help me help some of these?" I swept my hand out at all the cots, which were now filled.

"Yes," he nodded. "For you—and for Berel."

"Most certainly for Berel," I said and strode toward the cot which held the sickest young Sirenali.

∼

Queen's Palace, Le-Ath Veronis

Lissa

"Most of the kidnap victims hold an obsession," Aryn said as he took a seat in my private study.

"Kay will see to it," I waved a hand in dismissal.

"I am sorry for the loss of the warlocks," he said.

"Me, too."

"We cannot choose for everyone," he said simply.

"I know." I wiped a tear away.

"Here, now, my love." Aryn stood and came to me. I was lifted in his arms and carried to the sofa. I cried on his shoulder while he murmured soothing words.

∽

Avendor

Quin

Where am I?

His mindspeech was tentative. He was afraid.

"Love, you are on Avendor and are safe, now," I said, brushing short-cropped hair away from his forehead. Like every Sirenali that Kay, Opal and Lexsi had rescued, he had no tongue to speak aloud.

Will they come after us?

He was terrified of those who'd created him.

"They are dead. None can harm you here."

How? How are they dead? How was I saved?

"Young one," Ashe knelt beside his cot, "You were chosen by the Guardian of the Sirenali. You are quite special," he smiled.

He means Kay, I mused. She should be pleased to be named such. Before, she'd been somewhat timid, and perhaps incapable of saving so many.

"Not all is as it appears on the surface," Ashe beamed at me before standing and walking toward Kay.

He embraced her, surrounded as they were by cots and healing Sirenali young. Leaning down, Ashe placed a kiss on Kay's forehead.

For the first time in days, I relaxed.

∽

Carek Prime, Moon Thyppas
> *Recent Past*
> *Zaria*

I knew the exact day and time that Carek Prime was destroyed. It was time for me to catch up with Vardil Cayetes and V'ili, his chief of mayhem.

Carek Prime rotated peacefully in place bare moments before its destruction. I watched carefully from Thyppas, Carek Prime's largest moon, as Cayetes' ship appeared and fired.

Folding space, I landed on that vessel and rode with it to Paricos I.

~

Paricos II, Present
> *Revis' Rock*
> *Ilya*

Two more High Demons arrived while we waited for Weir's attack —Lexsi's parents, Reah and Torevik, came to see their daughter.

They held a private meeting to catch up, or so I assumed. Opal was also invited, although she wasn't family.

"I'm planning a night of drinking after this is over," Bleek set a mug of tea on the small table in the library, then pulled a footstool toward him so he could prop his feet up when he sat.

"I imagine Barc will need some time, too. This mess with Berel and Edden," he shook his head and settled heavily on the chair.

"Yeah."

"Did you know that Quin is pregnant?" Opal walked in, chose a chair and joined us with a sigh.

"What?"

It took a moment to realize I'd spoken; I was so surprised. "I thought," I floundered.

"I think it has to do with Zaria, when she brought Quin back."

"She can do that?" Bleek asked.

"Looks like it. Kevis told Reah that Quin was sterile before—the

Larentii confirmed it. That's no longer the case. She's pregnant—with Justis' baby, looks like."

"I imagine the royals on Karathia are breathing big sighs of relief," Bleek observed.

He was correct—if Bel Erland were to produce an heir, it would have been with someone else or through medical wizardry, until now.

"You think Bel Erland's child could have wings?" I asked Opal.

"No idea," she grinned at me. "Would it matter?"

"Probably not."

"So, family reunion?" Bleek asked, changing the subject.

"What?"

"Lexsi and her parents."

"Oh. That. Sort of, and to discuss some of the family property and what's been done with it recently."

"EastStar, right?" I asked.

"That's not the property discussed, no. It was just something that was given to Reah a while back, for services rendered. Few knew about it, actually, and she hadn't done anything with it. She ended up giving it away—for a worthy cause."

"Are Lexsi's parents staying to help?" Bleek asked.

"No. Reah said this isn't their fight. She and Tory left a few minutes ago. Besides, two High Demons should be plenty."

"Weir's on the move," Travis, with his brother Trent right behind him, strode in to the room. "Grandpap wants everybody in position right away."

"On it," Bleek dropped his booted feet to the floor and stood.

"Ready," I said.

"Me, too," Opal said.

⁓

Carek Prime, Recent Past
Zaria

Waste not, want not. That old saying ran through my mind as I *Pulled* the sphere from the soil of Carek Prime. It was needed elsewhere, instead of flying through space once Vardil's ship destroyed the planet.

I'd bent time so much in my recent history, and each destination had to be carefully timed and measured, so that it wouldn't interfere with the timeline.

Deaths had happened.

Some that should, and some that shouldn't. I identified with and had sympathy for the fictional Lady of Shalott, who'd gazed at images in a mirror to rebuild the world she saw there in woven threads. A curse was upon her—as there could be upon me when I completed my plans.

I'd been given a death sentence by the Larentii before.

The gods themselves could place it this time.

My next stop was Siriaa again, just before a nasty, red-winged princess chose to destroy an ancient book.

❧

Avii Castle, Avendor

Quin

I wouldn't have gone back to Avii Castle willingly, except for this; I was there to plead the case of the Sirenali young, who had no voices to plead for themselves.

They needed a home.

As did I, once.

Then, my only supporters had been Gurnil, Ordin and Dena. My naked wings back then had been a terrible distraction. My white wings and pregnancy served much the same purpose in this council meeting.

Justis was angry, that was easy to see. We had more than enough room for the Sirenali young, and Gurnil was willing to help teach them. They'd never been allowed to hold a book or read a word before.

In fact, most of them didn't have names; that's how ephemeral their existence had been.

Kay had come, too, to witness the Avii prejudice against outsiders.

I was thankful the Sirenali hadn't been brought to this meeting; they'd have thought their old torturers had arisen to make them suffer anew.

Terrett stood behind me, his hands on my shoulders as Gurnil and Ordin presented my case. I was shaking too badly to do it for myself. Lafe was nearby, sending mindspeech now and then to comfort me as another guild master presented his case against those who needed help.

Even with offers from SouthStar to provide assistance in the way of funds and other necessities, the guild masters were sure that the disruption of their lives by these strangers wasn't worth the risk— they could be criminals, or turn into criminals.

The guild masters had met before the King's Council, and decided the case before any argument was given on behalf of the Sirenali.

"Don't worry, I expected as much," Ashe appeared next to me. I blinked up at him. Had he been there all along?

"Yes," he answered my unspoken question, while Farisa kept railing at Justis against those who needed our help. "They can't see or hear me—only you and Kay have that privilege at the moment. It's strange, actually, that people who believe in the gods can't seem to believe that those same gods may be watching them in moments like these."

"Do you think some of them still believe in Liron?"

"Perhaps. That no longer matters. What matters is when they deliberately choose to mistreat another, who has done nothing to them."

"One of my lost feathers is growing back dark," I confessed and dropped my eyes to stare at the floor. I have no idea why that erupted from my lips, although it had concerned me ever since I'd noticed it.

"It is not growing back dark, Quin. It is growing back red—as will your other feathers. It is a gift—from the Guardian of the Avii."

Ashe disappeared as I dropped to my knees and wept with joy. Lafe and Terrett were beside me immediately. The others there imagined I wept for the Sirenali. I had—and would—weep for them. For now, I wept for myself.

~

Cloudsong, Seven Years Past

Zaria

I'd searched the ASD records to arrive at this date and time.

Marid of Belancour, already suffering from poison sickness (as was the planet beneath his feet), shouted at his eldest son, Morid.

Terrett huddled in a corner of the abandoned castle ruins, waiting for Marid to finish what he was doing.

A large crate, filled with leaking containment spheres, stood at the center of the broken stone floor.

Those spheres were the cache Marid would hide—the ones he intended to return to, in order to continue selling the filth.

Lining the top of the box were the bones from an entire Sirenali skeleton.

"Father, the ASD is here," Morid hissed. "Give yourself up and beg for leniency. Surrendering to them is preferable to capture, torture and death at Cayetes' hand."

"Surrender yourself. I don't intend to hand myself over to the ASD or those criminals," Marid snapped. "I have another place to go and plans to carry out. I care not what you and the rest of my family do."

"They are weary of running from the ASD, and even more weary of looking for Cayetes' thugs at every turn," Morid said. "They have no guilt in this matter."

"But you do," Marid's eyes narrowed. "Do you wish to die at the Vampire Queen's hands? She hates us still, you know."

"If you'd been honest at the beginning," Morid pointed out.

"Faugh, what would that have gotten us? We'd be dead."

"Cloudsong might have lived." Morid swept a hand out to encompass the husk of what Cloudsong had become, due to his father's incompetence and interference.

"How was I to know the bastard warlock would tap the core?"

"Give up, Father. Ask for mercy from the Founder, then. It will keep Cayetes away."

"He believes everything that witch tells him. She was a witch, you know, before she was vampire. That's why her son sits the throne of Karathia."

"We don't have time to discuss lineage," Morid complained. "They are getting close. They've already tripped my two outer sensing spells."

I realized at that moment that I had little time. Marid was about to leave and take the containment spheres with him. Taking a deep breath, I did what I'd come to do.

"Then stay and face their justice," Marid said. "I'm leaving. Come, Geng," Marid motioned for Terrett to follow him while pulling a leather bag into his arms. "Good luck, Son. I hope you live past sundown."

Marid, the crate and Terrett disappeared.

As did I.

~

Queen's Palace, Le-Ath Veronis

Lissa

"You rescued us." A kidnap victim sat beside me on the swing in the arboretum.

"I only followed up on someone else's lead," I said. "Two who were with me paid the price for your freedom."

"Odgun of Mildenis," he held out a hand. I took it. "Does the Queen of Le-Ath Veronis often involve herself in rescue efforts?" he asked as we shook. "I've never heard of such. Most leaders I know send someone else."

"I do when it's necessary," I said. "It's not often necessary, nowadays."

"Most of us had given up hope," he said.

"I know."

"I thank you for allowing us to communicate with our families. We all understand how this rescue must be kept secret, as our kidnapper still lives."

"I'm hoping that won't be for much longer," I said. "Until then, we can't leak this information."

"I'm grateful for everything you've done. My family says that you were able to remove half my wealth and hand it back to them, all while pretending it had been stolen by pirates."

"That's true," I smiled at him. "Your kidnapper has focused his anger on them—and a few others, I imagine. He's not the forgiving type, either."

"I know that well enough," Ogdun snorted. "We watched several of our fellow victims die because of it."

"I know. We've notified their families—discreetly, of course."

"I'm sorry about those two deaths. Who were they? Soldiers from your guard, perhaps?"

"Distant relatives," I sighed.

"My condolences for your loss, Lady."

∾

Command Ship Slayer, Destroyer Class

V'ili

"Order him to speak the truth," spittle flew from Vardil's mouth as I gripped the navigator's uniform in my fist, my eyes locking with his.

"No," the navigator whined. He knew the damage my obsession would do.

"Speak. The. Truth," I hissed at him.

"Paricos I has been destroyed," he parroted the message received from the one remaining sat-bot. "Our spy-bot tapped into the nearest Alliance Science Vessel and confirms."

I let him drop to the floor, where he lay in a heap.

"Weir," Vardil's eyes were hard as he gazed at me. "I don't know how, but he's behind this."

"It must have been by accident," I said. "We were invisible to any who came looking."

"Accident or betrayal, I no longer care," Vardil snapped. "Weir will receive a taste of his own medicine. How close are we to Paricos II?"

"We will be within firing range in a few moments," the ship's captain replied.

"Get me as close as you can; I wish to see his compound blown to bits before the rest of the planet follows."

"What about," I began.

"My friend, you offered something of yourself to create those clones. Scientists we can find and pay. I regret the additional pain, but it must be done."

"I will endure it," I said. "I wish to see Paricos II die."

Queen's Palace, Le-Ath Veronis

Lissa

"You mean Weir finally got off his ass and started the war?" I asked.

"I got word from Dragon to that effect," Tony acknowledged. "Here, we have a camera placed on the ramparts if you want to see," Tony placed a comp-vid on my desk. "You can zoom in and out, or move the camera with," he reached in to touch the button.

"I know how," I slapped his hand. "Wow, Dragon and my boys are doing damage."

"Let me see," Tony came around my desk to watch as five dragons flew over Weir's army, blowing fire and crisping everything in their path.

"There's Kordevik," Tony pointed off to the side. Kory was busy tossing a vehicle at a line of other vehicles. It exploded when it hit and began to burn, causing others it had landed on to explode and burn, too.

"What's Lexsi doing?" I gripped the comp-vid in both hands.

"She's sucking up the fire," Tony said. "I don't believe it. Wouldn't it be better to just let those things burn—oh my God."

Lexsi had released her fire, burning everything within a quarter-mile radius.

"That's my granddaughter," I said proudly.

"Wait," I whispered and stood immediately.

"No!" I shouted as my skin itched and burned so badly I wanted to claw it from my body. The screen had gone from clear to gray and then black.

Paricos II had just been destroyed.

∼

Command Ship Slayer, Destroyer Class
  V'ili
"Fire again," Vardil chortled.

"What?" I said.

The envelope just dropped in my lap—from nothing. My name was clearly written on the front.

Someone would die for playing this joke. I clawed the envelope open and withdrew the message.

Are you familiar with Liffel's Proverb? the message read.

"Liffel's Proverb?" I said aloud.

"Oh, it's that stupid saying about things going wrong," Vardil waved away my concern. "I said fire again," he demanded.

The crew fired our ranos cannon. What was left of Paricos II blew up.

And outward.

"Get us out of here," I shouted.

CHAPTER 18

Queen's Palace, Le-Ath Veronis
Lissa

When I lifted my head from my desk after spending the last fifteen minutes crying my eyes out, I found Bree, Charles and Ashe sitting together on my sofa.

"There will be a ceremony at SouthStar in three days," Ashe said.

"But," I begged Bree with my eyes to make this right.

To bring everybody back.

"Not my job," she said.

I wanted to strangle her.

"Three days," Ashe repeated. "Bring Devarr with you, and any others who wish to come. Trace will transport your party."

All three disappeared.

Avii Castle, Avendor
Quin

"The reports say that Cayetes and V'ili are dead, but I won't believe it until I see a body," Justis fumed.

He was angry.

Extremely angry.

Many of those lost on Paricos II were his friends—and mine.

Lissa lost mates, children and grandchildren. Ilya was gone. Kooper was gone. Bleek—gone. We hadn't told Barc yet—the pain was too raw.

"The ceremony is tomorrow," Justis turned away from the view off his balcony and frowned at me.

"I know. Justis?"

"What?"

"Do you think Zaria was there with them? At the end?"

"I don't know." Justis turned back to his view of the river and countless groves of gishi trees.

What will we do without them? I sent.

I don't know.

∾

Queen's Palace, Le-Ath Veronis

Lissa

"Ready?" Trace appeared in the library, where my group waited. Gavril and Ry stood at my side. If somebody wanted to thin the ranks of my mates and relatives, they'd done a spectacular job.

Devarr was nearby, looking guilty as hell.

Perhaps he should.

Hulce's device had no doubt allowed Cayetes to bring his fleet to Carek Prime without anyone knowing.

Word had it that Cayetes and V'ili were dead.

If they weren't, I was prepared to hunt them myself, to make them pay for their sins.

I was ready to sharpen my claws and go after them.

The envelope dropped from above and landed on my head before floating to the floor.

Zaria.

Trace, who watched as it fell, lifted an eyebrow as I leaned down to snatch the note from the Serendaan carpet at my feet.

With a slightly extended claw, I slit the envelope open.

Smile, Mom, the message read. *All is not lost.*

Travis and Trent.

~

BlackWing VIII

Captain Meric

"There soon," Nenzi, the helmsman of BlackWing I, informed me. I was coming to appreciate his abbreviated speech. We'd been traveling for three days—from wherever it was we'd been flung to when Paricos II exploded.

"How it feel to be legit?" Nenzi's voice came through clearly on the com.

"I feel like a free man—for the first time in my life," I replied.

"That good. Turn new page. We fight together, now."

"Has anyone seen Zaria?" I asked.

She'd gotten me out of Weir's clutches. Without her help, I'd be dead.

"Not see. Not know where."

"That's too bad. I wanted to thank her."

"You and others."

He was right. There at the last, just as things began to disintegrate around us, all eight of the BlackWing ships had been packed full with Tamp's army from the surface, and the ships flung to the far reaches of the universe.

Three days at our best speed it took, to get where Nenzi led us.

"Where are we going? I've never been in this part of space before," I said.

"Avendor. You see. May not want to leave," he chuckled.

"Where the gishi fruit is grown?"

"Yes. Kifirin grows other. Avendor first."

"Good enough," I leaned back in my chair and relaxed for the first time in days. I hoped the gishi fruit was in season. It was the best thing I'd ever tasted—next to freedom.

~

Avii Castle, Avendor

Lissa

Trace dropped us in the huge bowl at the center of Avii Castle. Still clutching the note in my hands, I looked about me. "Those are new," Corent made his way through my crowd to stand beside me.

Trust him to notice the new gardens and groves within the bowl while I was distracted.

This note—did it mean? I slapped it against my palm in irritation. I wanted answers and I wanted them now.

"All the Avii have been commanded to come," Bree appeared at my side. "They'll be here in a few."

I guess if you could fly in from wherever you were, it wasn't such a big deal. No crowds would be jostling along in hallways or down steps to get to the bowl.

"What is this?" I held the note in front of Bree's face.

"Looks like an envelope."

An impish grin lit her face—I'd seldom seen her smile before.

"You know what I meant," I said. Hell, she could read everything about me in a single glance.

"It's Hope. Love. Strength. Wisdom. Guardianship."

"Here they come," Charles appeared beside Bree and placed an arm around her.

He meant the Avii. Wings of all colors filled the air as they flew in and landed. I noticed—for the first time, perhaps—that the wing colors tended to band together on the ground.

Front and center was Farisa and the other Brown Wings. The Black Wings that remained waited near the base of the castle—Justis would enter from there with Quin. Gurnil and Ordin arrived together; Blue Wing and Green Wing—their friendship had been long and loyal.

Yellow Wings had left their chores and kitchen duties behind to attend. Their talk and whispers filled the bowl.

"What kind of ceremony is this?" I asked, frowning at my sister.

"You'll see," Ashe arrived with Kay at his side. "We only need the Avii King and Queen to arrive."

~

Quin

"Are you ready, my love?" Justis asked.

A Yellow Wing had helped me dress that morning—I wasn't feeling well, although a visit from Ordin and Kevis assured me that the baby was fine.

"You look beautiful," Justis assured me. I didn't feel beautiful. My clothes were, but I felt like a fraud in them.

Instead of attending the ceremony, I wished to go to the tent hospital and visit the Sirenali.

I felt as if I could help them, which in turn might serve to make me feel less helpless in the face of recent events.

They are waiting on your arrival, dearest. Mindspeech came from Daragar. Until then, I hadn't known he was coming.

Many Larentii are here, he replied, as if reading my thoughts. *Nefrigar is holding young Barc, and Valegar is holding Liron, so they will see and hear everything.*

We're coming. I couldn't keep the weariness and depression from my mindspeech.

I'm bringing her, Justis' mindspeech informed Daragar and me. Until then, I hadn't realized he'd been included in Daragar's messages.

For a brief moment, as Justis lifted me in his arms, I recalled the first time he'd carried me.

Then, I'd had little in the way of feathers.

With the molting, I felt almost the same way.

"I love you," I told Justis as he made me comfortable in his embrace. "I've loved you since the first time you carried me."

"I felt as if you belonged in my arms even then, my love." Justis kissed me.

Come on, time's wasting, a familiar voice entered my head. My eyes, which had closed with the kiss, flew open and I gazed in wonder at Justis, who'd obviously heard the same thing.

A happy sob escaped—Bleek was alive.

~

Lissa

The moment Justis and Quin arrived, a flower-covered dais rose from the grass at Justis' feet. He carried Quin up three steps and settled her on one of two ornate chairs that appeared from nothing.

Ashe, Bree and Charles had planned this carefully—that was evident.

The volume of conversation at my back suddenly increased. I turned quickly, to see that the crowd of Avii was parting—much like a sea of feathers might.

Like the others around me, I couldn't hold back a gasp. Kiarra, Adam and Merrill came as the giant unicorn, gryphon and snow leopard they could become. Dragon, his sons and grandsons strode in behind them, leading what looked to be a procession.

Behind them came Ilya, Rigo, Halimel, Bleek, Turtle, Flyer and the others who'd volunteered to go to Paricos II.

By that time, tears were running down my cheeks—happy tears. As they came closer, Drake and Drew winked at me.

I bounced with joy and blew them kisses.

More were coming—many of whom I didn't recognize. If I'd had Bree's talent, I would have known who they were.

Or Zaria's.

Wait—she wasn't with Ilya and the others. What had happened to Zaria?

~

Quin

Justis blinked at the endless parade of people who strode toward our dais. Following the mighty unicorn, gryphon and snow leopard were Dragon, Drake, Drew, Travis and Trent. They'd split up and took the stance of guards around us.

Joining them were Ilya, Bleek, Rigo, Halimel, Turtle, Flyer and a few others.

Still, there were people coming.

From where? Justis turned his head to look at me.

I was overwhelmed and couldn't answer because of who came next —or what, I couldn't decide.

One man marched in front of more than a thousand others, and behind him, those others transformed from men to trees to animals and everything else in between.

Pod'l-morphs, Bleek's voice sounded in my mind.

"Pod'l-morphs," I breathed aloud. "How wondrous."

And then—*Justis,* I sent. *Those following the pod'l-morphs. Those are— Sirenali. Whole Sirenali.*

There were roughly a thousand of those. Whomever these were, surely they'd been deemed trustworthy.

And then—I was standing and screaming with everyone else in the bowl as Avii swooped in from nothing—led by Ardis and Dena, who held her baby in her arms as she flew.

I was in Justis' arms and he was weeping, just as I was, when those three landed on our dais. Ardis knelt at our feet.

Justis let me go and raised Ardis, before embracing him.

Dena came to me; we embraced, with the baby between us. I knew not how this miracle was achieved, but I was grateful for it anyway.

"I missed you so much," I whispered in Dena's ear.

"We were never really gone," she whispered back. "I still don't understand it myself."

I wanted to ask her who was responsible, but she didn't know.

It didn't matter. My friend was back, and my tears were accompanied by laughter.

~

Lissa

Yes, the screams and cries were happy ones as a huge, family reunion took place in the bowl of Avii Castle. Avii hugged and laughed and shouted as their lost friends and family found them.

"You should see Cloudsong right now," Bree said.

"Huh?" I whirled to face her.

"You wouldn't recognize it," she shrugged. "It's a restored world, and all those people from Carek Prime are there. Devarr still has a kingdom—if he wants it."

"But," I said.

"I'll explain later," she chuckled. "Or, I'll let her do it."

"Her?" I blinked at my sister.

Bree pointed behind me.

I turned back—I thought the return of the Avii was the last miracle we'd witness in the bowl.

I was wrong.

A tall, blue Larentii woman walked in. The crowd that arrived parted to let her through.

Behind her walked four that I knew. Or had known.

I stopped breathing for a moment.

Berel and Edden spread wide, blue wings as they flanked Zaria.

On the opposite side, red wings spread.

Wellend and Warlend.

"Their lives as Karathians and Siriaans have ended. Their lives as Avii are just beginning," Bree's sigh sounded happy.

Then, perhaps the most wondrous thing of all happened.

Zaria's wings—shining in Avendor's sun, spread out. White and gleaming, they were blinding in that brightness. In her arms, Zaria carried a large book.

The First Ordinance.

As Zaria began to pass the crowd of Avii, the change started.

"Oh, my God," I whispered in awe.

"Exactly," Bree laughed.

∾

Quin

Dena's wings changed, even while we embraced.

I stepped back, my mouth open in wonder. "How?" I asked. Her wings—were now multicolored.

Beautiful.

They carried all colors belonging to the Avii—except one.

There was no red.

"Quin, your wings," Dena breathed, wiping wetness from her cheeks.

I spread out my left wing to take a look. My feathers were growing back, and those I hadn't lost to the molt were—*red*.

Except for a thin band of white, which separated the bands of copper, silver and gold at the ends of my primaries.

Ashe said it was a gift from the Avii Guardian. Kay had accomplished the impossible, I think.

It wasn't me, dear, Kay informed me. *Look up. You will see her.*

~

Zaria

"Hi, baby." I smiled down at Quin.

"Zaria?" Quin and Dena blinked at me, Dena with worship in her eyes.

"Yes, it's me," I said. "How are you feeling?"

As I was in Larentii form, it was no trouble for me to lift Quin in my arms and give her a warm hug.

"You changed their wings," Quin said.

"I did. Liron was an asshole who thought people belonged only in their own little niche. Now, the Avii get to choose who'll they'll be. Except for the royalty, of course. I left Gurnil and Ordin's wing color alone, too—they're two of the few who deserve to stand out.

"Quin?"

She looked down to see Berel standing beside us, with Edden nearby.

"Berel, you have blue wings," Quin stuttered, as if she imagined herself to be dreaming.

"I do. Justis said I deserved blue wings. Zaria says so, too."

"I love you," Quin said.

I set Quin in Berel's arms—they had a happy reunion to hold.

Yes, I'd been afraid the whole time I was collecting souls inside the spheres I'd stolen.

I'd carefully placed them in stasis, and laid a powerful spell for them to be released if I weren't alive to do it myself.

I couldn't imagine that the Three would eliminate those lives afterward; I was doing my best to save everyone I could, including Hulce.

I'd stood on the bridge of Cayetes' ship, shielded by my own power and by the power of the device I'd taken. Cayetes had built devices large enough and strong enough to hide an entire fleet of ships—even from the most powerful gods.

All those devices were destroyed when Paricos II exploded—I saw to that.

And, just to make sure of things, I'd released V'ili's and Vardil's particles, right before their ship was consumed by the final blast that eliminated Paricos II.

I'd packed the core of the planet with explosives and enough power beforehand, to make sure the job was finished.

I'd also considered Liffel's Proverb, and decided not to take any chances.

"What about Cayetes and that filth, V'ili?" Justis tapped my arm.

I looked down at him. As a winged Larentii, I could do that.

"Dead, and it was such a pleasure to see it happen," I smiled at him.

Lissa

Zaria was in her smaller form at the reception that followed the ceremony. This was a smaller crowd, comprised of those invited by Ashe to the big house.

"Zaria is the Guardian of the Avii, Sirenali, the pod'l-morphs and those of Cloudsong," Connegar smiled down at me. "It is a great honor for a Larentii to be designated as such."

"I can't get over the wings," I said.

"She only has wings as a Larentii," Connegar pointed out gently.

"I think she'll have wings any time she wants," I snorted a laugh.

"Shall we?" Charles placed a glass of wine in my hand. "I know you have questions for Zaria. We'll retire to the solarium, so you can have your answers."

Zaria

Lissa's first question was straightforward and to the point.

I almost didn't want to answer it.

"Yes, they would have died," I said bluntly. "All of them." I couldn't stop the shiver that went through me. "Those larger devices Cayetes built—they were powerful enough to hide him from anybody, including the most powerful among us."

"You were willing to risk a final death at the hands of the Three?" Lissa asked. She was right—if the Three had chosen to destroy me, I would never be reborn.

"Yes. I felt it was worth it."

"The wing colors—that's a stroke of genius," Ashe lifted a glass to me from his place near the door.

"I can't tell you how many times I watched Dena sighing after black wings," I stated flatly. "Others were much the same—they desired something besides what they'd apparently been born to do. It disgusted me, as did Liron's decision to do it in the first place. Now, they get to work for what they want and wing color be damned."

"You went back to that time?" Lissa asked.

"Yeah. I watched as Ranos destroyed itself at the last, with weapons it shouldn't have had. Speaking of which," I turned back to Ashe, "I've destroyed those devices and taken the memory of them away. Hulce doesn't recall making them, I'm sorry to say. He'll never create another, either. Kooper, those replication bots were also destroyed—with Paricos I. Those bots were making the larger devices there at the last—to cover entire fleets of ships."

"I have no problem with that," Kooper waved a hand.

"Neither do I," Ashe agreed.

"What about Lexsi, Kory, Kell and Opal?" Lissa asked.

"Sent back to Earth in the past. Opal and Kell remember, but Kory and Lexsi won't until they return to this timeline. They agreed to that, by the way. They understand how this could interfere with the past if we're not careful."

"Good," Lissa nodded. "Thank you."

"What about the containment spheres Marid hid?" Bill Jennings asked.

"I took those off his hands and replaced them with harmless, empty ones," I said.

"Where are those spheres now?" Gavin wanted to know.

"In the safest place imaginable, with so many shields around them they'll never get out again."

"Are you sure?"

"Absolutely."

"What about Cloudsong? Will it be isolated, like Carek Prime?" Trajan asked. "After all, Cloudsong was refused membership in the Alliance—in perpetuity—by Ildevar Wyyld."

I smiled at Trajan's question. "The Reth Alliance isn't the only Alliance," I said. "Ildevar offered to nullify that decree, but I told him it was all right. Cloudsong will petition the Campiaan Alliance for membership, soon. I'd suggest," my gazed settled on Gavril, who sat near his mother, Lissa, "that you seriously consider that request. Hulce has plenty of good ideas—aside from making those devices."

"Are you kidding?" Gavril shrugged. "Come have coffee with me some morning. We'll hammer out an agreement."

"Good enough. I'll bring Devarr, although he prefers tea."

❦

Ilya

I'm sure most people feel uncomfortable under the gaze of the Mighty Heart. She'd passed judgment on me once, and I'd served a sentence lasting thousands of years.

I'd been called into her presence again, once the meeting with Zaria ended. Most had gone to the hospital tent to visit the young Sirenali.

We stood on the flagstones surrounding the pool outside the big house. Breanne studied me for several minutes, which only served to increase my discomfort.

"How much do you love her?" she asked.

"I would give my life for her."

"Sincerely?"

"Sincerely."

"Good enough."

I felt the change, although there was no pain. "How?" I blinked at Breanne when it was finished. "How has she lived with this?"

"Ask her yourself."

Zaria

I walked among the cots, tables and beanbag chairs scattered beneath the tent. The young Sirenali appeared to have a thirst for knowledge; many had made themselves comfortable on the beanbags and leafed through books containing words and pictures. Many of Gurnil's former blue wings went from child to child, helping them read their first words.

"Zaria?" he said, his voice sounding tentative.

"Ilya?" I turned toward him.

My heart stopped.

"Cabbage?" he held his arms open. I was in them immediately.

I wanted to ask him how much of both lives he remembered, but I'd already seen the answer in his face.

He remembered everything.

~

Quin

"We have six this time," Lissa smiled at me when she arrived to receive a new batch of saving spheres.

"I have them here," I set a hand on the spheres lying on the library table. "Zaria brought us so many more," I added. "All those spheres she took from Liron to save so many, are now in the hidden room. We should have enough with plenty to spare."

"I don't think much gets past her," Lissa smiled and took the chair opposite mine. "How are things going here?"

"There has been some confusion regarding wing colors, but Justis is sorting things out," I ducked my head to hide the smile. "We've had several who wish to train with the guards instead of making beds. Dena is one of them."

Lissa threw back her head and laughed.

~

Six Eight-days Later
Avii Castle, Avendor
Phrinnis Tampirus

"You're prickly tonight." Zaria stepped onto the outside balcony and passed my cactus as if she were used to seeing such every day.

My heart was full after receiving the gift she'd given me—the entire grove of pod'l-morphs we'd found on Siriaa.

I was no longer alone.

Soon, she promised, *we'll find a place for all of you to grow and thrive as you wish. And, since you're immune to the Sirenali obsession, I imagine you may share a world with the few of those I saved.*

For three centuries, she'd allowed the rescued pod'l-morphs to sleep as trees in the soil of Avendor. It had taken that soil and the wondrous atmosphere surrounding SouthStar to bring them back from Liron's curse.

I'd met other Larentii, too, when she carried me back to the

Larentii Archives. There, she'd placed a crate of poison spheres, which were so heavily shielded that none of it would ever escape.

The type of sphere I'd been hunting, to destroy myself.

Nefrigar, the Archivist, had taken that crate and hidden it somewhere inside the Archives' massive structure, so none would ever find it.

I'd also been told that I was welcome in the Archives whenever I wished to visit. I wanted to visit often, as a world of learning had opened that I never thought to see.

"Zaria, my love," I became humanoid and went to wrap her in my arms.

"Phrinnis Tampirus, you make me happy," she sighed and melted against me.

EPILOGUE

LARENTII ARCHIVES

*N*efrigar, *Chief Archivist*

"What will happen, Father, when Quin reads those commands in the First Ordinance?" Valegar asked.

"Those commands were meant for a puppet," I answered. "Love and Wisdom found her when she was roughly six years of age, as humanoids count time. They gave her a part of themselves—a soul. After that, killing Zaria would never have occurred to Quin, because she was no longer wholly Liron's. When Zaria *Changed What Was* and brought Quin back from death, she was completely freed from him and his meddling."

"Will those words upset Quin, then? That Liron commanded her to kill Zaria?"

"She understands who and what Liron was, my child. She is grateful that he is gone and that Zaria has been named Guardian of the winged ones. I may find it amusing, however, when those of New Fyris learn that Zaria is also Guardian for them."

The End

ABOUT THE AUTHOR

Connie Suttle lives in Oklahoma with her husband and a conglomerate of cats. They have finally banded together to make their demands, which has proven disconcerting to all humans involved.

For more information:
    Website and Blog: subtledemon.com
    Facebook: Connie Suttle Author
    Twiter: @subtledemon

www.ingramcontent.com/pod-product-compliance
Lightning Source LLC
Chambersburg PA
CBHW071731190726
48292CB00003B/715